Alone

A novel by

K.B. Horricks-King

Thank you, and I hope you enjoy.
-K.B.

Filidh Publishing

First Edition, Soft cover

ISBN: 978-1-927848-26-5

Cover design by K.B Horricks-King & Danny Weeds

Filidh Publishing, Victoria, BC

filidhpublishing.com

Dedications

To everyone who kept me sane while my mind tried to unravel.

To my dentist, Dr. Huynh, who fixed my mouth so I would have a chance to read my work, eventually. When I finally finished writing it.

To my family, who put up with my borderline psychotic bullshit when I hit a wall.

To everyone else who I have forgotten, because who am I kidding, I can't remember everyone.

And to my daughter, who I hope never reads this because it will give her insights into my psyche that she doesn't need.

Thank you.

Table of Contents

Pronunciation Guide

Character Names (according to their own preferences)

Alecto – Ah-lec-toh	also goes by Lecto
Aphrodite – Ah-fro-die-tee	also goes by Dite
Apollo – Ah-poh-low	
Arcturus – Arc-ture-us	
Ares – Air-ees	
Artemis – Are-teh-mis	also goes by Artie/Arty
Athena – Ah-thee-nah	
Demetre – Dem-eh-ter	
Dyonisus – Die-oh-nigh-sus	also goes by Dyo
Eros – Err-ose	
Gaia – Guy-ah	
Hades – Hay-dees	also goes by Hade
Hephaestos – Heh-fest-ose	also goes by Phaes
Hera – Hair-ah	
Hermes – Her-mees	
Mageara – Mah-jair-ah	also goes by Maggie
Mnemosyne – Neh-moh-seen	
Persephone – Per-seph-owe-nee	also goes by Seph
Prometheus – Pro-mee-thee-us	
Psyche – Sigh-ch (NOT sigh-kee)	
Poseidon – Poh-sigh-dun	also goes by Don
Rylynne – Rye-lynne	also goes by Ry
Tisiphone – Tih-sif-own	also goes by Tis
Zeus – Zoo-se	

Fiona Amina Seratie Morovica – Fee-owe-nah Ah-mee-nah Ser-ah-tee Moh-row-vih-kah

Muses – Healers/Scientists

Clio – Clee-oh	
Erato – Eh-rah-toh	
Calliope – Cah-lee-oh-pe	also goes by Callie
Melpomene – Mel-poh-mee-ne	also goes by Meenie
Polyhymnia – Poh-lee-him-nee-ah	also goes by Poly
Terpsichore – Terp-sih-kore	also goes by Tiki
Thalia – Tah-lee-ah	
Urania – Ur-ah-nee-ah	also goes by Raini
Euterpe – You-terp	also goes by Terpsi

Pertinent Translations

Metaria (meh-tah-ree-ah) – mother
Gisareh (gee-sah-ray) – guide
Bradoro (brah-doh-row) – brother
Sisania (sih-sah-nee-ah) – sister
Dara (dah-rah) – daughter
Doros (doh-roh-se) – son
Patronie (pah-trow-nee) – father
Vrastefa (vrah-steh-fa) – abandon(ed)
Chshara (ch-shah-rah) – family
Moren (moh-ren) – my
Dur (du-re) – but
Dies (dee-es) – love(s/d)
Forto (for-toh) – hate
Ma (mah) – you
Aye (eye-yuh) – I
Mero (meh-roh) – us
Esa (eh-sah) – and
Sec (seh-k) – the
Tomos (toh-moh-se) – heart
Dama (dah-ma) – will
Nie (nee) – never
Gorro (gore-oh) – steer
Sesava (seh-sah-vah) – wrong
Cahr (kah-r) – how
Kie (kee) – it
Sav (sah-v) – was
Meerah (me-rah) – time
Careno (cah-reh-no) – need(ed/s)
Mora (more-ah) – me

Ayediesma (eye-yuh-dee-es-mah) – I love you
Ayefortoma (eye-yuh-for-toh-mah) – I hate you
Medara (meh-dah-rah) – my daughter(s)
Midoros (mee-doh-roh-se) – my son(s)

Preface

In our world, children are sacred. They have a special status and even the Hunters leave them alone. Their mothers are also left in peace until the children are at least twelve years old. It is very rare that a Hunter goes after a mother and young child – so rare in fact that he or she is swiftly tracked and terminated. To put it simply, to kill a child is to invoke the wrath of the gods.

When my family line first started in its current form over a thousand years ago, we were still technically human. We had a couple of extras, but we flew under the radar of the Hunters. They understood that some people were a little different but not shifters, vampires, demons, or other beings. It has just been the last couple of generations that we have been hunted, and all because my grandmother fell in love with an angel.

Morganna Selene and Margeurite Alice Hartley were the last humans born to our line. Margeurite followed in the footsteps of her aunts back through time, dying mere months after their mother when Morganna was fourteen. She was reborn as one of the most lethal creatures on the planet whose sole purpose was to protect her sister until her youngest niece, my mother, celebrated her fourteenth birthday. Josephine Isabella and Gabriella Elaine Hartley were the first ones hunted, and when they died the curse of not being human fell upon my sister, Serenity, and I.

It has been years since the death of our mother. We have been running, hiding, fighting to survive for years, but things are about to change – I can feel it. The universe is shifting, and the Hunters are finally going to get their due.

Every story has a beginning, but where that beginning truly originates is a mystery we have yet to unravel. The logical beginning would be what my big sister and I are. In all honesty, we don't know, and no one has been able to tell us – or willing to if they did know. All our mother told us (or me at least) is that our father was a half-breed like her, but from the 'dark' end of the supernatural spectrum. He was born of a vampire's line, and cursed us to a life of bloodlust and misery.

1

I don't know where to start. What age is most important in my life. I suppose starting at the beginning would be going too far back, but not telling anything of my life before my amazing daughters would be a failure to provide pertinent details of my life. I cannot go back to the death of my mother, consciously at least. It seems a middle-ground would be my final years of school, and the last few years I was hunted. I am Amelia Mystaya Hartley, and this is how my life was supposed to end. A couple of times.

December 6. Another day. Another erased identity. Serenity paused by the powder blue door of my most recent school and offered me a half-smile before adjusting my blonde wig. She knew I hated the itchy contraption, but it was necessary since most of the students had witnessed me beaten to the brink of death by Hunters who had finally caught up with us. According to the carefully manipulated news, Rhianne Alexander had succumbed to her injuries within hours of arriving at the hospital. I wasn't technically dead, but my brother-in-law did a hell of a job selling it once we were in the OR. James, bless his possibly damned soul, was a magician with a scalpel.

"Five more minutes, sweetie, and we'll be free for a while. We just need to erase the paper copies of this existence," my sister murmured before opening the door and stepping inside the bland beige building. Following quietly, I raised an eyebrow at the new, bubblegum-haired receptionist. Slipping into a skin of pure sophisticated snobbery, Serenity smiled.

"We have an appointment with Richardson," she drawled in an amazing South Texas accent. "We need to make this quick otherwise we'll miss our flight."

The receptionist blinked slowly. "His class ends in two minutes; he will see you then. His office is open if you would like to wait there for him."

I tapped my foot twice, knowing Serenity could sense my slightest movement. No real receptionist ever allowed someone into the administrator's office without their presence and permission. Two fingers of her right hand twitched deliberately, and out of the girl's sight. She knew something wasn't right, but that we had to proceed and erase our tracks.

"Be a doll and tell him Ella and Marlene Alexander are here," Serenity drifted past the desk and down the short hallway that led to the offices and 'sick' room. She pulled up short and crouched in front of me. "Tripwire," she dropped the accent. "Stay here."

"Yes ma'am," I mock-saluted, leaning against the wall to my left as I twiddled with a set of bracelets a guardian, of sorts, had given me as a child. She had said they would protect me from harm so long as they both touched my skin. They worked, too. Getting impatient, I moved to follow my sister when an explosion sent me through the cinder block wall.

Dazed, mildly confused, greatly bemused, and registering multiple throbbing injuries that should have been much worse, I silently thanked Artemis for her bracelets, and slowly began testing the mobility of my limbs. All eight fingers, two digits and ten toes were attached and wiggling – it couldn't be that bad. Frowning at my off-character levity, I shook my head (immediately regretting said action) and attempted to roll over so I could stand and take stock of my surroundings. My vision swam, and I managed to turn my upper body enough to avoid vomiting on myself as pain shot through my hip. Pushing up on my elbows, I frowned at the severed mandible embedded in my right side.

"You alive in there bè-be?" my sister called, her vibrant red and gold eyes glowing in the swirling dust.

"Just peachy, 'mia. Won't be walking straight for a week or so though," again with the odd lightness. By nature I am not a cheerful...creature. Fire and brimstone is more my speed.

Serenity drifted lithely through the rubble to my side and frowned at the thing sticking out of me. Squatting down, she jerked it unceremoniously from its perch in my bone; ignoring my string of profanity as she inspected it.

"If I'm not mistaken, this belonged to a Lazarus," her frown deepened.

"Lazari are gatekeepers, though. How could they have caught – let alone killed – one?"

"Hell if I know. It's a question to ask at our next stop," she tucked it gently in her bag. Grabbing my hands, she hauled me to my feet and brushed the dust off my clothes, fixing my wig again, and checking my eyes to make sure the tinted contacts were still in place. "I torched all the files and dropped a worm in their system that will erase all photos and mentions of you from every device hooked into their Wi-Fi."

"Thanks, Sere. I know you hate having to do this," I took her proffered arm and she 'helped' me to the door.

"You're right, I do. But you do it for me, and we made a promise to Mom before she died," she stopped at what was left of the door. "Why aren't there students screaming and making for the exits?"

I frowned at her. "That is a very good question. An explosion like that should have had emergency responders here a long time ago."

"You still have those knives in your boots?"

"Never leave home without 'em. Fat lot of good they do sometimes though."

"Might be wise to have them handy. That funky feeling Mom taught me to always trust is telling me to bail town right now."

"You sure that isn't just the tourist you ate this morning coming back for revenge?" What is it with this sudden personality shift? I hate jokes.

"Bè-be, he'd be eating you too, if that were the case. Besides, we didn't kill him so what's there to get revenge for?"

"Good point. Carry on. Ignore me. Bubblegum-hair is crawling on the ceiling."

The 'girl' hissed at me and dropped to the floor as I pulled the titanium carbide blades from the sheathes hidden in my boots. In the unlikely event she made it past my sister, she would not have fun with me.

"You're like a cockroach; you just don't seem to want to die," she sized us up.

"Dying's overrated," Serenity shrugged off her white leather coat. "Been there, done that, burned the souvenir t-shirt."

"You burned that thing? Sheeze, here I was thinking the monster under the bed stole it while I was sleeping," I sighed, shaking my head.

"Darling, I am the monster under your bed, remember?"

"Good point. Carry on."

"You two are unusual. If there weren't a Terminate on Sight on you, I'd consider keeping you as pets. Maybe I'll keep the next one," she lunged at us, catching Serenity around the waist and heaving her into what remained of a wall.

The jagged edges crumbled as my sister growled and lost some of her carefully crafted control. Nails turned to talons as she dug into the huntress' side and pulled. The young woman screamed, falling back as Serenity stood, straightened her clothes, then licked the blood off her fingers.

"Does the Hunters Council even tell you guys what you're up against when they send you out? They may be a new institution, but you are seriously under informed," Serenity squatted by the whimpering creature. "Amelia? I'll need a little blood."

"What for? Are you going to poison me?" she asked through clenched teeth.

"My blood, in particular, has spectacular curative properties when I spill it myself," I shrugged. "Take it by force and it's about as useful as tits on a bull."

"The Council you serve doesn't differentiate between good, bad and neutral. It kills for the sake of killing," my sister eased her forward as I tucked one knife away and made a small incision in my left hand with the other. Closing the distance between us, I placed my bleeding hand against the deepest of her wounds. Images flashed through my head at the contact, and I pulled away quickly.

"You're a Lamashtu," I pressed my hand against my jeans.

"How would you know that?" her voice was stronger.

"We are memory readers. When we aren't actively using it we have a tendency to pick up certain thoughts and images," Serenity ripped part of the girl's shirt and used the strip to tie her wrists together. "A full-blooded Lamashtu would never have gone down this easily so what are you? Half? Quarter?"

"Eighth, on my father's side. He couldn't be one himself, but he held the genes, and they were passed to my sister and me."

"What happened to your sister?" I asked, watching my own sibling.

"She was killed eight years ago by a Lazarus-"

"Lie," Serenity hissed. "The Lazari are gatekeepers, non-combatant."

"Then why did the Council tell me one killed her? She was barely thirteen years old," the semi-demon glared at us with glazed orange and green eyes. I sort of felt sorry for her, even though she had tried to kill us.

Serenity stood and pulled her coat back on. "You must have an ability that they saw as too valuable to destroy. The Council knows that the only way to turn one of us against our kind is to pin the death of a loved one on one of a different species. Personally, I need to brush up on my Sumerian demonology, so would you mind listing any and all major abilities that are common to your particular family line?"

"Why should I tell you? You could be lying to me," suspicion crept into her faintly gritty voice.

"Unless we have to, we don't lie," I shrugged. "Besides, we could have just killed you and walked away. Instead, we're still here, talking to demonikyn, while we could, and should, be moving along to our next hidey hole." Not that they're actually *holes*...

"My great-grandmother is one of the seven original Lamashtu, though she prefers to be called a Dimme. Since no male can be Lamashtu, she taught my sister and I the gift of her line after our father died since we were the first ones born with the ability to use them," she scooted against the wall and relaxed an iota. "She taught us how to cast a glamour over the minds of humans so large and powerful that war could be going on around them and they would not know anything was wrong; even if they were missing a limb, dying, or already dead."

"Ouch, no wonder they wanted you," I winced. "How long have you been a Hunter?"

"My sister was murdered eight years ago," she shrugged as though she had become a Hunter soon after.

"And would you like true vengeance? Against those who really killed her?" Serenity asked, placing a hand on my shoulder. She was doing as Aunt Gabi had taught her; using our combined energy to project an image that had never been rejected by one of the blood.

"Yes," the Lamashtu's eyes developed a haze, and her voice became faint.

"Will you join us?" Sere's voice took on a slightly breathy quality.

"Yes," her mouth was still slightly open when glass shattered, and my sister hit the floor with me beneath her; the demon's head no longer intact.

"Well fuck you too, asshole," Serenity growled, grabbing her phone from her pocket and auto-dialing James. "Mind coming in to save our asses, chère?"

"Of course I don't mind, love," he appeared at the other end of the hallway in his six foot, two inches, light brunette glory. "Where do you need me?"

"Anywhere that will keep one of us from potentially taking a bullet."

"Like this?" he appeared above us in the blink of an eye. Lifting us at the same time as though we weighed nothing (which I assure you, we do not), he flitted back to his original position and set us on our feet. "Good?"

"Marvellous," Sere pulled his head down and planted a teasing kiss on his plump lips. "I don't know how we survived before you came along."

"Half-ass job with a lot more injuries?" I suggested, avoiding looking back down the hall as I fiddled with my sister's bag.

Their laugh was cut off by a scream from the main foyer. Exchanging a look, we booted it past the student and used the panicked kids as a shield to hide our escape from the remaining Hunter, or Hunters, wherever he, she or they were hiding. Like most abilities, the glamour had evaporated with the death of the demon girl.

Sirens rent the air as we ducked into James's jeep and peeled away from the mass of confusion. With his near-indestructibility, he made no bones about driving safely or near the speed limit. We were far from the school and on our way out of town before we saw the faintest flash of emergency lights in the distance.

"So much for a clean in-and-out," he joked, slowing slightly as trees began to appear along the sides of the road.

"Can't always be a clean escape, unfortunately," Serenity caressed his face.

I gagged a little at the display of affection. Lovey-dovey crap nauseated me.

James pulled off the road and waited for what little traffic there was to disappear. When it was clear, he turned and drove through what should have been a copse of solid trees. Instead, their image wavered as we drove over the projectors hidden just beneath the ground.

"We'll leave just after dusk," he announced before hitting the brakes. Rolling down the windows, he sniffed the air, and I barely caught the look he exchanged with my sister before the acrid stench of smoke invaded my nostrils.

He was out the door and running toward the safe house before I could blink; back less than ten seconds later. He hopped in, shook his head, and peeled away in reverse so fast I had to hang on for dear life or be thrown out the side. Tightening the lap belt, I shrank in the seat out of habit. It also helped me listen in on the conversation up front.

"Based on how far gone it was, they hit it while we were at the school," James hit the brakes and swung the jeep around when we hit the main road.

"How did they know about that place? That she didn't die?" my sister had her phone out and was furiously typing away.

"They may have been after you," he dropped into drive and sped away from town. "The mark they carved in the ground was Old Celtic for 'one down, one to go'."

"How many people in this day and age still know Old Celtic?"

"Darling, do you really need to ask that?"

"I supposed not," she smiled, looking up from her phone. "How about I rephrase? How many *Hunters* do we know that actively use dead or nearly dead languages?"

"Last I checked, none," he eased off the gas a little. "I'll ask the elders when we arrive. Have you heard from our contact yet?"

"No, and neither has his handler. She emailed me his last known location, so we'll start looking when we get within walking distance."

He nodded and shifted most of his attention to the road as my sister fidgeted with a ring I had somehow failed to notice on her third finger. It was a beautiful piece, sedate, but it probably cost a fortune. Though, how one calculates a fortune depends on how long one has been amassing it and at what rate. In James's case, he had been collecting for over five thousand years. He had witnessed the rise and fall of empires; the birth (and occasionally death) of religions; the advancement and devolution of the human condition. Politely, he was old as dirt and twice as handsome. Not the oldest supernatural I knew, not by a long shot, but up there with the best of them.

Unbuckling my belt (illegal move, I know) I curled up in the backseat and passed out. A cool hand touching the back of my neck jolted me awake hours later. The jeep was still and silent; the full moon sitting lazily in the sky as a small smattering of clouds dropped the last of their load of snow and dissipated. We were on the edge of a cliff, and a vast forest of unknowns stretched before us.

2

I checked my watch and frowned as my sister told me we were on Vancouver Island. Don't ask me how, but we had somehow driven from Calgary to Vancouver in time to catch the last boat to Victoria. In a lot less time than we should have. My stomach rumbled in a protest of hunger and a feeling as though my internal organs were being turned into molten lava heralded the early onset of my particular brand of bloodlust.

Serenity held a semi-recently microwaved gas station burrito out to me, followed by a giant cinnamon bun and an even bigger coffee. Devouring it all and chugging the coffee, I licked my fingers clean when I was done.

"Sorry about the hungers. I had to borrow a lot of energy from you to get us here faster," my sister tossed the garbage in the far back of the jeep. "We have a problem though. Our contact for safe passage to Sanctuary hasn't been heard from in long enough that his handler is about to have their security protocols tightened."

"Tightened how?"

"Total lockdown until he is found, which could be never."

"Shit."

"Indeed," James muttered, holding up a finger to silence us. "Hellhounds."

I frowned. Hellhounds were the pets of Ares, god of war and embodiment of fertility of mountainous areas. None of the other deities had ever figured out why he had created the mutated mutts. Not that they cared to get close enough to ask. Like the matter that he had been created from, he was unforgiving at the best of times; and a raging lunatic the rest. Not that you could really blame his after nine hundred and eighty million years. Give or take a couple of millennia.

"Do you think Ares has a hand in this?" Serenity whispered.

"Doubtful," James shook his head. "We have invoked sanctuary, and it has been granted. If he tries to harm us, even indirectly, he's done. There was, however, a rumour of a theft from his home a couple of decades ago, though. We always thought it was just someone trying to talk themselves up in the underground."

A lot of the concepts they tossed back and forth were over my head, or before my time. Ignoring them for the moment, I pulled off my shoes and socks and wiggled my toes in the near-freezing grass. Not that it actually felt cold to me, given that my natural body temperature is around 8° Celsius.

Extending my senses out through the soles of my feet, I ignored the heartbeats closest to me and searched for the ones not familiar. The closest ones were slow and steady in sleep, but there was a cluster down the cliff and a short distance into the woods that were rapid and moving. Pulling my extra "senses" back, I opened my eyes and let out a small whimper as the bloodlust ate away the last of my control and the pain of it multiplied.

"Near the estuary, off the cliff and in the woods," I gasped. "Two dogs, eight humanoids and a snake moving. One humanoid near an ancient cedar."

"How much energy do you have left?" Serenity set a hand gently against the back of my neck.

A shuddering set in then abruptly stopped as I felt a shift in my eyes. It felt like the red ring was expanding, but I couldn't be sure. "Not nearly enough," the demonic tone mocked me. "Let me feast or watch this world burn until nothing is left alive."

"Uh, yih, no. No way in hell. Amelia, if you can still hear me bè-be, think moderation. A little bit from each to tide you over, then we'll make sure you get some of the good stuff soon, okay?"

The two immortal aspects of my being warred while my humanity sat on the back burner. Personally, I've never seen it, but when the good and evil parts of me decide to have a powwow over control, the red and purple in my irises play tag until one engulfs the other. Purple eyes mean the angel won and I can keep from causing unnecessary deaths. Red means my internal vampire was in too much of a mood, read: starving, to not indulge in some homicidal mayhem. Blue would mean pure humanity had control, and that hasn't happened as I have never renounced my non-human heritage. And silver, the final ring in my quad-coloured eyes, which has also never happened, would signify the unity of my three aspects for a single purpose. Standing there on the cliff top, I could feel the all-consuming hunger win out as my demon beat my compassion into submission.

I cocked my head to the right and studied my sister through predator's eyes. Her veins lit up and I could almost taste the coppery tang of her pulse on my tongue. Shaking my head, I grinned at James as my canines elongated and I took a single step backwards; pushing off with my other foot and falling over the edge.

The *whoosh* of air rushing past my ears was exhilarating; free fall made my blood sing in warning that trees were approaching. The first tree's upper branches brushed my legs and my muscles bunched; curling my arms and legs in as I twisted so that the ground was visible. Outstretched tree limbs careened past and slowed my descent as they grew closer together. My arms extended at random and grabbed a bough my heightened senses instinctively knew was strong enough to halt my momentum and support my weight.

My pulse danced on my tongue as I brought my feet up and crouched, hidden in the trees. Two seconds later a soft *womph* came from a couple trees over, followed by the branch in front of me swaying on impact. Fangs and eyes of electric blue fire flashed a smile before James silently monkeyed his way over to my sister. Taking a peek at them, they nodded in my general direction. Waiting for me to make the first move.

There was still about thirty feet between us and the ground. The scent of pine whisked along the breeze...blowing the wrong way. Serenity and James realised it the moment I did and we dropped from branch to branch as quickly as we could. The rough bark bit into my feet and left my toes raw as I ran out of branches and had to slide down the last twelve feet.

The ground was soft and loamy, silencing our landing. They split off and disappeared into the darkness as I bolted to the left. Trees seemed to be outlined in silver as I flew past them; logs on the ground there but not obstacles. We were silent in our approach and I smiled at the carnage to come.

I could smell them and came to a stop about ten feet away. Undoing a couple of buttons on my blouse, I fluffed my hair a little and stepped into view. The man did a double-take and lowered his gun, taking his hand off it. Perfect.

"Are you lost, miss? The woods aren't a safe place to be at night," his voice was a deep bass.

"I was here earlier with my friend but we got separated and I lost the path," my voice was sweet as honey as I moved toward his six-foot-eight frame.

"Where are your shoes? You could get hurt out here," he stepped in my direction.

"Back at our campsite. I've been wandering for hours, trying to find my way back," he was almost within arm's reach. He took another step and I pounced; wrapping my legs around his barrel chest and getting a death grip on his head, my fangs tearing through his throat.

The hot tang of his blood, pumping furiously down my throat as he struggled, kicked my bloodlust higher and I snapped his neck. Riding him to the ground, I bounced up from his silent landing and pasted myself to a tree as his radio chirped a useless warning and screams sounded in the distance.

A branch snapped behind me and a little to the left. I waited for the person to step into view, see me, see my eyes and realise he was going to die, before grabbing his gun and pulling his short, skinny frame to his knees. He was young, like he hadn't filled out completely. Old enough to know better, though, which meant he was probably a Blue-Blood Hunter.

I didn't feed from him. No, being a generational he didn't deserve the honour of being food. Instead I ripped his arms out of their sockets and used them to beat his skull in. His screams were pitiful and a demonic laugh escaped my blood-speckled lips. Part of me pulled away in revulsion as I dropped the limbs and walked away, toward the fighting. Years of anger and frustration surged and I tore through everyone and everything that got in my way; a haze clouding my mind to the details.

My demon sated, someone, likely my sister, hit me in the back of the head hard enough to knock me out. Oh the dreams I had, of blood and death and carnage of aeons passed. Had it not felt so real and familiar, it may have been a good tactical study. As it was, a single, final death sent me back to the real world in a cold sweat.

The probable concussion I likely got as a result of waking up I claim full responsibility for. Especially since I sat up straight into the back of Serenity's head. Flopping back down, I draped my left arm over my eyes and tried to ignore the new throb near my right temple.

“Full?” her voice was disembodied above me.

“As a well-fed kitten,” I licked my lips.

“I'm never going to look at my cat the same way again,” a new, vaguely feminine, but distinctly male voice came from the front seat.

“If you die in a locked apartment or house and a cat runs out of food, it will eat your decomposing body to survive,” the fun fact burst from my lips in a deadpan tone.

“If that delivery were any creepier, I'd jump to the side of the road right now,” the passenger seat creaked as he shifted.

“Don't worry, I won't kill you. I don't like killing people,” I sat up, slowly this time, and pulled the seatbelt into place.

“Could have fooled me. You shredded those Hunters and almost started dancing in their parts.”

“That was only one part of me. Normally I'm not like that.”

“If you think so.”

“I have to believe it. Otherwise I'm just another monster.”

“Sometimes, being a monster is the only thing that will keep you alive.”

“If being a monster, giving in, is the only way to stay alive then I'd rather die and get it over with.”

He had no comeback for that. Not many people do. We drove in silence for hours, and if you asked what I saw outside the window, all I could tell you is darkness. The few traffic lights we passed were magically green as we flew under them. Cities, if you could call them that, gave way to mountains and pure silver moonlight reflected off of snow so clean it could almost have been midday.

Mindless drifting, detachment even, caused me to miss a quiet exchange as we slowed. A sign appeared at the side of the road, indicating that we weren't too far from a town. Hanging a right at the intersection, if you could call it that, we drive through where a town should have been.

“Wha-” I shook my head, unable to complete the thought.

“The corner back there is the current boundary of our destination,” the passenger answered. “We slid through a sliver of an anomaly in space.”

“How do others not find this place then?” I eased back into my seat; the motion of sliding forward in the first place being an automatic gesture.

“We have a guardian, trained by the four gods of air, who can feel the approach of all her disciples. She opens the portals for a bare moment to allow us entry,” his voice held a note of reverence mixed with cult-like fervour.

“The guardian would be whom, exactly? And guardian of what? Prison?” Snide sarcasm, that's not me.

“The Lady Arcturus. She is the Guardian of Sanctuary, and protector of the air.”

“Never heard of her,” I shrugged. “Why is this sanctuary special enough to have a guardian? All the others are just on specially consecrated ground.”

"This specific sanctuary is not a fixed location. It is known to our kind as *Insula Templum*," James glanced in his rear-view mirror. "Because it can move through space, and on very rare occasions time, it needs supernatural safeguards. All residents of Sanctuary are vital to the balance –"

"Not yet," Serenity cut him off.

"She'll find out soon enough," he pulled the jeep slowly to a stop on a wooden platform. "She needs to know."

"Not fucking yet," she snarled.

"Why not?" he growled back.

"Because she'll flare and every creepy crawly that has ever hunted us will be able to find this place. So long as it is anchored, it can be found if there's a signal," she snapped back. Wow, a fight in paradise. Mark the calendar.

We lurched forward as James cut the engine. The air around us got thick and fuzzy as the temperature rose. No one else seemed to be affected as I broke out in a cold sweat. Black spots appeared in my dimming sight before darkness pulled me under.

There were no dreams for me that night, pleasant or otherwise. Just blackness, suffocating, unending blackness. Nowhere to run from or to. No Hunters bent on total destruction. No Hellhounds. No mom or Serenity. Not even a whisper from dad. There was absolutely nothing. I screamed at the darkness; tried to hit it with my fists but they found nothing but air. Eventually I collapsed to the dark 'ground' in exhaustion. I gave up trying to avoid the nothingness and smiled when it enveloped me in a warm, tender hug.

3

A cold draft caressing my skin and hushed whispers, barely louder than a murmur, woke me. My eyes opened a crack and I surveyed the room before opening them fully. A small fire flickered in the black and white marble fireplace about fifteen feet from the foot of the canopied bed I lay in. The Whisperers were standing in the shadows by the open floor-to-ceiling window. Serenity sat curled into a chair between the bed and the door; James not far from her, but not far from the others, either.

"You're awake," one of the shadow people spoke up. His voice was like velvet rubbing against the back of my eyes. He and his companion stepped into the dim light. Sitting up, I frowned at them.

I was taken aback by their beauty. And they were beautiful. One had hair a mix of gold and bronze, the other mahogany mixed with ruby red. They had skin made pale by the inability to create melanin in sunlight, much like albinos in their colour. What truly struck me was their eyes. Their vibrant blue, tri-coloured eyes.

"We are like you."

"Yet different."

"Where you are unique."

"We are...simple."

"Your ancestry is well known."

"To us, but not to many."

"Fuck off you two, speak normally," Serenity grumbled from her chair. "You're giving me a headache."

"As you wish, my dear," the dark-haired one chuckled. "I am Blair. This is my brother, Colby. Welcome to Sanctuary."

"Home of the orphans, misfits, and dumb asses who just don't know any better," Colby added.

"You'll be safe here for as long as you wish to stay. Classrooms are on floors four through twenty-three; the food court is in sub-basement two. Floors twenty-four through thirty-six, this one, is housing for our guests and the thirty-seventh is ours," Blair took a chair near the fireplace. "The first floor is the atrium that has a bulletin board to inform of cancellations and special activities. It is also the access to our grounds. Floors two and three are common areas for gaming and relaxation. Sub-basement one is our main medical floor and the main basement is supply storage."

"That's a lot to remember," I grimaced.

"It's all in the pocket book in your nightstand," Colby draped himself over the chair to his brother's right.

"Handy," I glanced at the oak table.

"Also, the thirty-fifth floor converts to an overflow ICU in case of training accident."

"Do those happen often?" I asked, shuddering.

"They don't happen often, but they aren't uncommon either," Colby shrugged. "This place isn't, strictly, a rigid structure in the common world."

"It's bigger on the inside that it looks on the out?"

"Indeed. From the ground it looks to be no more than eight storeys," Colby smiled, flashing fangs for a moment. "Some of the floors have twenty-foot ceilings; others are the current standard of eight."

"Nifty. Where's the library?"

"Separate building on the grounds. It has two doors, but one of them will only open if you've been granted special permissions in the security system," James supplied. "The secure library here makes a mockery of every library I've seen in the human world. Hell, the Dead Sea Scrolls are in magnificent condition for their age."

"A little piece of home?" I teased. He was older than the scrolls by at least three thousand years.

"Almost. They have the contents of the Library of Alexandria in there, though. It's absolutely beautiful."

"A little homesick?"

"If only. My people were the Neolithic druids, not the Sumerians," he shrugged. "Modern science hasn't caught up to the concept that we were civilized and didn't need a written information system."

"That's enough for now," Serenity eased out of her chair. "Amelia needs to get up and moving if she's going to attend any classes today. And she needs to read the handbook of rules to abide by."

"Very true," Colby nodded. "We shall leave you to it and check in after the dinner hour."

"Also, Amelia, if you feel any hint of bloodlust, let someone know. We have very strict rules about feeding on the unwilling here," Blair added before standing with his brother and disappearing out the open window.

"Those two are just a little creepy," I raised an eyebrow at my sister. "What are they?"

"Vampires, very old-school vampires," she shuddered. "No one but them knows how old they really are. They're older than Jamie and fully developed, that's all I know."

"Fucking weird."

"You get used to it," she replied lightly.

"Really?"

"No."

"How long was I out this time?"

"A week, give or take. Maybe two. Stopped counting."

"Still 2008?"

"Not long until Grinchmas."

"Solstice pass yet?"

"Tomorrow."

"Ritual sacrifice?"

"Next year. Didn't have time to find one this time."

"Damn."

“I know. You have about two hours before the sun rises and breakfast is at eight o'clock sharp,” she moved toward the door.

“Have we been here before?” the question was out of my mouth before I could stop it.

“Technically, no. Mom brought me here once when I was seven; you hadn't been born yet. We stayed for a few days and she signed something that Blair and Colby gave her, but she never told me what it was. After we got home and you were born she and dad had a huge fight about it and she kicked him out,” James wrapped an arm around her shoulders as she rested a hand on the doorknob.

“Why do I feel like I've been here before then?”

“I have no idea. Latent memory from a previous incarnation, maybe. Get dressed, read the book. We'll be across the hall if you need anything.”

“Thanks.”

She nodded as they slid through the door. I flung the light sheets off and eased out of the insanely comfortable bed. The room was surprisingly warm for having a massive window open in the pre-dawn hours. Somehow, it didn't feel like winter in the northern hemisphere. The air didn't taste right.

I ducked through the open closet door and ran my hands over the carefully organized clothes. They were colour-coded according to material and style. Pants, capris, shorts, and varying styles of skirts were on the left; jackets, coats, and shirts on the right and shoes on the back wall above an antique dresser.

I went to the dresser first and opened the drawers. The socks were still in their packages and the underwear still had the tags attached. Price section removed, though. They were all my size and very soft. I picked a pair at random, a bra that didn't match, and black ankle socks. Off the wall, a set of beautiful knee-high, black suede high heels found their way into my hands. On my way back to the main room I grabbed a pair of loose black capris and a long sleeved blood red shirt.

Sitting on the edge of the bed, I got dressed before reaching into the nightstand and retrieving the guide book. It was small and bound in very old leather. Opening it, I smiled.

Rules: Read, Understand, Obey – or Die!

(Someone definitely had a sense of humour.)

1. Do nothing that may bring harm to another.

Almost all other rules are simplifications of this.

a) No feeding on the unwilling.

b) No reading thoughts without permission.

c) No absorbing memories without permission.

d) No attempting to heal without supervision and extensive training.

e) No mental bonding without consent.

f) No soul bonding. Period. That's it. Finito. End of discussion.

g) Betray another who has been granted Sanctuary and you will die.

2. Certain areas are restricted. Don't try to go near them. It could get very ugly.

3. Sanctuary is a floating fortress. Days are twelve hours long. Breakfast is at 8 am sharp. Classes start at 9.

4. Gym lockers shift dimensions based on which class is in. Do not forget anything in your locker as you cannot retrieve it until the next day.

Most of the rest of the guide was just where classes were, who taught what, and a great list of consequences for those who broke the rules. A gentle chime came from everywhere and nowhere, only stopping when I looked at the clock. It was an antique table clock, sitting on the mantle above the fireplace. Something about it made me smile. I looked away until the chime sounded again. I frowned until the time registered in my mind. I had fifteen minutes until breakfast. Putting the book back, I climbed out of bed and went to the door. The lights behind me dimmed as I stepped into the long, decadent hallway. And decadent it was.

The feeling, the warmth of the hall was like liquefied velvet running down my spine. It felt like home, and I liked it. It may have been a trick of the eyes, but the gilt elevator doors seemed to be a good thirty feet closer than the blink before. My mind hazed a little at the illusion, but I shook it off and moved to the now-open doors. The interior was a rich red that seemed to be illuminated from within.

Stepping inside, I frowned at the smooth walls. Not a single button interrupted the perfect surface.

"Breakfast?" a light, chipper male voice echoed in the empty box.

"Umm, yes?" I raised an eyebrow.

A lithe figure appeared before me, like a slow fade-in. He started as nothing more than a vague outline and filled in quickly. Clearing six feet easily, he had auburn hair and electric green eyes.

"Hermes, messenger and punching bag of the universe, at your service," he inclined his head. "The elevator operates on a telepathic interface which only activates if you're over sixteen million years old."

"That would suck if you all happened to be sick at the same time," I smiled. "Amelia. My first, conscious, day here."

"Hartley?"

"Yeah."

"Serenity come with you?"

"Never go anywhere without her."

"How's she doing? Did she go through the change?"

"Three years ago. She's good. Engaged. Pain in the ass."

"Sounds like good old her."

"You know her?"

"I met her before you were born, when your mom brought her here. We kept in touch while she was growing up. The little sprout was the best part of my week when she was here."

"Hmm." The doors slid open. I hadn't felt us move at all.

"Breakfast hall. If you ever get lost just look for the elevator doors. Whoever is on shift will help you without question."

"Thanks, Hermes."

"Anytime, darling."

4

I stepped out of the gilded box into a comparatively plain hallway. It was a shade of peridot that was almost gem quality. It was less than ten metres to a set of oak double doors that were engraved with the scenes of a festival. It was a gorgeous piece of work.

"Tweedle Dumb-bum."

"Yes, Tweedle Dead Dee?"

"I have to pee."

"So go pee!"

"I can't."

"Why not?"

"There's a human type thing blocking the way."

I looked around for the source of the high-pitched conversation. I almost missed the pair of eight-inch tall fairies hovering by my left shoulder.

"Well?" they looked at me expectantly.

"Well what?" I replied slowly.

"Are you going to fucking move or what!"

I frowned at them, taken aback by their language, and was about to step out of the way when the elevator doors opened. The aura hit me first. It was a pulsating, living wall of energy that wrapped me in a cloud of warmth. The body that followed was flawless. Orange and yellow eyes sat in a face of early Greek perfection, tanned a light gold.

"Draconis," he inclined his head before frowning at the tiny creatures. "Back to your gardens you twits." His voice was deep and smooth.

The fairies vanished with a shrug.

"Name or species?"

"You're new here," his plump lips twitched up.

"First day," I shrugged.

"My apologies. The guide book doesn't cover everything," he nodded to the doors behind me. "Let us eat and we shall talk. As for your question, Draconis is my species. The simplest version of my name, that is pronounceable, is Daniel."

"Pleasure to meet you," I followed his broad shoulders into the surprisingly quiet hall. Everyone within thirty feet of the door looked up, and I immediately felt like fresh meat. Half of the gazes were obviously predatory, and they set off my unfed, angry, vaguely evil other part. "Ye might not want to stand right in front of me right now."

"Eyes on your food, or you will be food," Daniel barked, a wave of iron-fisted control splashing over me, and possibly the others. It calmed my hunger and left me feeling...satisfied. Everyone looked away immediately.

"Thank you."

"Do not thank me yet. You will need to satiate your blood hunger before the day is out."

"It hasn't been fed in a week, ish, so quite probably," I shrugged.

"And you are not feeling the madness?" he raised a perfectly arched eyebrow at me.

"I'm a mongrel hybrid. Old Fangy is the least of my parts."

A short, sharp laugh escaped his lips. "Old Fangy?"

"The gift of my father's side," I followed him to the buffet style food area. Dishing small amounts of everything that looked good onto a handy plate, I grabbed a fork and made my way to an empty table. Daniel followed silently.

"Do you know your species?" he asked after cleaning his plate.

"No. If there's anyone alive who knows, I either haven't found them, or they've been unwilling to tell me," I paused before finishing my eggs.

"What are your parts then?"

"Half human, quarter angel, quarter vampire."

I caught a flicker of recognition in his eyes before he hid it. "The angel accounts for your control. The mix is vaguely familiar, like a legend from the ancient stories of my people."

"Your people?"

"Guardians of the ancient races."

I raised an eyebrow at him. "That doesn't tell me much."

"The Draconi were the original guardians of the Earth-Bringers. Until we came to be feared by the humans, legend says we kept the Ancient Ones safe. When they vanished, their descendants became the charges of the lesser shifters, like the wolves. Now we exist only as guardians of the fledgling gods."

"Why that much of a shift?"

"We were considered too powerful to protect the diluted ones," he leaned back. "You, however, make my bones ache with the need to supplicate."

I laughed at that. "I don't see why. I'm nothing."

"You are young. Your power will come under your control in time."

A frown stretched my face. "How can I have power and not feel it?"

He closed his vibrant eyes and breathed deeply for a moment. I felt the faintest brush of power along my spine before he relaxed.

"Your power is nested. It will remain dormant until it is either awakened by need, or ripped to the surface by Persephone."

"Will it hurt?"

"It almost always does."

"Can I ask – "

"Why I'm here? I'm the last of my kind," he shrugged. "My family was massacred by the Hunters almost four hundred years ago, human time."

“How?! Creatures who guard gods should be damn powerful.”

“All creatures have a weakness. We took an injured human into our home. She had been beaten, badly. Our healers treated her, gave her food. She was with us for a month when they came. She had told them our weakness, stolen the secret by watching the death of one of our elders. No matter what we did, we died. Colby found my sister and me three weeks later. She was still a hatchling, couldn't control her shifting. Because I wasn't old enough, I couldn't freeze her form long enough for her to eat. She died three days after we arrived here.”

“I'm sorry. Losing everyone you care about is hard to recover from.”

“After four hundred years, you get used to it. I can never thank the Elders enough for everything they have done,” he shivered, as though shaking off the past. “As for our original conversation, the guide book is incomplete.”

“So you said,” I sat straighter.

“When you're new, you'll be greeted by all staff and senior residents with their species. The proper reply is your species, but since it is unknown 'hybrid' will do. A sect of vampire halflings do live here, and they walk the halls in cloaks. Do not engage them. They have limited control over their hunger.”

“Sounds like a pretty good warning.”

“Indeed. There are those like me in all rooms except private rooms and bathrooms. We are there to keep the peace. We will not interfere unless Ares is being an asshole or Dyonisus tied on one too many and mixed up his volatile chemicals.”

“Does that happen often?”

“With Dyo? More often than not. We trade shifts as to who is going to watch him for the first few classes of the day.”

“And Ares?”

“Only when he has a wild hare up his ass.”

“Nice image,” I chuckled. He grinned and was about to reply when a gong rang.

“Fifteen-minute warning bell. You'll need to go to the first floor and get your class list before anything else.”

“Thanks. What about supplies? I had to leave everything behind.”

“Books, pens and paper are all in the classrooms,” Daniel smiled a little. “And watch Hermes in the elevator. He has an impossible-to-break habit of peeking into thoughts of a...sexual nature. One would think being married to Mageara would keep his ass in line, but he's a glutton for punishment,” he chuckled before vanishing as people got up and made a push for the door.

Shrugging, I stood and joined the faceless masses headed to the elevator. The doors stood open, and people filed in but it looked empty when it should have been overloaded. I looked around before stepping in.

“This is a dimensional null point. Unless you're going to the same place, you ride the lift alone,” Hermes grinned. “I can also make exceptions to that rule.”

“My brain is feeling a little overloaded,” I rubbed my temples.

“I know. It takes a couple of weeks to get used to it. Atrium. To your right is your class list if you want to just reach out and grab it.”

I poked my head out and a piece of paper with my name on it was indeed within reach. Grabbing it, I looked it over and frowned. I recognized the names, but had not had the pleasure of meeting half of them.

“Athena, English and Literature, floor fifteen. Coming right up,” Hermes read over my shoulder. “Have fun.”

“Thanks,” I muttered, still looking at the page when the doors opened. Stepping out, I walked right into a set of very solid, broad shoulders. “'Scuse me.”

The person moved without saying anything and I kept moving toward the front of the room. Putting the paper in my pocket, I looked around for Athena and found nothing but confused stares.

"Did you know that you used to be knee-high to a grasshopper?" a tinkling, melodic voice came from behind me.

"A mutated grasshopper, maybe," I turned, smiling. "Long time no see Athena."

"What's it been? Eight years?" the auburn-and-honey tressed goddess wrapped her long arms around my shoulders.

"Almost to the day," I hugged her back. She felt...safe, like my mom used to. "How have you been?"

"Good, sorry. I've been well," she pulled away. "For being a know-it-all, sometimes I forget to switch between colloquial and proper English."

"Speak colloquially," I laughed. "Class hasn't started yet."

"True," she smiled. "We should toss some of the required materials in your general direction, though. Just a warning, we are doing an in-depth study of Hamlet right now."

I cringed. "I love Hamlet, but I just did him."

"You did the human bastardization of him," she replied, smiling sweetly. "Who do you think Shakespeare got his spark from? I pointed at some general source material, put the bug in his brain, and locked him in a room with food, water and a good old chamberpot."

I groaned. "How long was the original?"

"Eight hundred pages, plus or minus a paragraph."

"And we have to read all of it?"

"You have to *act* all of it."

"Fuck me sideways..."

"Thanks for the offer, but I'll just fuck your mind," Athena laughed. "You don't have to do the first hundred and fifty pages since we already covered them. We'll be reviewing the next two hundred over the next week, and starting on the next hundred and fifty pages the week after that."

"My brain is going to explode."

"I know. Once we start you should be able to settle right in."

"I hope so. With all the moves I've been having trouble concentrating."

"It's okay. Some of our residents arrive here unable to read or write because the Hunters broke their own laws and chased them from birth."

"Shitty deal."

"Indeed. You'll catch up, in time."

Soft chimes broke in on our conversation. I almost jumped out of my skin at the sound, while Athena just smiled.

"Second row from the left, third seat from the back. Pen and paper are waiting."

5

Taking the seat she assigned me, I picked up a pen and scribbled my name in the upper left corner. Athena jumped right in and selected random people to answer questions that had me lost by the third sentence. My brain was fogging out when two notes appeared in front of me in two vastly different sets of handwriting.

The first one was short and semi-sweet; *'Bored yet?'*. The other was in a more elegant script, though quite blunt: *'You smell different'*. The first one I scrawled back *'More like lost'*, the other one I followed Daniel's advice and just wrote *'Hybrid'* back. They vanished and reappeared a few moments later, same sets of writing on the pages.

'Hybrid what?' I frowned at that. *'I know the parts but not the whole.'*

'Want help finding the way?' My frown flashed into a smile for a moment. *'The light that leads need not always be a brightness in the dark.'*

The first one, with the elegant writing, didn't come back again. The other one came back with a frown and a question mark. I tucked it under my half-full page of random notes I didn't realize I was actually keeping. My hand started moving of its own volition, taking notes of the highlights. I frowned, unable to reclaim control of my arm.

A new note in the sloppier handwriting appeared. *'Your arm shouldn't be doing that'*, it read. *'Notes that detailed take a long time to make a habit of.'*

I shrugged at the room in general, not knowing who kept writing the notes. By the scrawl, the owner was male, other than that he could have been anyone. A new one arrived, and it was fairly simple. *'Look right. My name is Graham.'* I did, and had to stifle a giggle as he mimed dying over his books. Flat-ish brown hair was buzzed short and left otherwise impeccable ears stranded on the sides of his slightly oblong face. He was not handsome, by any stretch of the imagination. His eyes, though...they were disconcerting. One was green and blue; the other was blue and brown.

Chimes broke in and Athena stopped mid-sentence, my arm with her. I put the pen down and was about to grab my notes when a thick binder appeared around them.

"It's automatic for all new students," the orange-haired girl in front of me nodded at the binder. Her kaleidoscope eyes were bright, intelligent, in her semi-feline face. "My name is Nicole."

"Amelia," I responded automatically. "I'd shake your hand, but I might absorb some of your memories, and the guidebook said that's a major no-no."

"It's okay. Do the Caretakers know about your memory reading?" she asked, offering me her fully covered arm.

"Yeah. It's genetic on my mother's side," I took it and stood, grabbing the binder with my free hand. "She and my sister came here before I was born."

"They should have left you with gloves then, to avoid accidents," Nicole steered me to the elevator.

"They forgot, I guess," I shrugged. "Do you mind my asking your species?"

"Chymera-human hybrid."

"The Chymera are analysts, aren't they?"

"We are. I haven't finished my training yet, but I can tell that you are new, yet ancient," she stopped us at the back of the elevator line. "Your species has not been seen for thousands of years, and from you all others descend."

She vanished into the crowd before I could press her for more.

"She does that," a faintly gritty voice rumbled in my ear, making me jump.

"Graham," I fiddled with my new binder. "Word to the wise, never come up behind me if you value the current placement of your head."

His odd eyes widened and he took two steps to the left. “Sometimes I forget that most new arrivals are still in survival mode.”

“It's not survival mode, so much as an ingrained habit,” I shrugged, stepping into Hermes's Highway to Hell.

“I heard that,” the god muttered in my ear. “Getting in or what, Graham? Next stop, Ares on eight.”

He joined us, and I'm fairly sure Hermes blew the dimension wall on purpose for the thought he shouldn't have been listening to in the first place. I sent a very rude mental image his way as a 'thank you' for the bumpy ride as soon as the doors opened. His answering laugh was darkly playful.

Stepping into the classroom of my least favourite immortal, I frowned at the lack of seating. Daniel appeared from thin air on my right and held out a pair of fitted black leather gloves.

“The Elders apologize for their oversight. They can block a reader from accessing their memories, and so often forget that others can not,” he smiled.

Taking them gingerly, I tucked my binder between my knees and pulled the supple material over my hands and half-grinned as they molded to my skin.

“I will be the safeguard this class. If you feel the hunger, let me know,” he vanished between blinks. The rest of the class assembled and removed their shoes. Following their lead, I took my boots off and placed them on my binder. A door on the other side of the room, across the sea of blue mats, opened and Ares strode through in his 7'2", stick-up-his-ass glory. His red eyes were blazing in semi-controlled fury.

“Mats, partners, now!” he barked, his dark cheeks mottled.

No one hesitated as they paired up into, probably, familiar groups. Mats were filled until there was only one left, and only I had no partner to join me on it. Looking around, everyone was watching Ares, waiting for his next orders.

He watched me carefully for a moment. “Why the fuck are you here? Mongrels like you don't deserve Sanctuary.”

Daniel cut in from the wall before I could answer. “The Caretakers open our doors to all in need, not just those you choose.”

“Fuck you Dragon.”

“In your dreams, wide ass.”

A couple of people choked back giggles. Smart on their parts. Ares was/is/probably always will be, a very unforgiving, short-tempered, closeted asshole.

“Are you still sour over my killing that mutated mutt you sent after my mom four years ago?” I taunted him, just for shits and giggles. Probably a bad idea, in hindsight.

His fist connected with my jaw before I could blink. Whether it was his hand, or the bones in my face that went *crunch*, I'm not sure, but the force of it snapped my head back and dropped me on my ass. Laying there for a moment, I gingerly tested my jaw with a fingertip. It wasn't broken, but it hurt like hell. Old Fangy reacted to the pain and the trickle of blood coming from the inside of my cheek.

“You hit like an untrained leprechaun,” my demon laughed. “When did you turn into such a wuss?”

“When did you start drinking blood?” he countered.

Standing slowly, I smiled at him, and it wasn’t pretty. “The day my mother died,” I lost my cool a little and launched myself at him.

He barely moved out of the way in time. Turning, I barely avoided him landing another blow to my head. Grabbing his arm before he could pull it back, I used it as leverage to land a kick to his throat. Ares stumbled, but didn’t fall.

“You’ve gotten better,” he wheezed. “Too bad you’re still going to die a horrible death.”

I bit him. Fangs, fury, I made it hurt. It was just on his forearm, but his muscles seized and he collapsed to his knees.

Extracting my teeth, I was about to go for his throat when new, fresh, heavenly smelling blood tempted my olfactory towards a new target.

Daniel had his left arm out, a thin line of deep red, luscious blood trickling from a shallow cut just about his wrist. Between blinks I was to him, wrapping my fingers around his hand and elbow as much as I was able; watching carefully for any sign of reticence. Seeing none, I slowly licked the coppery-sweet trail from its end to its source. The slice had already started to close, so I nicked it with the tip of a fang and fresh blood welled out.

His right hand stroked the back of my head as I fed. He was very careful to close off his memories, seeming to understand that I could not control the 'download' when I was not actually in control.

"Send Hermes for the Caretakers," Daniel addressed someone behind me.

"No need." Colby's voice broke my single-minded need for blood. "We were monitoring this class just in case this did happen."

Colby stepped into my line of sight and held a hand out to me. Breaking away from Daniel's arm, I took it and stood.

"We should have known that Ares would start something," Blair's voice came from behind me. "His only reason for hating your family, aside from the fact that he hates everyone, is your ties to Persephone, and through her, Hades."

"He hates knowing that hurting you hurts Seph, and would result in Hades nailing his ass to the rock up there with Prometheus," Colby didn't seem to notice my shiver at the titan's name. "Your classes are cancelled for the rest of the day. You need to feed fully, and we need to have a talk with Seph. Everyone else, you now have this period free until Ares is fit to teach again."

Cheers went up at that announcement. The class dissipated quickly until only Colby, Blair, Daniel and I remained.

Colby still had my hand, but they were all looking at me like I had sprouted a second head.

"We were not expecting such a violent reaction to His Assholishness," Blair finally broke the silence.

"Neither was I," I shrugged. "Must have been tied to my being hungry."

"Perhaps," Daniel shrugged himself. "Your power flared when he hit you, as though it recognised him as more than just a threat."

"Serenity would kill you for telling her that much," Colby chuckled. "She tried to shelter her too much. It's dangerous."

"Why would my power recognise him?" I asked Daniel.

He glanced at the ancient vampires before answering. "There is a myth, an old legend from my people, of a being called the All Mother. She was impossibly old, yet eternally young. It was told that she was the one who created the immortals, and some of the guardian races to protect those who did not understand how to protect themselves."

"Guardian races like yours?"

"And the Lazari. The dimensions used to be open for access to all, until she crafted a solution. Too many innocents were falling through into other worlds, so she narrowed their access points to well-hidden doors. Over time she drew away from her creations, until one day, about ten thousand years ago, she vanished."

"What happened to her?"

"Not here," Colby's fingers tightened momentarily on my hand. "This room, as secure as it is, is not secure enough to continue speaking of Her."

"Where is?" I asked as they led me to the elevator. Daniel picked up my boots and binder on the way. Hermes wasn't in the elevator when we arrived.

"When class is in session he goes to the library," Blair supplied. "Colby and I have a little over five million years on him."

"How old are you two?" I raised an eyebrow at them.

"At last check? One billion, nine hundred and thirty-five million, two hundred and seventeen thousand, eight hundred and eighty-one years," Colby grinned, with just a hint of fang.

"Eighty-three," Blair corrected.

"When did I lose two years?"

"The sixties."

"Ah. The sixties were fun."

"Indeed they were."

The doors opened to the thirty-sixth floor and a new door came into existence on the opposite wall. It looked sturdy, even from a distance. The ancients led me toward it in near silence. Daniel knocked on my sister's door and waited for her and James to join our party. I could feel when they joined us, but they didn't speak as Blair opened the new room.

There was a circle carved into the stone floor, symbols of what could have been a cousin to human Enochian inside it. The room felt safe, warm. Leather chairs sat about a foot outside the circle's edge. Colby released my hand as the others took random seats.

"Do not step inside the circle," a female voice came from the shadows to the left of the room. "It reacts to power, both active and dormant."

"Why do I get the feeling we aren't in Kansas, or in this case Canada, anymore?" I followed her instructions and carefully kept away from the cage.

"Welcome to Hades," lights came to life around her. "My name is Persephone."

6

Persephone was beautiful. Blood-ocher hair highlighted moonlight skin, with purple and blue eyes sitting like sparkling gems in her delicate face. Barefoot, she looked to be around five feet, eight inches tall.

"Danielseraphnietzurgatezranasoph, you feel it, don't you?" she was watching Daniel closely. He nodded but didn't speak.

I stifled a smile at his name. No wonder he shortened it to Daniel.

"Sit. Hades and Tisiphone will be here soon," she stayed across the room from me as I moved to an empty seat. It half felt like someone was guiding me to the one that was slightly darker than all the others. As soon as I sat two people popped into chairs beside the vampires.

Hades was unmistakeable; white hair with a black statement-stripe at the front fell to his shoulders, framing his angular face and startling purple and yellow eyes. If it were possible (which, apparently it was), he had less colour in his skin than the near-albino blood-suckers. I couldn't be sure with him sitting, but he looked to be at least six and a half feet tall.

The other figure was a mystery; their entire body covered by a thick, dark cloak. Nothing peeked out for even the barest moment as cloth redraped itself.

With no chairs left, Persephone perched on her husband's lap and the lights dimmed enough that we could still see, but not in great detail. I looked around at our secret assembly and wondered what the fuck I had gotten myself into.

"Before we begin, I would like to make it clear that I object to this," Serenity broke the silence that had fallen.

"We know, and understand why. However, she needs to know and the time is long past for keeping secrets from her," the cloaked figure, woman, spoke with a honey-rich voice. Tisiphone.

"But why now? Why not next week?" Sere continued/complained.

“Because Ares struck her, and the power she contains recognised him, tried to reabsorb him,” Daniel sat forward in his chair. “Never in my life did I ever think I would meet one, let alone two.”

“Two what?” I looked at him and my sister.

“Creators,” Hades’s deep, bassy voice rumbled through my bones.

“Creators?” I raised an eyebrow at that.

“The ancient race that my species were guardians of,” Daniel studied me.

“They vanished from the Earth a little over ten thousand years ago,” Persophone twined her fingers with Hades’. “Their lives were directly linked to that of the All Mother. When she disappeared, they went with her.”

“What’s this got to do with me?” I asked.

“Only she who created us has the power to reabsorb all that we are. We felt the loss of her down to the bottom of our souls. For millennia, we searched for a bare trace of her and found nothing. After a while, we returned to the duties we had been derelecting during our search,” Tisiphone spoke in clipped sentences. “When Ares hit you, we all felt it; all of us who she herself created.”

“Again, why does this involve me?” I rephrased and repeated.

“You and Serenity are the first Creators to walk this planet in over ten thousand years,” Blair spoke for the first time since entering the room. “You are the only ones to have actually been born on this planet, not created by a remnant of the previous universe.”

I shook my head. “I don’t understand.”

“I believe what they’re trying to say, whilst indulging in a history lesson, is that the All Mother needed a host to return from wherever she disappeared to,” James summed it up and simplified it nicely. “With no Creators left, she had to wait for one to be born the old-fashioned way.”

“If she’s so powerful, why can’t she make herself a new body?”

“Because it would crumble,” the Fury sighed. “This planet is dying, long before its time. Any body she crafted from the elements we have here would destablize before she has a chance to use it."

"Where Creators walk, Gaia gains new life and can more easily repair damage," Hades glanced around. "We used to have a saying, a very long time ago, that where Creators walk, the Earth renews itself. We have been working for centuries to find a way to slow the decay, but have been unsuccessful. We finally realised that it is because we are a patch, a bandage. We are a short-term solution waiting for the long-term cure to arrive."

"Let me guess, Serenity and I are the long-term cure?" I sat back, away from them all.

"Among other things," Colby piped in. "It is you, Amelia, that we are most interested in."

"Why? I'm a mongrel hybrid with no home, and no special talents."

"There, you are wrong," Persephone stood. "So very wrong. You are – "

She didn't get to finish her sentence as her eyes rolled back and she collapsed. Hades caught her before she could land inside the circle, but she started seizing as he gently laid her on the floor.

"Serenity, how far did she get in your training?" Hades glanced at my sister.

"Far enough that I can stop the seizures for now, but not permanently," she replied, joining him on the other side.

"For now it is enough," he took her left hand and placed it on Persephone's forehead. Power crawled up my skin and left goosebumps in its wake as warm, golden light burst from my sister's skin. Bright white wings with obsidian tips ripped her shirt as they erupted from her shoulders. The power amplified and I watched as the gold band in Serenity's eyes swallowed the thick band of deep red. She muttered something in a language I had never heard before a bare moment before the magic, for lack of a better term, forced itself into the goddess.

Persephone took a shaky breath as Serenity fell backwards, her wings dissolving into nothing. James was at her side and offering his wrist within moments. Her fangs were already out and she bit into his proffered appendage immediately.

"I think this is enough for now," Tisiphone stood. "We have much to do."

"Amelia also needs a full feed," Colby and Blair spoke in unison.

"Who will feed her? Most of the donors need to know the ones they're feeding on a personal level," the Fury watched me.

"On a side note, I prefer feeding on women so that I don't have to have sex with them afterwards," I stood and carefully walked away from the etching in the floor.

That earned me a puzzled look from everyone except Serenity and James. I shrugged at them and went for the door. Touching the handle, I yanked my hand back as it burned my fingers. Pulling away, I stared in confusion as blood flowed from my hand. A shiver ran up my spine and I turned without meaning to.

It was like I was being pushed into the passenger seat in my own body. I tried to move my hands but couldn't as I spoke. "Years have passed, empires have fallen. The human race has become a stain, a blight, a disease, that must be eradicated if the planet is to survive. Time is close. Soon my return will be permanent. I will come. I have seen. I will conquer."

As it came, so it left; this time the shiver went down my spine instead of up. I wound up panting on my hands and knees as my semi-quashed bloodlust roared to the surface. Nothing rose up and tried to stop it, and I sniffed the air. Three scents did nothing for me. One pulsed with familiarity that prevented me from launching myself at it. The four remaining...flavours tempted me with their ripeness. One I had already tasted, but it didn't call to me as strongly as the others.

"Amelia?" Persephone watched me carefully. "Can you hear me?"

"You smell like cinnamon and chocolate," I studied her. "With a touch of sickness."

"I know."

"The ill are not good food."

"Stop thinking with that stomach. Channel your hunger into something else," she attempted to reason with every part of me. "Drinking us without permission could kill you."

"What is there but the hunger?" I cocked my head, curious.

"Love, lust, curiousity, passion. They feed different stomachs, and often just as well."

"She doesn't understand, Seph. She won't be able to until she's had her fill of blood and this genie goes back in its bottle," Tisiphone swung my attention over to her. An opalescent hand and forearm appeared from her right sleeve as she moved towards me. "Drink. Remember who you are."

I was up and biting into her wrist between blinks. She didn't tense, but her left hand stroked the back of my head as I absorbed her surface memories. Some were flashes, others snapshots, but all featured a woman who could have been me, if I had wings. Her past poured through me as sage, pears, and the salty brine of the sea ran down my throat. It didn't take as long as normal to fill my reserves and I stumbled back from the goddess.

"What the hell *was* that?" I sputtered, angry and confused.

"That, Amelia, was a very angry, very old Creator," Tisiphone's arm disappeared.

"The All Mother." They nodded. "Why do I look like her?"

"We don't know," Blair shrugged. "Our best guess is that she inserted dormant gene sequences into some angels and vampires in hopes that this would eventually come about."

"So I'm supposed to just sit back and let her take over my body whenever the hell she wants?"

"No," Hades shook his head. "To host her is to share willingly, unless there is a clear and present danger that must be eradicated. For her to possess you like that while still nested beneath your soul, she is angrier than we have ever seen. She was the ultimate arbiter for peace before she vanished."

"Sometimes the most peaceful people are the ones who break the hardest when they get shoved over the edge."

"What could have pushed the Benevolent One this far?" Daniel asked, watching me closely.

"Death of a loved one usually does it. Ergo, who died?" I was blunt, and probably shouldn't have been. The answer, unexpectedly, came from Tisiphone.

Her cloak slithered to the floor to reveal a five foot nine beauty with blood, deep blood, red hair and golden eyes. A single tear trailed from her right eye. "My daughter, Rylynne, was murdered twenty years ago. She was the first goddess ever born, which made her precious in more ways than she could imagine."

"I'm sorry," I wanted to hug her but resisted. Ancients often had trouble with touch if they didn't initiate it.

"I had almost six hundred and eighty million years with her," she smoothed imaginary wrinkles from her black Grecian-style dress.

"Bonds like that hurt when they're torn away," Serenity came up from James's wrist. "It hurt when my mom died and she only had twenty-one years to make my life beautiful."

She just nodded.

"We need to speak with the others," Hades stood, lifting Persephone with him. "They need to know of the impending return."

Hades, Persephone and Tisiphone teleported out with that. Or would stepped out of our dimension be a better way to put it? Serenity and James stood and followed Blair and Colby to the door. I fell in behind them, and Daniel brought up the rear. As soon as Colby touched the handle, it swung open on well-oiled hinges. The hallway on the other side was almost too bright and I flinched away from it. A hand found my shoulder and I focussed on the warmth of it rather than the light.

"We apologise, Amelia," Blair's voice cut through the fog.

"For what?" we had arrived outside my door.

"We should have given you time to adjust before you started classes, or at least made sure you fed before going down," he shrugged.

"It wouldn't have stopped what happened. Ares is a coward who likes to pick on those that he doesn't think will fight back," I resisted the sudden urge to scratch my left eyebrow, even as it began to drive me the tiniest bit crazy.

"Yes, but we could have delayed it," he sighed. "Would you allow Daniel to stay with you? For your protection? Word will spread, whether we want it to or not, and there is a very old, but very valid price still in play for the heart of a Creator."

"Hunters have been around for that long?" I gave in and scratched.

"Longer. They've been around since Atlantis was destroyed," Colby flicked his wrist and my suite (because who am I kidding, it was more than just a bedroom) opened.

"He can stay, but his clothes must remain on at all times," I acquiesced. Tired. I was tired.

"Done," they nodded.

Leaving them to their business, I went to the bed and fell face-first onto it; passing out almost immediately.

7

"Hello," a voice a bare octave below mine, though otherwise identical, came through the darkness.

"Hi," I responded automatically.

"My apologies for my outburst earlier," she materialised in front of me. The only difference, as in Tisiphone's memories, was the set of opal wings protruding from her shoulders.

"We're all entitled to them," I shrugged.

"My name is Fiona," she held out her hand. Hesitantly, I took it. "I know most of the events of your life, Amelia, but you have a vault in your mind that I cannot penetrate. It radiates pain, sorrow and suffering. Enough that it could drown you and all those near if you ever let it out."

"That's where I shove things that all the free therapy in the world won't help."

"Therapy?" she rolled the word like alien candy on her tongue.

"Therapy is a fairly modern concept. Basically, you tell someone a whole bunch of really personal shit and they try to find ways to help you deal with your issues."

"That is both intriguing and disturbing."

"Blame Freud. He made a killing out of spilling bullshit. Some came before, many came after, but his debunked theories remain."

She was silent for a moment. "The world has changed since the last time I was here. People are no longer localised pockets of life."

"Took a couple of thousand years," I shrugged.

"Once the human race paused their squabbles for a time, they indulged in discovery."

"Blame religion for a lot of the fighting."

"Religion?"

"Worship of a deity who may or may not exist in hopes of gaining entry into a possibly mythical afterlife of peace and happiness."

She did one of those long blinks of confusion. "Humans believe that worship will gain them entry into *Vrai Morte*?"

"*Vrai Morte*?" It was my turn to be confused.

"The place where all souls rest between incarnations. Those who cause harm are stripped of their misdeeds by Hades before being granted entry."

"Heaven and Hell are real, then?"

"After a fashion. Some must pass through fire before they can find peace in the well of forgiveness."

"Was this place always there?"

"No. When a being of any kind died, its soul was released. They often wandered, lonely and scared, until a new vessel could be found. I created the angels to collect the souls before they could get lost; to take them to the collectiveness so they could heal surrounded by unconditional love. When they felt it was time, they were returned to this plane to inhabit a new form."

"What are souls then? If they don't cease to exist with the body they were living in."

"I have never been able to answer that question, unfortunately. They already existed on this planet when I arrived, billions of years ago."

I raised an eyebrow at her. "Exactly how old are you?"

"My consciousness predates this universe," she shrugged. "I was there for its creation, and I was there for the destruction of the previous one. In many forms I have traversed time and space, to be here on this day."

"Why this one?"

"Because it is the winter solstice. Today you are seventeen years and six months, and you are finally ready to embrace your future."

Something ripped me awake as soon as she said that. I sputtered and coughed, wondering why I was cold. Glancing to the fireplace, it was dark and cold, but shadows danced along the walls to either side.

"Goody goody!" A high pitched voice squealed in delight.

"It's awake! Can we eat it now?" Another, just as high, joined in.

"Our orders are to bring it back alive," a slightly deeper, more normal tone responded. "Kahlia would have our heads if we ate it."

I had a moment to think 'Where's Daniel?' before pain slammed into my right temple.

"Not to put a damper on your fun, guys, but I'm not going anywhere," I winced.

"It thinks it has a choice! How exciting!" The first one spoke again.

"I do have a choice. And I'm not an 'it'," I snapped.

Shadows moved again, but they were formless and no light cast them from physical forms. One seemed denser than the others, but it wasn't moving either.

"Why can't we eat it? It smells so good! Just a little nibble – please!"

"Kahlia gave us orders," darkness rose up like a wave and solidified at the foot of the bed. "Once he confirms what it is, you can eat what he doesn't dissect."

A sliver of fear ran up my spine. People willing to abduct and dissect others, presumably while still alive, usually weren't the nicest out there. Power I neither recognised nor understood ran down my arms and pooled in my palms. I could feel my eyes shifting – not to angel, not to vampire – to silver, and unity of purpose. It felt…different…good. I could 'see' my would-be captors, and found them lacking. An unpleasant smile curled my lips.

"You are not shadow walkers," my voice was a rolling, harmonic mix of all my parts. "You use borrowed, stolen gifts to perform your evil deeds. I weigh you, measure you, and find you lacking. We order you to be gone."

My hands rose; the power forming bright white suns around them to chase back the creatures. They seemed to shred, but the energy latched onto them as they vanished. I felt it slam into their bodies and nestle inside them; creating a warning beacon of sorts telling those who could see it to stay away.

Swinging my feet over the edge of the bed, I meant to walk but wound up floating to Daniel's awkwardly slumped body. They had tucked him in beside the fireplace. His neck was at an odd angle, and I touched it gently.

'I can save him,' Fiona's voice whispered through my mind.

'Do it,' I thought back.

'Give me your hands,' she coaxed.

I nodded, not really understanding. I thought about her, her moving my hands, arms, body. I didn't resist when they started moving, nor did I try to stop the, to me, gibberish from falling from my lips. A short, sharp pain bowed my spine as the skin on either side split. It eased as quickly as it came, and Fiona placed my hands on either side of Daniel's neck. With a quick jerk and a sickening crunch it straightened, and she brought my lips down to his; breathing energy and life into him with a chaste kiss. He inhaled sharply before she wiped a fine powder off his eyes and tasted it.

"Crushed pearls…loadstone…sapphire…belladonna? They know what you are, my dragon," she purred a little.

"All Mother," he dropped his gaze from our face.

With a still-glowing finger under his chin, we brought his eyes back up as the door to our room crashed open. "Fiona will do."

"What in high hell happened in here?" Serenity's voice somehow cut through my connection with Fiona and her power. She retreated and left me as alone as she could to control my – no, our – body.

"Sanctuary has a leak," I shrugged. The motion felt off, like there was an extra weight pulling on my shoulders.

Daniel stood stiffly, using the mantle as a support. "They knew what I am, and how to kill me. However, I do not understand why they waited for her to wake."

"Basic rule of teleporting. Unless you've jumped together before, you can't take an unconscious person through the dimension rifts," James paused halfway between my sister and my guard to look at me. "Are those wings?"

I frowned at him. "Are what wings?"

"You don't know?"

"Know what?"

"Turn around, Amelia," Serenity gestured at me.

I did as she bid and frowned even harder. Two bright white wings rustled as I moved my shoulders up and down. Turning sideways, they protruded from where I had felt the skin split.

"What the…" I reached back and grabbed a feather.

'They'll dissolve soon,' Fiona chuckled at me. *'Some abilities need parts of all that you are to function properly.'*

'How often will they do this?'

'Only when I choose, for now. With time and practice you will be able to use them at will.'

I gave a mental nod to her. "Fiona needed them to save Daniel," I spoke aloud.

"They aren't permanent?" Serenity queried.

"Not for now," I shook my head. They began to dissipate from the bottom up.

"I must speak with the Guardians. You will be able to guard her better that I can until we find a way to neutralise my weakness," Daniel bowed before moving gingerly to the door. He exited silently with barely a glance backward.

"We may need to leave here," I rotated my shoulders as the weight vanished.

"Give Colby and Blair some time. They can speak to Arcturus about closing down the doors," James took one of the plush chairs and steepled his hands with his elbows on his knees.

"Whoever contacted the Hunters will be dealt with," my sister attempted to reassure me.

I shook my head. "Who is Kahlia?"

They paused, and it was a pause that lasted too long. Finally, James spoke.

"Kahlia was my little brother. After I 'died' he tried to find out what happened to me, but I made sure there was nothing to find. He was supposed to have died fifteen years after I was turned."

"So why does he want to dissect me, if he did figure out how to cheat death?"

"Maybe he found a temporary fix and needs something to make it permanent, I don't know. He was always a gentle boy. His path was religious where mine was warrior."

We fell silent. I'm not sure any of us knew what to say after that. For the most part, the dead are supposed to stay dead. Particularly if they're family and you made peace with their passing millennia ago.

Wind ruffled the drapes by the floor-to-ceiling windows. It was a warm breeze, but it held the faintest scent of tropical rain; almost like an afterthought for the senses. Turning to the massive panes of glass, I frowned at the dark outline that seemed to float. Approaching warily, I smiled a little. It was just a gargoyle standing on a balcony I had previously failed to notice.

"Good to know that this place has gargoyles," I chuckled.

"Amelia..." the hesitation in my sister's voice turned me to the delicate frown on her face. My smile slipped. "Gargoyles, real ones, aren't that big, and Sanctuary doesn't have any."

"Then what's – " my air supply was abruptly cut off and claws gripped my neck.

"Try to follow and we kill her," the grave words were the last I heard before darkness took me.

8

Bright, impossibly bright, light tortured my eyes until my brain caught up with the sensory input. My throat hurt, but there was no niggling feeling in the back of my head to say that I was in any sort of danger. I tried to turn my head, but a pinching at my neck stopped me. Whatever held me was cold and unmoving. Opening my eyes slowly, I frowned at the frozen faux-gargoyle.

Its face was stuck somewhere between a snarl and intense agony. Glancing around as well as I could, the mirror over the mantle showed the room to be frozen in time. It was unnerving, to say the least, but as soon as I acknowledged it the fingers at my throat crumbled. The drop to my feet was a few short inches, but it felt like it took forever to hit the floor. I poked the statue gingerly, and it collapsed in on itself.

"What the hell," I stepped away. Moving toward Serenity and James, I was afraid to even breathe on them in case they crumbled as well.

The door opened to show Athena in the hall. She hurried inside and gave me a half-smile. "Unfortunately, I can't let you remember this. Your mind will believe that you went to bed and slept until morning. No interruptions, no breaches in security. You will remember what was discussed in the room that does not exist, and why Daniel must always be with you. You will not remember the name Kahlia."

"Why?"

"Because knowing makes you a target. If someone reads you and tells others that the kidnapping failed they will just kill you. If they believe it hasn't been attempted yet then they may slip and reveal their entire network."

I nodded slowly and she placed her fingertips gently against my temples. Closing my eyes, I felt a slow, pulsing warmth before I was out again. Though, this time it was restful.

I woke to a semi-uncomfortable bunching around my ribs and knees. It took a few seconds to remember that I had passed out with my clothes on. I grumbled to myself, stripping silently, and went to the closet to find fresh clothes. Grabbing runners, a t-shirt, jogging pants, a light sweater, socks and underwear, all in black by accident, I just about shrieked when I stepped back into the room.

"Good morning," Daniel kept his back to me.

"How much did you see?"

"More than I will willingly admit to," his tone was carefully neutral.

"What time is it?"

"Nearly seven-thirty. You have time to dress and hit the training room before breakfast and your first class."

"You'll be with me all day?" I pulled the clothes on hastily and laced the shoes.

"By order of the Guardians. If I am unavailable then a deity will escort you."

"Do you have any problems with being a bodyguard? Taking orders from other people all the time?" Curiosity made me ask.

"It is what I was bred for. Now that you exist I have a true path and purpose to follow," he shrugged.

"And you're just okay with that?"

"Yes."

"Why?"

"All my life I have felt like a piece of debris caught in a hurricane; tossed hither and yon on a whim. Now, I am anchored with a clear goal and I can understand the path set before my feet."

I nodded slowly, more to myself than his still turned back. "Shall we?"

"Indeed," he turned on his heels and marched to the door. Opening it a crack, he peeked out before opening it fully and stepping into view. When nothing tried to kill him he waved me over.

"Where is the training room?"

"Ares's classroom. Until he has his shit together he isn't allowed back within Sanctuary's walls."

"Good," an edge of dark glee coloured my voice.

The elevator doors opened and Hermes produced a sweeping bow for us. "Off to work out some excess energy?"

"Need to get rid of it somehow," I nodded.

He flashed a merry, lecherous grin. “I can think of a couple other ways.”

“Of course you can,” I couldn’t help but smile. “But I’m not a fan, so you’ll have to find a different play-partner.”

“Aw,” he pouted. He perked up again almost instantly. “How about you, Danny-boy?”

“You know I would rather do your wife. Maybe your sister,” Daniel chuckled. “You, Herm, are not my type.”

“Why? Too tall?”

“You don’t have a certain –”

“Just say boobs,” I laughed, stepping out of the doors as they opened.

Daniel followed, smiling widely. “Laps after stretches, followed by knife-work with a finish at weights?’

“I can skip the weights. Serenity doesn’t like people to know, but I can repeatedly bench press a lion without breaking a sweat.”

“Impressive.”

“Only when the people after you aren’t using a vehicle of some sort. Or can do the same thing.”

“Touché.”

The lights were slowly coming on across the room, and it looked nothing like it had the day before. The mats were gone and a full gym with Olympic running track was in their place. We stretched in silence until we were limber enough to run. Pausing to make one concession to his arsenal, Daniel placed his sword in one of the lockers by the elevator.

“You set the pace. I’ll keep stride and let you know when ten minutes is up,” he rolled his broad shoulders as he walked back to me.

“Light jog with slowly increasing speed?”

“Sounds good.”

As soon as he was back beside me, we started. He shortened his strides so that he could keep pace and after a while he held up his index finger with his thumb half-curled to indicate a minute and a half had passed. Nodding and keeping my breathing deep and even, I increased our pace gradually until the room outside of my direct path was a blur. Daniel finally held up just his thumb and we slowed, allowing a cool-down lap, or three, so our muscles wouldn't seize when we stopped. I was panting and my legs burned to high hell. He seemed barely winded.

"We'll need to work on your stamina," he grinned.

I grinned back. "My stamina is just fine, thank you. I excel at being lazy."

He gave a full, deep laugh at that. "Let's test your knife work. We'll use dummy knives for a while so you can see the hits you're making, and those landing against you."

"What's the tracer on them?"

"Hephaestos crafted them with dull edges that excrete a white powder on contact."

"Nifty."

"Indeed."

Daniel led me from the track to the weapon chest between the boxing ring and a conglomeration of fall mats. Leaning over the chest, he picked out four dagger-length knives as I shed my sweater.

"I'm going to assume you know how to hold these?"

"Up the arm, not out from the hand. Makes you harder to disarm."

"Very good."

"Indeed," I parroted his seemingly favourite line with a smile.

Handing me two, I followed him to the centre of our practice area and got them sitting in my hands the way I liked, that felt good.

"No holds barred. Fight me like I'm trying to kill you."

"Understood," I nodded, taking a step back and bending my knees a little to shift my centre of gravity.

He feinted, and I fell for it; bringing my left arm up so he could land a shot to my ribs.

"Watch body language before committing. A person cannot move without it showing in their torso first."

"I forgot that. Serenity doesn't let me fight enough."

He nodded and reset. We nodded to each other and I dissociated; shutting off my doubtful, gullible, side and acting on pure instinct. We both landed blows and called it when a gong sounded. Putting the knives away, I grabbed my sweater from the floor and looked at all the white marks on my clothes. Either he was just that good, or I was that bad.

"Like you said, Serenity doesn't let you fight much," Daniel appeared in front of me with a soft smile on his face. "If it makes you feel any better, had those been real knives, and I susceptible to death by exsanguination, you would have killed me a couple of times over. What you lacked in number, you made up for in accuracy of placement."

"If you say so," I shrugged, pulling the sweater on. Even at my best I wasn't good enough. I would never be good enough to face my enemies on my own, and most of them were human. "Had those been real knives, you could have carved me up into little bits for my enemies and saved them all the trouble." I picked at it. I had to. It was an old compulsion.

"Amelia," his voice held the faintest edge of what I could only think of as a growl.

"Face it, I'm not worth your time to protect," I turned to the oddly open elevator. "Go protect my sister."

"She can protect herself," his voice was calm, though not right behind me.

"And I can't," I mumbled, a single scalding tear escaping my left eye as I hung my head.

"Want to change?" Hermes asked quietly.

I nodded and we rocketed skyward. Our arrival was smooth and I stepped into the hall without looking up. Opening my door, I went straight to the closet and exchanged everything with powder on it for something identical, though clean. Adding a black, hooded pea coat, I was leaving my room when I ran into Colby.

"Privacy?" he asked, undoubtedly already knowing about the training fiasco.

"Library," I shrugged.

"Too crowded. Class is out today for the solstice light-up."

"Where else then?"

"The back gardens. No one would think to look for you there."

"Thanks."

"My pleasure."

I was walking back to the elevator when he called out "Amelia?"

"Yes?"

"Self-doubt affects us all. Eventually you overcome it and see things without a biased haze."

I gave a short, curt nod and the elevator doors opened in front of me. I didn't need to tell Hermes where I was going; one minute we were in the elevator and the next we were by a massive fountain surrounded by a lush garden and thick woods. The air was crisp, cold, fresh.

"I'll be back to bring you to the light-up."

The absence of human-ish contact was welcome when he vanished. I pulled the thick hood over my head and was happy-ish to find it was lined with thick, soft, faux-fur. My ears definitely enjoyed the warm softness of it.

I sat on the fountain edge, studying the floral masterpiece. It was intricate, and with some colour it could have looked real. It took me a little while to realise that there wasn't a single tool mark on it, as though someone just froze the arrangement as it was so they could always see its beauty.

Time seemed to fade away as the softly bubbling water coursed through its endless journey down the fountain. Trees occasionally waved in the imaginary breeze, and some of the flowers in the garden seemed to open and shut at will.

For something to do I trailed my fingers through a small fall of water. A flash of memory hit me and I jerked back in surprise. Curiosity got the better of me and I put my hand back in; this time with my palm up so I could actually 'see' the memory.

Someone was screaming. It was dark, so dark.

"Arya! Arya where are you?" It was a woman screaming, her voice so familiar.

My back hurt. I couldn't move. Where was my mommy? She was supposed to come find me before the bad men arrived.

I yanked my hand out of the water before I could see any more. The flower that particular water cascaded from looked a little less like stone. I couldn't put my finger on what, specifically, but it looked…softer.

“This is the Fountain of Sorrow,” a small female voice came from within the stone.

“Fountain of Sorrow?” I repeated, wiping my hand dry on my pants.

“This is where the waters of Acheron and Styx come from. Mnemosyne created me so that there would always be a record of unjust losses.”

“Losses as in deaths?”

“Yes.”

“How is the fountain so small then?”

“I am a fractal. If you were to look at me from above you would understand.”

I nodded, not sure if – it? – could see. Not wanting to touch the water again, I stood and walked out through all the flowers. There were species I had no name for; shapes I had only seen in books. Poisons and their cures. Small plants with huge flowers; huge plants with tiny flowers. It was beautiful, and walking through those flowers I forgot everything but the moment.

9

A quick flash of light at the edge of the woods caught my attention. It was like the flash from an arc welder across my retinas; almost blistering in its intensity. Blinking slowly, a figure appeared, just a dim, dark outline at first. Slowly it got sharper, clearer, until I could see a woman with leathery wings beckoning to me.

Her hair was a flaming red, and the wings on her back were a few shades darker with streaks of forest green. I went to her warily, both trusting the island to keep me safe, and not trusting the woman I had never seen before. When I got close enough and could finally see her eyes, I frowned.

"I thought Daniel was the only dragon left."

"He is," her voice was high and melodic, like chimes in a breeze. "I am the spirit of the first Draconis. I came to see the charge that has my last child praying for guidance."

"And do I measure up?"

"It is not my place to judge. Fiona never needed a guardian, but I was her companion through many ages. From her I received untold tomes of knowledge, much of which I passed to my children so they could protect others of The Blood."

"Others of 'The Blood'?" I repeated. "Other Creators?"

"Yes. Fiona never had a biological child in this universe. Those she created became her children, and the lesser Creators were her only vulnerability. Each one was formed from a single drop of her blood, as a manifestation of a specific ability. Those that held power over life and death were reabsorbed into her, understanding that their existence was too dangerous and could upset the balance."

"Why tell me all this?"

"So you can understand why…Daniel must protect you. Your sister, though a Creator born, has been altered. She is a creature of death, as well as life. You are a being of life; pure, unadulterated life. You can kill, yes, but more parts of you than not find it distasteful."

"So?" I grit my teeth, trying to avoid sounding snarky. And likely failing.

"You are the razor's edge upon which life balances. If you die before your time comes, all with half-blood heritage or greater will die with you."

The same shivery feeling as the night before came over me and Fiona took over control of our body. I felt her smiling as she pushed me to the side.

"Svetanyasieemay," she held our arms out.

The spirit stepped to us and wrapped both her wings and her arms around our shoulders. She was much more petite than she seemed, with barely an inch on our height. A teasing scent of cinnamon and roses drifted past our nose.

"Tell the young dragon to have patience," Fiona spoke. "The neuroses of this age take time to overcome."

"I shall pass the message," she responded before evaporating.

'Amelia?' she thought to me, receding like a tide back into passenger-hood.

'Yes?' I thought back, not sure how I felt about single-entity telepathy.

'Why do you not feel you are good enough? That you are undeserving?'

I thought about it for a moment. Though I'm not sure "thought" is a good term. If she listened in on my mental gymnastics, she didn't let me know as I finally settled on an answer I was happy with.

'I guess it goes back to when my mom died. Serenity lost her, too, and because of that she wasn't there for me as much as I needed her. We were always running from place to place, almost as soon as she died, and I had to bury my grief. I never really dealt with her death; I've never had enough time. I mean, Serenity did as good a job as she could, but she's not a mom. She's not my mom.'

'She couldn't encourage you the same way your mother was able to.'

'Yes.'

'Why does that make you feel that you are unworthy of compassion?'

'Because I haven't earned it. If I can't protect myself then I'm useless. If I'm not smart enough, I'll fail. If I can't pick

myself up, why should anyone waste their precious energy helping me?'

'Everyone needs help sometimes. You don't need to be the strongest, fastest, smartest, or best. You just need to be you, and the rest of the world will fall into place.'

'I wish I could believe that.'

'You don't have to.'

'Why not?'

'Because I believe it. I believe that you will find your place and realise that what you have been fighting for was always yours, and had been to begin with.'

I had no smart-ass comeback for that so I let it go. She either sensed that, or understood that I needed time to think so she retreated. I stood there, right between the woods and the flowers for what seemed like hours. Colby eventually startled me with a tap on my shoulder.

"I thought Hermes was going to retrieve me," I frowned at him.

"He was held up by his wife," the vampire shrugged. Smiling, he held his hand out to me. Taking it, he winked before teleporting us back to the main building.

No one looked twice when we appeared at the edge of the crowd. We joined the press of bodies heading out the door. I was surprised by the age of some of the other residents. Most were in their mid-teens, but there were a few babies with their mothers and some toddlers holding the hands of what must be siblings.

"I thought Hunters were forbidden from hunting children and their parents," I whispered to Colby.

"Their mothers, yes; their fathers, no," he whispered back. "Some of their mothers stood between their mates and their pursuers and died because of it. Because they broke the laws they set down for themselves they didn't try to hide when we took vengeance on them."

"And the orphaned children come here."

"Yes. We bring them in ourselves so they don't have to worry about finding a guide like you did."

"Your guides seem a little obsessed with someone called Arcturus."

He smiled. "She was our first resident. Arcturus is completely human, and the exception to our rule about her species. From birth she has been able to control all air in a spectacular fashion. Like she did for Psyche, Persephone stopped the calendar of her life so that she could protect future generations from the pain she went through."

"How long has she been here?"

"Fifty thousand years, I think."

"Can't keep track?"

"After almost two billion years, I stopped trying. For the most part."

We were outside, squished in the press of bodies waiting to watch the solstice light-up. Colby didn't have to stay with me, but he did. I wasn't expecting the *boom* that came with the sudden brightness emanating from the building. I jumped and caught him stifling the smile that likely came at my expense.

Once the flare spots faded from my eyes, I could finally see the carefully crafted tableau set against the side of the building. It was beautiful, with the main theme being the lunar cycle and the solstice. Homage was paid to all the world's religions, but they were secondary; afterthoughts almost.

"It's beautiful," I murmured absently.

"The lights are all fairies," Colby apparently caught the comment. "They rehearse the image they decide on the moment they finish their act at the summer solstice."

"Amazing."

"Indeed."

We fell into silence and just watched the epic image transform into something indescribably beautiful. It felt like forever and a day later, but the glimmering shine finally started to fade and people began making their way back inside; presumably towards dinner. A couple of the fairies drifted down and floated with really little children to the doors and I had a really uncomfortable thought.

"I don't want kids," I whispered to Colby. "I know I'm going to have two, thanks to that fuck up a thousand years ago, but I don't want them."

"You're seventeen; that's understandable."

"It's not that. I'll die when the younger one is fourteen, like my mother before me and hers before her, *ad nauseum*."

"You don't want to abandon them."

"No. I know how hard it is to live understanding that I will leave them and fuck up their lives and have them do the exact same thing when it's their time."

He was silent for a moment. "There is a difference this time. When your consciousness passes on, Fiona will still be in your body. She will be there to help your daughters finish growing, and all the children after that. She will be the guardian of your family until the end of time."

"Why would she do that? She has bigger fish to fry."

"It is her nature. She will view your descendants as her own, and protect them as such. Though she is a warrior, she was a mother first."

"She didn't have any biological children though."

"Not in this universe. She had twins the day before the last universe was destroyed. Much of her time before she found this planet and created us was spent looking for them."

"Did she ever find them?"

"If she did, she didn't tell us," he paused, then changed the subject. "How are your hungers? Do you need to feed?"

"They'll be good for a while," I shrugged. "If given a choice between feeding on emotion and feeding on power, I'll choose power every time. It lasts longer and is ultimately more satisfying."

"Really?"

"Have you never fed off one of the gods?"

"No. When our services were not required, Blair and our siblings and I could turn off our need to feed so we would not over-hunt our food supply. It was a fail-safe so that nature would remain in balance."

"How long has it been since you last fed?" It was my turn to arch an eyebrow at him.

He actually had to stop and think about it for a full minute. Finally, he answered. "Eighty-eight years, five months, thirteen days, six hours and three minutes. It was a Hunter in Prague, one of their Council."

"You can calculate the exact time of your last feed?"

“I can remember the exact moment of every one of my kills.”

“I’m not sure if that’s creepy or useful.”

“At times, it is both. For now I will bid you *adieu*, as your guard has finally figured out where we are,” Colby inclined his head to the dragon.

“Good night, and thanks for the talk.”

“My pleasure, Amelia.”

He disappeared into the crowd and Daniel took his place beside me. We didn’t speak as we reached the elevator and Hermes brought us down to dinner with a group that looked to be around my age. They kept a careful distance from us, and made a hasty exit when the doors opened.

I frowned after them. “Are they afraid of you or me?”

“You,” Daniel chuckled, following them at a sedate pace.

“Why?”

“Because they were watching when Ares attacked you.”

“Why would that make them scared of me? All I did was bite him.”

“No. You beat him when he had multiple advantages over you. None of them have ever been able to even strike him when they had an advantage.”

“Are they trained killers? Or pampered rich kids who came here when they found out their parents lied to them about what they are?”

“They have never taken the life of another. They understand, in theory, what the psychological effects will be, but they have never experienced the nightmares or flashbacks. They do not have the self-doubt that comes from reliving it and questioning whether there were other actions they could have taken that would have saved lives.”

“Do you ever grow out of questioning your kills?” I asked quietly, slowly letting go of my flash of anger.

“Only when you embrace sociopathy, or quit giving a shit that killing needs to be done for survival,” he shrugged.

“There’s a difference?” I raised an eyebrow at him.

He smiled, a small smile, that was somehow mocking, appreciative, and appraising all at the same time. Finally, he chuckled. “Never let anyone see how smart you truly are. Let them believe the lie of your packaging – delicate, petite. They will not see you as a threat until you open your mouth and give them a reason to fear you."

"Delicate and non-threatening… I really don't know if I can do that."

"You can, it's wanting to that may be a problem."

I shrugged, not sure what to say to that. I didn't know when we had stopped to have our conversation, but we stood halfway between the elevator and food. My stomach grumbling decided which direction I was headed for. Steak, among other things, was calling my name quite loudly.

"Feed the physical hunger and you won't have to feed the other part of you as soon. When you catch it early you can channel the blood-hunger into less volatile and potentially violent pursuits."

"Like what?" I watched him from the corner of my eye.

"Sex, art, sometimes mediation."

"I'll pass on the sex, thanks. Not my cup of tea."

"May I ask why?"

I shrugged. I didn't like talking about it. It was one of those memories that was in the vault Fiona couldn't access. It was one of many things I liked to pretend hadn't happened over the last few years.

"Some things shouldn't be talked about if you want to be able to eat," I finally said as we entered the dining hall. "And I'm bloody hungry."

10

Tantalizing scents dragged across my nose to foods I had never seen before. Some were obviously regional delicacies, and others seemed to be species specific – with nameplates to match their purported diners. Sautéed moose slices with a rosemary-infused glaze seemed to be for Chymeras, while platters of beef titake were reserved for Djinn and succubi/incubi.

"Can I take a little of everything, or am I allowed to eat the unmarked stuff only?" I asked Daniel as I stared at the food in confusion.

He chuckled. "They really need to add an entry to the guide book about this. Unmarked first, and once all of one species has finished their plaque will disappear if there is any of their particular food left."

"Then it's a free-for-all?"

"No," he grinned. "Most are too full by that time, so those who need to eat more to maintain their physical equilibrium get it. And some people just don't like specific specialty items."

"Is there anything up here you refuse to eat?" I grabbed a plate and made my way down to the section of general foods.

"Anything with mushrooms or tomatoes. Feed me either one of those and I get supremely nasty abdominal cramps."

"So you're allergic."

"Allergic?" he rolled the apparently unfamiliar word around his mouth.

"Your body reacts to it as though something was attacking you from the inside when it's not."

"If you say so. I do not understand this 'allergic'."

I wasn't sure if I could explain it to him any other way so, I selected random items until my plate was full and looked around for an empty table. There didn't appear to be any, but the young woman from my English class, Nicole, was waving excitedly at me. I glanced at Daniel, who nodded, before making my way over and taking one of the empty seats. Graham was sitting with her and wasted a smile on me.

"Draconis," Daniel greeted them, taking a seat that faced the room.

"Chymera," Nicole replied, her eyes more blue and orange than the day before.

"Wolf," Graham nodded to him.

"Hybrid," I shrugged, not sure how many people knew what I really was by now.

"Everyone knows already," Nicole grinned. "It was all anyone could talk about before the light-up."

"How much do they know?" I ducked my head self-consciously, seriously hoping they didn't know about Fiona.

"You're a Creator, one of the first in thousands of years. What else is there to know?" Graham asked between mouthfuls of one of the reserved dishes. In his case, roasted veal flank with a whiskey glaze.

I shrugged and dug into my food after exchanging a look with Daniel. He seemed as relieved as I was that only my species was common knowledge. If anyone knew about the extra bits, chances were good that things would get really ugly, really fast.

We ate in silence until our plates were empty. I was fine with the silence, but Nicole apparently needed to ask questions.

"How long were you running before you were granted Sanctuary?"

The question made me wince internally. "Three and a half years. You?"

"Two years, six months and eight days," she responded. "My guides kept missing our meetings."

"What about you, Graham?" I was partially being polite and partly curious.

"I never had to run. Do you know the mechanics of shifter culture?"

I shook my head. "Haven't had the opportunity to learn."

"With werewolves specifically, only half-bloods and purebloods can shift, with the exception of twins who are quarter-blood. Their energies combine to allow for a stable transition," Daniel informed me.

Graham nodded. "I was the first male born of the ruling line in three generations. The moment I turned sixteen my grandmother was supposed to abdicate her regency. She instead played on my mother's instability, whispered lies to her, until she tried to kill me. The first time, I was nine. The Guardians brought me here before she could finish the job when I was twelve."

"Why wasn't your grandmother brought to justice?" I asked, fully curious now.

"Unfortunately shifters are more likely to believe purebloods that anyone else, particularly if they are expected to take seats of power, or already hold it and have for a long time."

"They're basically pretty speciesist then? Or more elitist?"

"Cross the two, with an emphasis on species," Daniel nodded. "Shifters are the bane of all supernatural creatures. We have ruling councils within our individual species, and they send one member, as their customs dictate, to the higher council. At the higher council, a record of births, deaths, and losses is kept. It is also where threat assessments, warnings, and occasionally high-profile assignments are done or handed out."

I frowned. "Am I supposed to be glad I'm not a shifter?"

"Yes," all three of my table companions answered emphatically.

"Do any of you know what a Creator is supposed to *do*? Are we combatants, or passive, or what?" The random thought burst from my lips.

Graham shrugged, and Daniel gave me a look that said he would speak in private, but Nicole actually paused; staring at me as her eyes shifted, collapsed, and recoloured themselves. Finally she blinked and they reset to the colour they started as.

"As contradictory as it sounds, you are a passive combatant. Your primary role is to heal, but some healing requires sacrifice. Based on your skin, you'll do your best work under the light of the moon. And that red-eyed demoness behind you, approaching with an aura of death, does her best work with the sun. You sister, I presume?"

I cringed and ducked my head. I really didn't want to talk to her. A slow ember of anger I didn't know I had been nursing roared to life. She had lied and kept things from me for so many fucking years. Her eyes found the back of my head the moment my fangs dropped and my eyes raced to red.

"Amelia," Daniel's voice was low in warning. I growled at him as my muscles tensed. Instead of reaching for me physically as I expected, his energy washed over me as it had the day before and doused my anger and hurt under a cloak of calm. The burning feeling that had been attacking the back of my head vanished and I turned to face my sister. Her eyes were closed and her head was tilted back with a look of supreme ecstasy on her face.

Serenity's hands unclenched and her fingers returned to normal. She sighed, shook her head, then opened her eyes. The red collapsed into a bare glimmer at the outer edge of the gold, and she walked the rest of the way to us calmly. She took an empty seat between Graham and me and looked curiously at Daniel.

"The Guardians said you could suppress strong emotions," she inclined her head. "I have no clue why I was so angry, though."

"Someone was trying to start a fight," Nicole's eyes swirled again, this time landing on red and green patterns. "They're testing for weaknesses."

"Can you see who?" Serenity asked her, eyebrow raised.

Nicole shook her head. "I'm not old enough. I won't be able to do that for another thirty years, at least."

"Always worth a try," my sister shrugged. "You up for more information? Since we aren't keeping anything from you anymore, there's a lot to catch up on."

I raised an eyebrow at her. There had never been full disclosure between us, especially over the last couple of years. "How will I know if you're actually telling me everything?"

"You can pull it straight from my memory. Anything I don't know, James will tell you if he can," she sighed. "You know I object to telling you everything. The less you know, the safer you are."

"Not always," Nicole interjected. "Sometimes the less you know, the less you're able to defend yourself."

Serenity shrugged. An awkward silence fell. I didn't know what to say to her, she didn't know what to say in front of Nicole and Graham. They didn't appear comfortable talking in front of her. It was a big pile of awkward until Daniel nodded to me and stood, the plates on our table vanishing.

My sister and I rose swiftly. I smiled at Nicole and Graham before following the others out of the hall and to the elevator. Hermes was leaning against the open door, pretending to look bored as he picked at his fingers. He smiled when we approached, and it seemed to have a vaguely evil edge to it.

"Y'know, Danny-boy, you don't always have to load the shotgun when someone's not a happy little camper," he chuckled.

"Like you would know the difference between surgical excision and total amputation," he shot back, stepping past the god into Hell's Express Delivery.

"I heard that," Hermes muttered as I passed him. I shot back a sickly sweet and angelic smile.

We rocketed upward and came to a sudden, jarring halt just as quickly. Possibly as retaliation for my snide thoughts about his 'ride'. The doors snapped open without a word and Daniel led us out. It took the doors almost closing on my ass to realise we were on the thirty-sixth floor, and it confused me.

"Why are we here? Isn't there somewhere else for us to do this?"

"This is the most secure floor, except for the Guardian's quarters on the thirty-seventh. The top two floors are spelled to other residents cannot come here without invitation," Daniel shot over his shoulder as he opened my suite.

James, Blair and Colby were waiting for us inside.

"Any problems?" Colby asked as I shut the door.

"Nothing major," Serenity shrugged.

We filled the seats in near silence. I sat cross-legged on one side of the couch while my sister perched on the other. I looked at everyone but her and found only patient stares coming back at me.

"Where should we start?" I finally asked.

"Where do you want to?" Serenity replied, eyes closed.

"You and mom, when you were here before."

"Done," she held out her hand. "Blair, Colby would you like to add your side of the memory to this? That way she won't get just my side."

"Of course," they replied in unison, rising and placing their hands over ours.

Instead of the normal falling sensation I had always associated with deliberate memory reading, it felt like I was being sucked under and drowned. The richness of the details assaulted my senses, and I floated above the scene instead of reliving the experiences of a single mind. It was…weird. We, or rather they, were in the same room but the furniture was different. My mom was sitting on a chaise with Serenity curled up behind her. Gods, she was so young, barely seven, and mom was stroking the mound of flesh that was hiding me.

'Thank you for seeing us on such short notice,' Josephine's soft, ringing voice surprised me. Her voice held an edge to it that I had never heard before.

'It's not short notice to us, don't worry. We were alerted to this possibility before you were born,' Blair smiled at her. He and Colby stood together a few feet away from the lounger.

'So you know why we're here.'

'Of course. You wish Sanctuary for your girls,' Colby inclined his head.

'Yes.'

'You know the restrictions, don't you?'

'I have to be dead before you can give it to them.'

'Unless something goes wrong, we will be there the moment you pass on.'

'Thank you,' she smiled.

The memory faded and I was thrown back into my body as they, Blair and Colby, pulled their hands away.

I looked at them. "What happened?"

"An unexpected complication in the form of me," a new male spoke from the door.

We all turned and looked. Hermes stood beside a very tall brunette. He was as pale as James, Colby and Blair, but his eyes were red and blue.

"You have no business here," James snarled, still sitting but his muscles tense.

"I have a right to be here," his reply was calmly cold.

"That's debatable," I raised an eyebrow at him. "Just who the fuck do you think you are? Aside from a vampire with a stick up its ass."

He grinned. "Stuart Oliver Hamilton, Esquire. Former Lord of Dovercourt and Greater Essex, born December 3rd, 1472."

"All that tells me is that you really do have a stick secured high in your derrière," I turned back to our circle.

"I'm your father, Amelia. Your mother and I met just after she opened a lingerie store in Greece when she was nineteen."

My face froze. I had no memories of him, and mom had been very careful to never think of him when she held me.

"How do I know you're telling the truth? Our father abandoned us when I was lcss than a year old."

"I did no such thing," he scoffed. "Your mother called your grandfather and he dropped me into an active volcano."

I bit my tongue. I desperately wanted to call him a liar, but I didn't.

"Read my memories, you'll see the truth."

James snarled and Serenity shook her head.

"Which line do you come from?" she asked, turning to him.

"I don't see why that's important," Stuart shrugged.

"It's important because different vampire lineages can do different things. You obviously have telepathy, but what else?" Serenity stiffened in her seat.

"Magellen's line. I don't know who turned her, but she turned my father," Stuart finally sighed.

"Magellen was bitten by Sophia, who was changed by Cleopatra, and so on back to Cassandra and her creator; my son Damian," Blair looked thoughtful for a moment. "You can trust his memories, Amelia. My line cannot alter what we remember."

I nodded. Stuart came towards us until Daniel stopped him with a hand on his chest. The unspoken warning was clear, and Stuart extended just his hand.

"I want to see this, too," Serenity watched him warily.

"Of course," he inclined his head, holding out his other hand.

We both took one, and the feeling I was used to swept over me as we dropped into his body and felt the overwhelming emotions of the scene before us.

She was angry, the dishes clattering together as she dropped them by the sink. She was much slimmer, but she looked tired. 'If you wake Amelia, so help me I will kill you.'

'Josephine, goddamnit, listen to me! I can protect them if you just let me take them into the underground. I can ensure they'll want for nothing.'

'Let you take them? And never see them again? Risk them getting killed by someone who doesn't follow orders? No thank you. I'll protect them where we can run. Sanctuary will be able to open its doors to them the moment I die.'

'And until then? What if they can't find the gatekeeper?' hurt rose up like a glove wrapped around our throat.

'They will. I've made sure of it.'

'Josephine, what did you do?'

'What I had to, Stuart. They'll only have to hide for two years, then they'll be safe.'

Betrayal and anger added their potency to the emotional mix. 'And if something goes wrong?'

'It won't.'

'You don't know that! I won't let you risk the lives of MY daughters.'

'You have no choice! All our societies are matrilineal and matriarchal, which means that what I say goes. Having a human mother does not excuse you from our laws.'

'Your mother was human, too.'

'Only by the thinnest of technicalities.'

He pulled away then, and I dropped my hand. I desperately wanted to be angry with him for leaving, for not coming back when we needed him. Instead I looked at Serenity.

"Do you remember any of that?" I asked.

"Sort of. I was upstairs with you, and I heard yelling but I couldn't hear the words. You weren't even a year old yet."

"As you saw, I didn't want to leave," Stuart stepped away, seemingly at the behest of Daniel.

"So why didn't you come back if you didn't want to leave?"

"I couldn't find you. It took me a year to crawl out of the volcano, and she, your mother, had moved you numerous times since then."

"Four different houses in that first year alone," Serenity confirmed.

"So. Where do we go from here? We're a little old for you to step in and start protecting us now. It's also a little late for it."

"I just want to get to know the women my daughters have grown up to be."

I sighed. "If you can wait I'll make time for you, but you interrupted something important."

"Impeccable timing then," he chuckled.

"More like terrible," I muttered.

11

"So where were we before this interruption?" I looked at the seated group brightly.

They all looked at me as though I had sprouted a second head.

"What?"

"You're being too reasonable. This is a lot of information to process," Serenity shifted a little.

"Lay it on me," I shrugged. "My mind will sort it out later if there's an overload."

"Are you sure?"

"Positive. Now, who started Hartley House of Fashion?"

"Grandma Morganna and her sister. It was originally financed by their inheritance, which came from the Russian royal family under Empress Catherine's daughter – Anna Petrovna, who was supposed to have died as a young child. Anna's grandmother Elizabeth hid her away for her safety and replaced her with a sick beggar's child. No one knew the difference as few people had ever seen the little girl. Elizabeth funnelled money to her keepers with strict instructions that half be hidden away until she reached her majority.

"She lived simply, and safely, until her grandmother died and her keepers left. She saved money by not having servants and living without frivolity. Cossacks raided her little town when she was in her late twenties. They were about to brand her as a slave when our however-many-time-great aunt finished transitioning and came out of it homicidal. Anna found our ancestor and took her in. When she died she left all her money to the girls."

"And they passed it down when they died," I nodded.

"Yes."

"The day mom died, why don't I remember it?"

"I took it from you, for your protection. One of the Hunters that time was a telepath, and your grief was projecting it loud and clear. They were able to track us because of it, so I took the actual memory and left just the knowledge that she was gone."

"Why didn't you give it back after we escaped?"

She paused for a moment. “I don’t know. Giving it back never really crossed my mind.”

“Why not? It’s MY memory.”

“It is, and it isn’t. When I took it from you it became part of a daisy chain that goes all the way back to the original sisters. The lives of our entire line were passed to me from Aunt Gabi, and to her from Great-Aunt Margeurite. It’s basically a living record of a thousand years of love, pain, heartbreak, and joy.”

“So I’ll never get to deal with it properly, rather than that shadow you left me.”

“You can access it through me; I’m just not sure if or how to return it.”

“It’s not the same as having it all the time, and you know it.”

“I do. But you need to understand, Aunt Gabi didn’t explain any of this to me. She absorbed mom’s memories then shoved everything into me right before she died. I don’t have enough control to do a specific search through the thousands of lives that are in my head,” she shoved her fingers through her hair and dragged it away from her face. “I need to find someone with gifts specific to memory to teach me.”

My hands itched as a memory from the afternoon came free. “Mnemosyne.”

Colby and Blair looked at me with faint smiles. Colby finally chuckled and Serenity looked at him, confused.

“I knew sending you out there would be a good idea. Mnemosyne would be the perfect teacher,” his smile turned to a grin. “We can have her here by next week.”

“Mnemosyne, the goddess of memory?” Serenity asked, puzzled.

“More like quasi-goddess. She is not a child of Fiona, and as such cannot be a true deity,” Blair corrected lightly. “Much like Arcturus.”

“I thought she was an old wives tale,” my sister looked around at us.

“That’s how she started out,” Colby nodded. “Enough humans believed in her and what she stood for at exactly the right moment. She was created in a pocket of errant magic by wishful thinking.”

"That's possible?" I frowned.

"It was, thousands of years ago. The magic has been used up since then," Colby shook his head. "Oracles delved too deeply into the mists and depleted everything."

"We are getting off track," James remarked lightly. "We should move on."

"Yes," Serenity nodded. "Back to task. We've covered Mom, Sanctuary, and where all our money comes from. What next?"

I paused for a moment and really thought. "The Change."

"Kevin killed me after I caught him in bed with some blonde hoe. He was hoping you would die so I could be his trophy wife."

I shook my head. "Stupid human."

"Indeed," she chuckled. "Next."

"Why do you have more control over your bloodlust than I do?"

She shrugged. "That is a question for our presiding experts. They've lived it for long enough that they can answer just about anything."

Blair and Colby glanced at each other. "What age were you when it first started?"

"It was the day before Mom died. Fourteen, basically."

"And you, Serenity?" Colby asked.

"Seventeen and a bit. If it makes a difference, it was early morning."

"It does. When did it hit you, Amelia?"

"Almost midnight. It this related to what Nicole said earlier?"

"Possibly," Blair nodded both to Daniel and to me. "We have noticed in the past, among those born not bitten, that time of birth makes a difference. Those born at night, who are triggered at night, have a harder time controlling the hunger. It has something to do with the moon and inherent power in the bloodlines. Day-born and 'activated', as it were, have the warmth of the sun to help them balance the need to feed."

"So I was screwed from the get-go," I sighed.

"Yes and no," Colby spoke. "It is a gift as much as a curse. The hunger started in you much earlier than it should have.

Normally it starts in the year after you turn seventeen, like with Serenity. It is a combination of stress and hormones. When it happens early, it's because your dormant vampire side senses danger and upheaval coming and needs you strong so you will survive."

"So I basically did it to myself because I knew my mom was going to die?"

"In a sense, yes. Your survival instincts overrode everything else and left you stronger, faster, and more deadly."

"A perfect killing machine," I said blithely as I picked at a loose thread in the couch's embroidery.

"No. Not that. A strong, capable adversary," Daniel stopped my fingers with his warm hand.

I didn't look at him. Instead, I changed the subject. "When did the Hunters first appear?"

"They go back almost to the beginning of modern civilisation. The first one that we were able to track back was from the last of the Cro-Magnon humans. He was an outlier, a blip in the chain. The rest were/are all homo sapiens and homo sapien sapiens of much later eras in human evolution," Blair glanced at his brother. "Hunters became organised factions around twenty-five thousand years ago."

"We have no solid proof, but we believe Prometheus was the instigator," Colby shrugged. "The one who could have looked into the past to check is dead."

"Rylynne?" I asked, remembering things I had never seen. Fiona's memories, most likely. Information poured into my head and out of my mouth. "Goddess of Time by birth; Blood, Battle and Sunshine by acquisition and evolution. Daughter of Tisiphone and Ares. She liked to dance."

"Yes. She could remove herself from time and watch, even change, things that were to come. The past she could look at with no problems from this plane, but she refused to change it because of consequences she could not see until it was too late," Colby indulged in a small biography of the deceased, though clearly beloved, goddess. "She was the one who destroyed Atlantis. She ripped it out of time and obliterated it."

"Why do you suspect it was that asshole who was the '*agent provocateur*'?"

"It fits his style and personality. He's a sore loser. Has been since he was exiled to that mountain. He should be thankful he wasn't killed with the others," Blair spat. There was an undertone of extreme animosity in his voice. "He created a lot of misery before he had his ass handed to him."

"I thought there weren't sentient creatures back then," I wracked my brain.

"Sentient or not, everything had a soul. Prometheus tortured many of them into metaphorical insanity."

"But they healed?"

"With time, as all things do."

"If it is him, what can we do? He's too powerful to kill, and the Hunters need to be eradicated so future generations of our kind will be safe and free."

"That's not feasible. Part of our safety relies on human believing us to be myths," Colby interjected. "If we were to live in the open it would be total chaos."

"You've tried to before?" I raised an eyebrow.

"It's part of why Atlantis was destroyed, though this is neither the time, nor the place for that history lesson," he nodded. "There is not enough time left in this night to properly explain the complexity of that…situation."

"How late is it?" I glanced at the mantle for the clock, but it was no longer there. "What happened to the clock?"

"Almost three in the morning. As for the clock, one of the gears picked up a speck of dust and started to stick. It should be back by next week," Blair stood. "We will depart until tomorrow afternoon. We will find you when it is time."

"Good night," I smiled at them.

"Good night," they echoed before disappearing from their chairs.

The abrupt departure of the Elders seemed to suck the energy out of the room. I studied my sister's face for a long moment and saw dark circles under her eyes, as well as a sickly sallowness in her skin. A tingling started in my right shoulder and ran down to my fingertips; itching there until I reached over and touched her upper arm. She sucked in a deep breath as her face filled up and brightened.

"What was that?" she looked at me.

I shrugged. “No idea. It felt like something mom used to do.”

“She did have a spectacular gift for healing,” Stuart piped in, startling both of us. “I never knew if it was her gift, or an inherited one.”

“If she inherited it, it would have been from her dad,” Serenity stood and stretched. “Grandma Morganna just had the memory reading, that I know of.”

“Angels cannot heal others,” Daniel shook his head. “They can be called upon to fight, but they are a last defence. Dismemberment will not kill them as their energy reforms with little effort, but they are guardians of the dead. They have no need of healing.”

“How would you know that?” Stuart watched him warily.

“I have had much time to study the archives here at *Insula Templum*. I know much about the many species of our realm.”

“What is your species that allows you to know so much?”

“Draconis.”

Stuart shut his mouth and backed away slowly.

“Is that a problem?” I asked brightly.

He choked a little. “Problem, no not a problem. The Draconi were thought extinct, that’s all. They were so exclusive no one could hire them for anything. They always said they had a higher purpose that precluded them from the petty needs of others.”

“Yes,” Daniel smiled, the edges more than a touch evil. “We are the keepers of the gods and their cousins. By the light of the darkness we protect the pure, the ultimate –”

“Creators,” his voice was a bare whisper of terror before he, too, vanished.

12

"Well that was interesting," I smiled, standing and stretching my back. After several satisfying pops, I moved to the windows to make sure they were locked. "Any idea how he got to the island, let alone on this floor, without an invitation? I thought this place was supposed to be magically sealed."

"No idea," Serenity shook her head. "Maybe being a direct blood relative gives him a loophole he can skip through?"

"If that were the case Graham's family would have killed him already," I shrugged. "At least in regards to the island."

"I don't want to think about it tonight. Even with that jolt of energy, I'm still exhausted," she yawned. "It's a tomorrow job. So is figuring out why Stuart was terrified of what we are."

"Eh, I don't really care. Takes too much energy to give a shit."

"I know. 'Night Amelia."

"'Night Serenity, James."

"Good night, Amelia," he smiled before taking my sister's hand and leading her to the door. Daniel followed and locked it behind them.

"When was the last time you slept?" I asked.

"Define 'sleep'."

"Brain and body shut down for energy recharge."

"Before your arrival. Now that you are here, I do not need sleep."

"How do you function then?"

"While on watch, if there are no threats, half of my brain shuts down to recuperate."

"Like a dolphin."

"Very much so. If there is a threat, or you are awake, both halves are fully functional until unnecessary."

"I don't know if that's neat, or creepy."

"At times it can be both."

"Ignoring the odd sleep pattern, what do you do in your downtime? I'm not the slightest bit tired right now."

"Meditation, war games, things like that."

I frowned a little. "Is your speech pattern changing? It was much more stiff and formal the other day."

"Yes and no. When near the Elders it maintains the stiff syntax, but when with you and your sister my instinct is to relax."

"Is there a reason for it?"

"It helps me blend with the changing societies. I have at least six centuries left in my life, and it allows me to pass for normal."

"Very useful."

"Indeed it is."

We fell into one of those awkward silences that happen in the middle of the night with people you barely know. It was vaguely disturbing so I went to the closet to change into something lighter. Jeans turned into light cotton pants; sweater became a long-sleeved v-neck. The coat was hung carefully back on its hanger so it wouldn't wrinkle.

Coming out, I glanced over at Daniel and saw him balancing a dagger in one hand and flicking a flame across his fingers on the other. The little ball of fire changed colour with each flick until it had run the rainbow twice. Finally it jumped to the knife and turned the matte gray metal a brilliant blue. He snapped his hand shut around the blade; the fire ran up his arm and neck until it formed two great, curved horns on his head.

"You're thinking too hard," his voice was deeper and held a rumble.

"Probably," I finally pulled my eyes away and walked to the bed. "Thinking too hard happens when I'm not paying attention to it."

"What were you thinking so hard about?"

"Truth or what I should have been thinking?"

"Both," he shrugged.

"Your ass looks great in those pants, and where the hell do you hide those horns?"

He laughed. It was deep and rich and jerked my stomach to hear it. "I do not actually have horns yet. What you saw is the promise of what is to come. They are the final mark of power for my species, and they are bestowed once I have taken the oath of protection."

"And when do you take that?"

"Whenever you accept that I will be there to protect you until the day one of us dies. Unfortunately, that is more likely to be you than me."

"What happens if you take it and I die tomorrow?"

"Everyone dies."

"Is there something I should be remembering about that? It feels like I've forgotten something really important."

"It is tied to you being a natural-born Creator. Most of your power is still contained, which means it's compressed beneath your life force. Your life energy is a stabiliser of sorts, and if it disappears then your power will explode over this planet and kill everyone who is half-blood or greater."

I sat. I couldn't help it as my knees gave out and my ass hit the floor. "Shit."

"Yes."

"Does it apply to vampires who were bitten, not born? Why didn't Serenity dying create that reaction?"

"Bitten, born, it does not matter as the head of the bloodline is their source of life. As for Serenity, she was dead for too short a time, and she had already learned some of the greater gifts. She also had the chance to cheat death that you do not," he tucked the dagger away as he approached. "Have you finally reached your information limit for the day?"

"I think I might have, yeah."

"Then it is time for you to sleep and find some peace," his large, warm hands wrapped around my ribs and lifted me easily. He placed me gingerly on the bed and made me lay down as though I were a child.

"This isn't in your job description, is it?" I asked as he moved my rubbery legs until they were no longer hanging over the edge.

"Everything is in my job description. Whatever you need of me, with the exception of a lover," he shrugged, grabbing a light blanket from the foot of the bed and fluffing it over me. "I cannot guard your body if my heart is unduly involved."

"Sounds reasonable," I yawned, my eyes getting heavy.

"Sweet dreams, Amelia. I hope you can find answers in your sleep," his voice faded as the darkness of blissful unconsciousness sucked me under.

My doppelgänger was waiting in the darkness with her hands clasped in front of her. She smiled and held one of her elegant hands out to me. I took it from what felt like aeons away. Seats appeared behind her and she sat me down.

"Am I actually asleep?" I asked as warmth flowed from her hand to mine.

"Functionally, yes. Your body and most of your mind are in the normal state of recovery that your human half requires," she nodded. "Until I am closer to the surface I have limited capabilities in your body. However, I can help ease your troubled mind and sort out questions for later."

"Questions like what?"

"How are you going to live with the knowledge that has been bestowed upon you about the potential destruction of all my 'children'. To name one."

"You have some ideas about that?"

"Of course. It is my place to craft solutions to problems that have yet to arise. Not all can be avoided, but greeting them rather than trying to run can ease the blow they land."

"What do you see as a solution to this problem?"

"Give the power of the words to me."

"What?" I raised an eyebrow at her.

"Words, both great and small, have immeasurable power. They stick to you, dig deep and taunt you. But if you are strong enough, or have me," she gave a soft little snort, "then you can shrug off the burden that comes with them."

"Why would you take it upon yourself? You have a lot to deal with as is."

"I can handle it. Unlike you, I am truly immortal. I have ages of untold knowledge and wisdom fused to my basic energy. What is one more molecule, to me?"

She had a point, I had to admit. "Will I still know what will happen?"

"Yes. However, you will not dwell on it. It will pop into your thoughts once in a while, but it will be for only a fleeting moment."

"And never when knowing might inadvertently kill me?"

"Correct."

"How do we do this, then?"

"Kiss me, and let go of your iron-fisted control. I will do the rest," she leaned towards me. I met her halfway and found her lips to be exquisitely soft.

I relaxed and let go of everything. She pulled away slowly, and it felt like a great weight was rising from my shoulders with her. Unfortunately, my total relaxation came with a price. A crack appeared in the door that hid memories I didn't want to deal with, or couldn't deal with. A sliver of sensation slipped out and hit us both. Old scars on my left arm reopened as new wounds appeared on hers in the same places. Ribs cracked and blood trickled from our mouths. We shared a look of…something before she held up her shaking hand and blasted the metaphoric door with ice.

"Memories are more powerful than words can ever be," she coughed. "If your mind is strong, and you have death magic in your blood, they can be just as damaging as the original act. I am sorry that even that much managed to escape."

"Shit happens," I shrugged, then cringed as my ribs crunched and the gashes in my arm tugged. "What aren't you healing yet?"

"I will not heal until you do. As the damage was done by a memory of assault, not an assault itself, my form here will not be whole until yours is."

"And how do I heal? Blood?"

"Blood, and dealing with the trauma."

I shook my head. "I can't deal with it. I won't. That's why I put it in there, so I wouldn't remember. I *refuse* to remember that day."

"Why? What happened that's so bad you hide from it?"

"Someone I loved died. Because of me."

"Why because of you? What makes you think it's your fault?"

"He was human!" I screamed at her. "He died trying to protect me! He knew what I was and didn't care. He wasn't even supposed to be there that day!"

"Why was he there, then?" she remained infuriatingly calm. It took some of the wind out of my emotional sail.

"I forgot my bracelet in his car. He found it and was returning it."

"How old were you?"

"Fifteen."

"He was your first love?"

"Yes."

"How old was he?"

"Seventeen."

"Did he ever feed you?"

"More than once. He was starting to show signs of bite addiction."

She smiled a little and straightened in her chair. "Feel better?"

I thought about it for a minute. "A little."

"Sometimes you can deal with the bulk of an event without reliving it. Pain and guilt can multiply over time, especially when we blame ourselves for the death of a loved one. Yes, you loved him. Yes, he died. But he made the choice to protect you of his own free will. Occasionally, the universe sets people up to die as a lesson to those who survive. Maybe this was one of those cases. What did you learn from it?"

"Humans are food, and you should never fall in love with a steak you intend to eat."

She heaved a sigh and shook her head. "What was his name?"

"Jeremy."

"What did losing Jeremy teach you?"

"Humans are stupid, selfish bastards who like to play hero and die on you."

"Good, but try again."

"Never love a human."

"Amelia…"

"Okay, okay. Just because someone you love dies, doesn't mean you'll never love again. It just means you have to cherish every moment because you never know when it will be taken away."

"Very good. Have you loved since Jeremy?"

"No."

"Why not?"

"I didn't want to lose someone else the way I lost him, and my mom."

"Loss is a part of life, though. It cannot be avoided."

"Maybe I'm just not ready to potentially lose someone else."

"No one is ever ready for a loss. That's why you grieve."

I shook my head. "Not me. My grief is a living, breathing thing that sucks everyone down with me."

"Hmm. Interesting."

"How so?"

"Mine never did. I could experience it, then shrug it off."

"You're also billions of years old. You have methods to cope with your emotions."

"Yes, but it took me a very long time to develop them. It doesn't just happen overnight, or even over a decade."

"But your emotions never came alive and tried to eat people, either."

"True," she laughed. "And trillions is closer to my actual age, not billions. With that little information nugget, I shall bid you *adieu* for the day."

I was about to say something witty when she disappeared and the darkness became the back of my own eyelids.

13

My body hurt. It felt like someone had worked me over with a sledgehammer. I opened my eyes, only to flinch and try to hide beneath the thick blanket. My mind stumbled on that tiny detail. The blanket had been light when I fell asleep. And there hadn't been a space heater against my back.

"Do not be alarmed," Daniel's voice came through the fog in my head.

"With an opening line like that, how can I not be?" I coughed, my lungs aching.

He chuckled. "The wolf is here. Your body went ice cold during the night, and he agreed to keep his hands to himself while we used him to warm you up."

I wracked my brain for a moment, trying to think of who 'the wolf' would be. "Graham?" it finally clicked.

"S'meone say m'name?" the deep, groggy voice scared me upright and out of bed, pain be damned. He chuckled. "Don't think anyone's ever gotten out of bed so fast."

"Happens when I go to bed alone and wake up next to a stranger," I wheezed.

"Not a common occurrence?"

"Not by a long shot."

"You do not sound well, Amelia," Daniel lifted a sweater from the back of the couch and brought it over to me. I shrugged it on gladly.

"I feel like crap," I attempted to shrug before sitting on a convenient chair.

"When was the last time you were ill?"

"Before I started considering the upright and furless as food. I haven't had time to *be* sick over the last few years."

"Then we should take you to the infirmary for a full physical," his tone was authoritative and brooked no argument. "Can you walk, or will I have to carry you?"

"Gods no! Hermes would never let me live that down."

"He doesn't let anyone live anything down, ever. Trust me," he grinned. "Graham, I trust you can find your way out of here in a timely fashion?"

"'Course. Glad I could be of service to someone," he sat up and flipped the blankets off his thankfully clothed body. He smiled, "they told me to keep my clothes on and my hands where they could see them."

"'They' who?" I frowned.

"Daniel and your sister. She left once she was sure I wasn't going to do anything."

"Hmm. Well, thanks for the help?" What are you supposed to say to someone that got drafted into being a walking space heater while you were sleeping?

"Anytime," his smile became a grin before he bounded to his feet and out the door.

"Doctor, then food if they say it's okay," Daniel held a hand up in an indication that we should follow Graham through the door.

I stood stiffly, and almost waddled because my joints were so stiff.

"Are you absolutely positive you don't want me to carry you?"

"Hermes's Hell-Gossip."

"Understood," he chuckled. He stayed close to my side in case I wobbled.

"Why is the elevator always here?" I coughed as we approached the open Hell Box.

"Dimensional null-point, remember?" Hermes chirped brightly. "You look like a giant pile of crap."

"Thanks for the update," I grouched.

"Infirmary, please Hermes," Daniel stepped between us a moment before my stomach jumped up to my throat and my feet felt like they were leaving the floor.

I hit the floor like a ton of bricks when we stopped. My joints screamed in protest, but I forced myself back to my feet so I could avoid looking like an invalid. Unfortunately, it didn't stop the immediate fussing of a few very beautiful women.

"Don't worry about our names," a brunette with topaz eyes smiled as she took my right arm. "We are the Muses, and that is all you need to know for now."

"Come sit."

"We will heal what ails you."

"If we can."

"And if not."

"We will help."

"You heal yourself."

My guide sat me on a bed and proceeded to give the standard instructions as one of the others tucked a stethoscope under my shirt. I did the breathing, then held still while they did the blood pressure thing.

"There's a rattle-y crinkle. Probably pneumonia," a redhead with amethyst eye stepped into my sight line. "It's most likely bacterial, so we'll give you one of our special blend antibiotics. Take them three times a day, with food, for three weeks. That will make sure it clears your system. However, you should expect a longer recovery. It will take a while for your body to heal."

"You can't just do a poof-presto?" I wheezed past the ache in my chest.

"No, infections that attack the lungs are too tricky for us. They can have weird reactions to our magic. Broken bones, cancer, most other infections we can do. Comas we don't. Too many things can go wrong since we don't always know if the person wants to wake up."

"Why isn't anyone else infected?"

"They probably are, but still in the incubation stage. You likely picked it up from someone you fed on recently."

"Shit."

"If you say so," the Muse chuckled. "Once the infection is gone you MAY be able to shorten the total recuperation time by feeding twice a day. I won't guarantee it, but I do recommend it as a precaution."

"I can do once a day, not twice. There aren't enough feeders here for that," I shook my head.

"How can you tell that?" one of the other Muses asked as she handed me a large bottle of pills.

"It's an instinct of sorts. Part of me is always searching out food, and it puts a tag of sorts on those it feels are willing donors," I looked at the pills.

"Neat," she smiled before walking away.

"Go eat, take a pill, and rest," my main Muse ordered. "Come back when the pills run out so we can make sure it's cleared."

"Will do," I eased off the bed. "What about quarantine?"

"Unless you cough right in someone's face, they should be fine," the redhead shrugged. "This may be hard for you, but don't exert yourself."

"Mhm," I nodded, not promising anything.

Daniel offered me an arm to use as a crutch and I took it. My body hurt too much for my mind to argue. He kept the pace sedate and didn't seem to mind. Hermes was waiting, quietly. Unusually quietly.

"Hermes, what's wrong?" I prodded his still form.

"Huh? Oh, nothing. Just a couple messages I need to ferry around. Where to? I promise I'll be gentle this time," he grinned his normal grin.

"Food, please."

"Coming right up," he closed the doors and, as he promised, brought us down one floor without his usual theatrics.

"Thanks."

"Anytime. But gentle only when you're sick or injured," he chuckled before letting us out.

I looked back when we were halfway down the hall and shuddered. It looked like he was splitting himself in two, then three. When the clones were complete they nodded to each other and vanished.

"Try not to think about it," Daniel tugged me away from the scene.

"That'll be a little hard."

"I know. Amelia, look at me," he ordered. I complied. "Sanctuary's rules are very clear, but some of our residents have instincts that override their common sense. If they see you with that bottle, they may attack. It is better if they think we are intimate than for them to know you are sick."

"It's better for them to believe a lie than know the truth because I'm a Creator?"

"Yes. Can I have the bottle, please?"

I held it out and he pocketed it quickly. "I'll put one in with your cutlery. If you sit with your back to the room no one will see you take it."

"Okay," I took his arm again and we resumed walking.

"Your stomach may not like the idea, but eat high-protein foods. It'll help you keep your strength up."

"Does that mean…" I paused for dramatic effect. "Bacon?"

He laughed that deep, stomach jerking laugh again. "Lots and lots of bacon."

"Yum," I felt like melting in my socks as my face fell into bliss.

"Is there something I should know?" he asked as we entered the dining hall.

"If you're asking if I'll leave you for a platter of bacon, the answer's no. That doesn't mean you won't find me eating it at three in the morning, though," I slipped right into our charade as some of the predatory eyes followed us.

"Good. I don't want to play second-fiddle to food," he placed two trays on the counter and slid them down towards the eggs and meat.

"But you are food!" I affected a high, whiny voice.

"Sh! If anyone else hears that I'll be the most requested chew toy here."

"Mm, they'll have to go through me first," I grabbed a vine of grapes as we passed the fruit.

"Don't tempt them," he stopped and piled food onto plates I had failed to see him grab.

When they were full, I lifted my tray and tucked my elbows into my side so my arm wouldn't shake and betray our ruse. He chose a table in the corner away from everyone else and guided me to a seat, with my back to the room as he suggested. He placed his tray carefully on the table, then moved to the big pile of wrapped cutlery. His arm twitched a little out of everyone's sight before he returned. He handed one bundle to me before sitting. Unwrapping it, I picked up the pill with my right hand and rubbed the back of my neck with my left. Daniel gave a short nod and I popped it in my mouth; following it swiftly with a fork of eggs.

"Not so bad, is it?" he murmured, eyes scanning the hall behind me.

"Not right now," I shrugged back. Raising my voice a little, I continued. "What are the plans for the day?"

"You have classes, followed by lunch, then a tour of the libraries, more classes, dinner, and the conclusion of yesterday's discussion," he listed everything off easily. "Some of that may be negotiable."

"Which part, or parts?" I cocked an eyebrow.

"The afternoon classes. After all, you are still transitioning from human life."

"Euphemism?"

"Could be if you choose to see it as one."

"Then I won't. Takes too much energy," I smiled. Something about him made me want to grin until my face fell off. I was startled out of a quasi- whatever it was as Nicole popped into my peripheral vision.

"Didn't mean to scare you. Seat taken?" she indicated the one to my left.

"All yours," I shook my head.

She sat daintily, her eyes rich purples and greens as she looked around. White and orange cascaded and swirled before her eyes reset and she spoke. "There's something wrong. Someone's not supposed to be here."

If it were possible, Daniel straightened in his seat. "Good, bad, ugly, or neutral?"

"Unknown."

"Leave it be," I sighed. "I want to eat without having to worry about finding a chunk of intestine in with my meat."

She shuddered. "I did not need that visual."

"I know. Just needed to say it."

"Point taken," Daniel nodded.

"Good. Until a threat is actually a threat, don't poke it. Today, we don't poke anything. Today we relax."

Daniel, however, didn't relax. He maintained a discrete alertness as we ate.

"What's Graham been so excited about? He was practically bouncing this morning," Nicole asked.

"No idea," I shrugged.

Daniel shook his head. "Has he mentioned anything?"

"Not that I heard. He was just oddly happy," she frowned. "I can't read you today. Why can't I read you?"

"Probably something one of the Caretakers did," I shrugged again and bit back a wince. The near-constant movement was really beginning to hurt.

"Mm," Nicole nodded and delved into her food.

We are in silence after that. It passed quickly and turned into a blur. I don't remember finishing, or getting through class. Lunch passed with no memory, and the afternoon was flying by before it jolted back into focus.

I was on my back in the grass. Not in the clearing from the day before, but the main area outside the building. People were lazing about in the sun; some with books open in their laps, others apparently napping. It took me a while to realise what jolted me from my fugue. Colby had a hand on an open thermos to the right of my nose.

"Wakey-wakey, eggs and bakey. Sort of. Not really. Just coffee," he grinned.

"Time for another information download?"

"Indeed. Shall we?" he held a hand out.

I took it stiffly and he jumped us from the grounds to my room. The shift from horizontal to vertical made my head spin, but Daniel led me to a chair as Colby went to let everyone in.

Blair melted into his chair from who-knew-where as Serenity and James entered, followed by Persephone, Hades and Hera. They all found seats in silence as the windows were closed, the lights dimmed, and a fire lit itself.

"So," I looked around. "Where do we begin?"

14

"With you drinking a large cup of coffee," Colby flicked a hand at my low table. "You need to perk up before we start, unless Fiona can give you a quick boost?"

I shook my head. "I can't hear her clearly most of the time, unless I'm asleep. She might not be close enough to the surface yet."

"Then hot caffeine it is," Hera nodded, her voice mellow and calming. It was a startling contrast to her electric purple eyes. As she blinked the thermos disappeared from Colby's hands and rematerialized over several cups on the table. Cream and sugar appeared beside them. Colby gave her a sulky look, and she cracked a very evil smile in return.

When the cups were full, the thermos landed on the table and spoons appeared in a pile in the centre. Followed by a tray of bagels and fruit. I frowned at the seeming afterthought of food.

"Contrary to popular belief, we do need real food," Persephone winked, reaching for a pomegranate. I raised an eyebrow. "They're my favourite. Hades didn't want me to eat the first one, but I couldn't resist. I was too young."

"Okay…I get that there's a difference between the mythologies and your actual histories, but where did things get mixed up? Was it intentional?" I had to ask. It was something I had always wanted to know.

"Part of it was us, but most of it was the humans of the time," Hades expertly opened the fruit for his wife without breaking a single seed. "Though many Greek civilisations had queens, they were very patriarchal societies. They turned Zeus into a power-crazed, bestial rapist who hated humans and was willing to trade his children for subservience from greater powers."

"Hence the myth that he sold me in exchange for Hades not overthrowing him as King of the Gods," Seph popped a few seeds in her mouth. "Zeus didn't want me to pursue anyone until I figured out my gifts. He was the over-protective big brother. Hades was gone, deep into the earth creating a home for souls to come to between lives. It was millions of years before I really *met* him."

"A hundred and seventy-three million, to be a little more accurate," he corrected.

"I was that old already?" she looked horror-struck.

"You still don't look a day over twenty-three," he kissed her cheek.

"Liar."

"But you love me anyways."

"I wouldn't put up with your dirty socks on the floor otherwisc."

I could see that it was about to dissolve into an 'uh huh', 'nuh uh' war so I cleared my throat. She blushed a brilliant scarlet and silently nibbled her fruit. Hades settled more deeply into his chair and looked around for anyone else to speak. When no one did, I reached out and fixed myself a coffee. Taking a sip, I sighed in happiness at the rich brew.

"Are we still answering all of my questions with no censors?" I balanced my cup carefully on the arm of the couch.

"We are," Serenity nodded. "What would you like to know?"

"How did our line get started?"

"The original sisters? That was partly my fault," Persephone exchanged food for coffee. "Anna was twenty-one, Kitren was fourteen. The plague had taken their mother, and their whole town thought it was gone, but it came back with a vengeance. When the girls died, their father begged and pleaded for someone to give them back. They were his only children, his life. I took pity on him, and found them before they could be sorted into their destinations. To bring them back I had to bond my blood to theirs. Unfortunately, there were side-effects. Hades didn't know that I was the one who brought them back, and he sent the Furies to retrieve them. Tis knew as soon as she saw them, and tried to warn Maggie and 'Lecto, but they wouldn't listen. They wanted to kill. Maggie killed Anna, but the bond was still settling in and it adapted. The damage shifted to me, and she absorbed parts of their shapeshifting abilities in return. She came back to life a third time, and did one hell of a job keeping them away from Kitren."

"Is our line still directly linked to you?"

"In what way?"

"Damage, pain, stuff like that."

"Yes," she nodded.

I froze. "Then you know."

"And it is not for me to tell. Until you are ready, it is no one else's business."

"Thank you."

"No thanks are necessary."

The other immortals seemed to be completely confused by our short exchange. I wanted to say something witty, but nothing jumped to mind.

"Trying to guess what they're talking about will give you a migraine," my sister warned them. "Now, on to a more pleasant topic."

"Are we slated to die like our ancestors?" the question leapt out of my mouth before I could stop it. Not more pleasant, but different enough.

"We don't know, honestly," Hera answered. "Creators born of this earth are different from the ones made of the All Mother's blood. Combined, you could have enough power to throw off the 'curse'."

"But it isn't set in stone anymore?"

"No. Only time will tell."

"I can live with that. How did my father get in here last night?"

"A loophole we didn't think of," Blair responded. "*Residents* need an invitation to the upper floors. Blood-related *visitors* do not. That oversight has been corrected."

"Ninety-eight percent of our guests are orphans, and those that are not have measures in place to prevent this sort of thing from happening," Colby added. "Had we known that Stuart was still alive, we would have done it for you as well."

"How did you not know? Can't the head of a bloodline feel all of their descendants?" I frowned.

"I have so many that it's hard to keep track," Blair shook his head. "Too many die and are created every day for me to sense them all."

"That must suck."

"It does and it doesn't. The more 'children' there are of my line, the more powerful I am, but the trade-off is that I am less connected to their lives, if that makes sense."

"It does," I nodded. "Are you able to feel Serenity and I, as we're part of your line? Or are we blind spots?"

"That is an interesting question. I have only felt you once, when you fed for the first time. Since then you have been disturbances in the field."

"The field?"

"The network, the web. This may need a demonstration…Hera?" He looked at the goddess. She nodded and held her hand out to him. He took it and little sparks started popping to life between us. "There is a light for every one of you, and a pattern of webs connecting the 'families'."

I swallowed. "There are thousands of them."

"Hundreds of thousands," he nodded.

"No wonder you can't keep track of them all," Serenity whistled.

"Whose line does James belong to?" I glanced at his silent form.

"Mine," Colby inclined his head. "I can feel him quite easily, as well as his few brothers and sisters. We number at only a few dozen."

"Why so few?" I arched an eyebrow at him.

"I have a problem with blood addiction. It passed to most of my lineage, unfortunately," he sipped his coffee nonchalantly. "We run the risk of forgetting to turn others every time we taste blood and its emotions. The more powerful the food, the more likely we are to kill them."

"But James can feed off Serenity and not go overboard."

"They have a bond that helps him control the urge."

"In my day, I slaughtered many thousands," James admitted. "Your sister fed from me first, and it left a trace of me in her that keeps my need to kill in check."

"So if you fed from me?"

"I would kill you, and enjoy every moment of it."

I swallowed hard. "No feeding you, then."

"Not unless you bite me first."

"And I have no plans to do that, no offence."

"None taken."

"Hera?" I looked at the mostly silent goddess.

"Yes?"

"What are you doing here? I though you and Zeus were never apart."

"He's negotiating a truce between a couple of factions of shifters. Someone accidentally killed a few deer on someone else's land during the full moon a couple of months ago, and they got pissy about it. I have no patience for these things, and wanted to speak with Mother."

"If I could help, I would."

"We had a thought about that, actually. Seph's amazing with abilities, hence her teaching position here, but she can selectively activate dormant gifts," she looked at her little 'sister'.

"So…" I prompted.

"So, she could bring out a few talents that aren't highly destructive. It would bring Fiona closer to the surface, and ease that ticking time bomb inside of you."

"You know?" I frowned.

"We all know, and have for years," Hades nodded. "Every time you have almost died things constructed by our magic began to crack and crumble. Magic always falls away before anything else is destroyed."

"Originally, we didn't know you were the source," Hera added. "We didn't know for a long time that Creators had finally been reborn, let alone into the curse you share."

"Why me, then?"

"Luck of the draw," she shrugged.

I sighed. "How many active abilities did you have by the time you were my age, Serenity? Anything useful?"

"Depends on your definition of useful. I had thirty-one active by seventeen."

"Thirty-one? How many are there?"

"Thousands, technically," Persephone piped up. "Some are superfluous, though."

"What ones will you try to draw out of me?"

"I don't know. Whichever are closest to coming out on their own."

"Will it hurt?"

"Probably."

"Do it fast, then. Before I change my mind."

She stood and moved around the table to my couch. Sitting on the edge, she placed her hands on the sides of my head and closed her eyes. Her lips quivered as her palms warmed. I was about to ask if it was working when my head snapped back and my teeth crashed together. The pain in my skull was intense, and I tasted blood before that tell-tale shiver ran up my spine.

Fiona moved my hands, almost as though she were forcing them through molasses, until she could grab Persephone's wrists. Energy poured out of me and into her as our head came down and halos of spectrally diverse light cocooned the others. A dark spot bobbed behind the golden glow of my sister and our left hand moved from the goddess's arm to point at it.

"You were not invited," the simultaneously ringing-rumble poured from my mouth. "You are not invisible to those who can see."

Heads snapped around as the illusion melted. Fiona stayed, but the energy faded and she sat straighter in our seat. Hades was on his feet, one hand around my father's throat, as Daniel moved in front of us. Persephone seemed to become a puddle of pure relaxation in her seat.

"Bring him to me," Fiona growled.

Hades obliged by throwing him at Daniel's feet. The dragon had a knife out and against his throat before he could gather himself. I want to say that he whined and whimpered, but he didn't, unfortunately.

"How did you get in here?" She/we glared at him.

"I never left."

"Why are you here?"

"To see my –"

"Do not lie to me. If you really think I'm that stupid then I'll just kill you."

"I was gathering information," he gulped.

"Good. For whom?" We pressed.

"That I will not answer."

"You're scared," we chuckled. "I created every being that you could fear. Their biggest nightmare is me coming because they have outlived their usefulness. Now, I ask, who do you serve?”

He looked around at our assembly, then inhaled deeply. I’m not sure whether he was pausing for dramatic effect or not, but it took him a long time to actually say it.

“Prometheus,” he exhaled.

15

If they had been still before, they became statues. Serenity and James were trying to look at *me*, while the others were waiting for Fiona. I could feel her rage, her fury, and it burned me. I thought I was quivering in my passenger seat, but I realised she was trembling, fighting for control.

"Amelia?" she spoke aloud.

"Yes?" I paused, confused. We were sharing an external voice.

"I need more power. You currently cannot wield the ability that can destroy that little weasel," she growled.

"How far down is it?"

"Deep. I can ease the pain, but it is not a gift I ever wanted you to suffer with. It will always be active, and it will be hard to control."

I sucked in a hard breath to keep from stuttering. "Do it."

"Why?" she sounded genuinely puzzled.

"Personal reasons."

"You'll tell me?"

"When I'm ready," I nodded.

Stuart was looking at us in horror. "You…you're…" he stumbled over his tongue.

We smiled, and it felt fangy and evil. She blended our voices and we spoke with one mind. "We are Alpha and Omega. From us all came, and to us all shall return. We will avenge the deaths of our children, and pain will be the only companion of their murderers."

Sparks bristled and bubbled along our exposed skin. "Serenity."

"Yes?" She startled, not expecting the change of focus.

"I have a gift for you, if you'll accept it," Fiona spoke alone.

"I will, but why?"

"Never bring destruction to the world without an act to balance the scales."

"Will you kill our father?"

She laughed. "Oh no, no, no. I have different plans for him. I hold a special place in my version of hell for those who betray their blood."

"Good."

"Come and take my hand," Fiona held one out to her. She rose and approached silently. The others stayed immobile, locked in place as the ancient acted. My sister took our hand and the sparks jumped to her arm; igniting a light inside her golden skin. She breathed in sharply as I 'saw' where Fiona was directing her innate energy. Fiona sent me a small mental smile as she blew out our wings, and my sister's; sending her eyes a solid, shimmering gold.

It was then that Colby lost it. He launched himself at us and latched onto Serenity's throat. We were still connected, and blood poured down my neck as he fed. Everyone got over their shock at the same time; Hera grabbed Stuart as Daniel and Hades tried to strong arm Colby off her throat. James's hands were on her waist, supporting her as they finally tore him away, unfortunately with a piece of her still in his mouth.

Our glow faltered and faded. Fiona brought our hand to our neck and touched the gaping hole that matched my sister's. "Oh," shock was quieting her. "I can't fix this. I can't remember why I can't fix this…"

"Colby!" Blair was yelling for the attention of his rabid brother. "Control yourself!"

"I can't," came the snarled reply. "They smell – they taste! – so good! Just one more bite. Let me have one more bite!"

"No. Remember Alexia, remember what you did to her when she offered you that one more taste," Blair wrapped a hand around his throat. "You killed her because you don't know how to stop."

James had a bloody hand against Serenity's ravaged throat. She kept trying to speak but it was nothing more than a gurgle. Blood kept pouring from between his fingers, but it seemed to be slowing.

"How can you resist them?" Colby almost broke free.

"I can resist because my first feeding was from the All Mother herself. Because of her I do not *need* to drink again. I have control because she was pure; she was not born of this earth."

That seemed to take the wind out of Colby's rabid sales. He went limp and looked around, blinking fast. "Oh god. What did I do?"

"Amelia?" Persephone's voice was faint beside me. Faces were becoming fuzzy. "Can you hear me, Amelia? Fiona? Nod if you can hear me."

I tried to turn to look at her, but everything was slowing down, turning gray. One moment she was struggling to sit up, and the next she had me on the floor with a hand over my heart.

"You are not going to die, not today, because my neck now fucking hurts and someone needs to die who only you can kill. Now wake the fuck up!" she shoved power into me, an invisible wind blowing her hair around her face. She grabbed something from a place inside me that I didn't know existed and I screamed at the feeling of being torn apart from the inside.

My world exploded into flames and streamers of neon colour. My hands curled into tight fists and my fangs extended fully as the vault in the back of my mind came crashing open. Everything I had been suppressing for years came flooding out, and the tidal wave of it swept over the room. I had just enough presence of mind left to direct what Prometheus had done to me into Stuart. He needed to know the perversions of his master, and I didn't want the others to know any of it.

When the mass exodus finished I was able to take a deep breath. Persephone was sitting back, laughing for some insane reason. Daniel and Hades set Colby on his feet, and they were watching for a reaction from her that matched the metaphoric pool they were standing in.

"Don't mind me, guys," she chuckled. "I'm enjoying feeling fabulous too much to pay attention to the history floating around.

"You're better?" Hades confirmed.

"Almost like brand new," she grinned.

I rolled over and coughed for an eternity. My body hurt more than it had when I woke up, and I had a feeling I was going to pay for what we had just done. "Note to self," I wheezed. "Never piss of Persephone."

Serenity laughed. "I thought you already knew that."

"I knew the theory, not the fact," I smiled at her as James helped her sit up.

She was about to snap out a witty response when Stuart screamed; all eyes finding him. Blood fountained from his nose and bones broke; welts and burns and cuts appearing as my memories copied themselves onto him.

"Make it stop, make it stop, please make it stop! I'll do anything! Please!" Tears were streaming down his face and I sighed.

Inhaling, I brought the memories back to where they belonged. With every breath I guided them back into their vault. I left his for last, but the moment they were in I slammed that door shut. Lying there, I enjoyed the moment of silence.

"Well, that was exciting," Fiona chuckled.

I paused. "Why didn't I feel you rise?"

"I never left," she shrugged. "I was pushed to a side seat by one of your survival instincts, and it wouldn't let me back in."

"Hmm. Are we actually speaking out loud?"

"Yes."

"We must look like I'm nuts," I giggled.

"To a human, we would be," she smiled widely, cutting our bottom lip with our fangs.

"I hurt."

"I know. It will pass. I need to teach you how to control this new ability before you accidentally kill someone."

"What new ability?" I frowned.

"Hera?" Fiona called.

"Yes, Mother?" her voice came from behind us.

"Can we use you as a guinea pig?"

"Of course. Do you need me to come to you?"

"If you don't mind. I'm not sure we can move very far yet."

Hera stepped into view silently, and I almost went blind from the ultraviolet sun beating in her heart. The more I looked at it, the brighter it got.

"Careful, Amelia. You're sending energy from us to her," Fiona forced our head to look away. "Intent is ninety-nine percent of this gift. You can use it to give and take life, without leaving a single mark on the body."

"Nifty. Can I relegate it to second sight?"

"With a little practice, possibly," she nodded.

"And until then?"

"Be careful who you stare at."

I laughed. "No problem there. How low is our reserve?"

"We'll need to feed by the day after tomorrow."

"So soon?" I arched an eyebrow.

"Dying and healing take a lot out of a person."

"Dinner then sleep?"

"Sounds like a plan to me," she managed to get us into a sitting position. "Hades? Would you mind holding Stuart in the dungeon until we can deal with him?"

"I don't mind at all," he inclined his head. Snapping his fingers, Stuart disappeared. "Shall we pick this up when you feel better? I think I need to take my wife dancing."

"Go! Have fun," Fiona grinned. Persephone leaned over and kissed our cheek before they vanished as well.

"I am going to flagellate myself until I feel like I'm not an abject failure," Colby melted away, Blair following silently.

"You needed to speak with me, my darling daughter?" Fiona smiled up at Hera.

"It can wait until you and Amelia are better," she smiled back.

"Are you positive?"

"I am. Send Hermes if you need anything before then."

"I will. *Ayediesma*." *I love you* in their original language. How I knew that, I'm not sure.

"*Ayediesma*," Hera replied before following the others out.

"Are you okay Serenity?" I asked, trying to keep my eyes up and open.

"I'll survive. Just need some blood and a lot of sleep," she nodded, yawning.

"Come get me tomorrow?"

"As soon as I'm up and able," she promised.

"Take care of her, James."

"I will," he smiled before lifting her easily and walking to the door. It opened as they approached, and closed behind them without being touched.

"So. You think any of the food is salvageable?" I asked Daniel as I surveyed the essentially destroyed coffee table and Fiona retreated.

"Politely, no," he shook his head.

"Damn. I have no energy to change and go downstairs," I sighed.

"I think you can skip food with this one," he opened the bottle of pills and handed me one. Swallowing it dry, it took a moment to go down. "However, your clothes are ruined and should not go within ten feet of that bed."

"Fuck it all to hell. I'll sleep naked. If you could be so kind as to help me up and cut them off me," I grinned, half teasing him.

He laughed, long and loud. "You're going to need a bath, and you need some form of food to keep your strength up."

I sighed. "Something warm-blooded would be easier than going all the way downstairs for real food."

"Bathe, and I will feed you," he squatted down and placed his hands under my arms; lifting me easily and putting me gently on my feet.

"Where's the bathroom?" I frowned. "And why haven't I had to use it since I arrived?"

"Through the door opposite your closet, and I don't know," he paused. "It may be something to do with the island."

"Creepy," I grimaced before heading stiffly to the bathroom. My joints were screaming at me, and I could feel a massive headache starting.

Lights came on as the door opened in front of me. The room was full of creamy marble, and the floor was warm beneath my feet. The bath was a massive claw foot tub and water was already filling it. I paused by the edge and dipped my hand in to test the temperature. It was perfect, of course. Like everything else in my suite.

Daniel was behind me in a moment, silent but for his breathing. He carefully pulled my sweater off and dropped it in the basket by the end of the tub. The soft *snick* of a switchblade opening startled me; a second later it sliced open the back of my shirt. He moved the knife to the waistband of my pants as I peeled the sticky shirt off.

"I feel like an invalid," I wheezed as I was left standing in my socks and underwear. My lungs felt way too heavy, and the water stopped flowing.

"Get in, you'll feel better," he patted my shoulder. "I'll be outside."

I nodded and the sensation of him behind me disappeared. Stepping carefully into the bath, I sank into the warmth and smiled as my muscles relaxed. I managed to bring my feet up and get my soaked socks off before the last of my energy faded away.

16

The water was the pink of diluted blood by the time I opened my eyes again. There were patches of itchy dry flakes on my neck and I dunked myself; rubbing them off while I was under. Coming up for air, I peeled off my underwear and dropped it by the socks. Blinking to clear my eyes, I noticed shampoo and body wash on the low table to my left.

I washed my hair with the lavender-scented shampoo first, and finished with the pomegranate scrub. When I was sure all the blood was gone, I pulled the drain plug and levered myself out. I grabbed a towel from the rack against the wall and wrapped its luxurious softness around my body. Another one dried my hair, but I left it on the counter by the sink.

I was dawdling, I knew it. I didn't want to feed again so soon. I hated feeding, even if the donor was willing. Sucking in a deep breath, I made my way back to the bedroom and stumbled at the door.

Daniel was reclining shirtless on the bed, and a jolt of lust shot through me. Followed by an impossible fantasy, which got steamrolled just as quickly by flashes of memory that made me cringe. His eyes were closed, but a small smile curled up the edges of his lips. A red and gold sunburned inside his chest.

"I can hear your brain running through all the reasons you shouldn't do this, Amelia."

"What's a good reason why I should?"

"You need it, and I volunteered."

"What about bite addiction?"

"Immune," he shrugged. It made his muscles ripple and my mouth water. "What's one of your reasons for not doing it?"

The words were out of my mouth before my filter crashed down. "I have a weird, random urge to jump your bones, and I don't like sex." I clapped my hand over my mouth to prevent anything else from falling out.

He opened one eye and looked at me. "My duties as your guardian preclude any sexual contact between us, unless explicitly stated by a power higher than me."

"Technically I haven't accepted you yet," I spoke through my fingers.

"True, but no. I would not break your trust by allowing it. It would also likely strip my ability to think objectively about your safety."

"And my safety is the priority," I dropped my hand and sighed.

"No," he shook his head. "Your sanity is. There is a shadow in your past that haunts you, and every time you think you may be ready it rears its ugly head."

My fingers curled into fists. "And how would you know that?"

"The scars on your back. I recognise the pattern, and can only imagine what Promethcus did to you," both eyes were open now, and he was sitting up. "There is no shame in surviving, Amelia. You are one of the lucky ones."

"No," I growled. "The lucky ones are dead."

He shook his head again, more vehemently this time. "They're just dead. They can't pick up the pieces of their lives and make something of themselves. This is neither the time, nor the place for this conversation, and time is wasting. You're tired, and hungry, and sick. Feed, sleep, do something tomorrow."

"You're lucky I'm tired and hungry," I snapped, stomping towards him even though it hurt my knees. Climbing on the bed, I shoved him back and straddled his hips; holding him down as my fans descended. His memories poured into my head from everywhere our skin touched, and I leaned over; biting into his left shoulder. Warm blood raced down my throat, and I drank greedily. He jerked involuntarily under me, but I ignored it, his taste, and the flashes of his life as they passed through my mind.

Pulling away, panting, I rolled off him and across the bed. I was content in my anger to just fall asleep, but his breathing was fast and shallow. I was about to check on him when he shifted and his hand rested on my waist.

"Gods, your fantasies are vivid," he shuddered.

I frowned. "I don't remember sharing."

"Your control was down and it came through," he convulsed a little. "Fuck, those images are going to be burned into my mind for years."

"You'll get over it." Fatigue and partial satiation were making my eyes heavy as I yawned. "Everyone does."

Sleep pulled me under then, and if he replied I missed it. Fiona was waiting for me with her arms crossed and a frown on her face.

"Show me your back," she demanded calmly. "I heard everything."

I was still in my towel so I turned away from her and loosened it until the back dipped low. Cool fingers traced the masses of scar tissue over and over, but she didn't speak. Eventually they disappeared, and I turned to look at her but she wasn't there. In her place was the door to my vault, and it slammed shut before I could stop it. I wanted to go in after her, but my cowardice kept me rooted to the spot. I couldn't open *that* door. My mind just said "fuck no".

I was shaken awake some time later, but she still hadn't emerged. I wanted to be worried, but something told me that she'd be more homicidal than anything else. Orange and yellow eyes were bright with laughter above me, and it took me a moment to recognise Daniel. A moment after that I realised he was beside, not above me.

"This is one scenario I would be at a loss to explain if anyone saw it," he chuckled.

I tried to sit up and found I couldn't. "What's going on?"

"You tried to strangle me in your sleep, then you attempted to get my pants off."

Horror crashed over me. "No… I didn't…"

"You did," he grinned. "I had to tie a sheet around you to get you to stop."

A knock, Serenity's knock, sounded against the door. I groaned.

"Fuck me sideways."

"In your dreams," he got up to let her in. She took one stop in and looked at him, then me, and started laughing.

"I'm sorry," she guffawed. "Am I interrupting something? Bondage of some sort?"

"Hurry up and untie me," I narrowed my eyes at her.

"This is priceless," she shook her head. "What did she try to do?"

"Strangle me and get in my pants," he chuckled.

She doubled over and it looked like she was going to pee herself from laughing so hard.

"I claim no responsibility for my actions while I was asleep!" I shouted, struggling as claustrophobia started to set in, and memories of being restrained edged up. "Seriously, get me out of this thing right now."

Daniel grabbed a knife from a chair as he came towards me. He sliced the knots and grabbed an edge of the sheet; yanking it and rolling me free. Pulling myself to the edge of the bed, I hung my head over and coughed until something came loose. He fluffed the remainder of the sheet over me to hide the fact that my towel had disappeared sometime during the night. I wanted to know exactly what I had done, but I didn't at the same time. Something told me it was extremely embarrassing, on top of my faulty-filter confession.

I could hear footsteps, both approaching and departing, but I didn't look up. Serenity squatted in front of me and ran her fingers methodically through my hair; first one side, then the other, and back.

"We shall never speak of this again," I muttered.

"Mhm," was her non-committal response.

"Breakfast?"

"And clothes," she brushed my cheek as she pulled her hands away.

"Clothes would be good," I agreed.

"Stand up?"

"In a minute," I nodded. She stepped away and I stretched; rolling over and securing the sheet around my chest. I got up and stumbled to the closet, going first for underwear, then for pants and a shirt; this time dark red. Changing as quickly as I could, I ran a brush through my hair and pulled it into a bun.

"Food?" I asked, rejoining them.

They nodded and went for the door, me trailing behind as clothes appeared on Daniel's body. He caught me looking and shrugged with a sly smile. He held out his arm and waited for me to take it before continuing to the hall and elevator.

Hermes, as always, was waiting. He was lounging against the wall, picking his nails with a look of contentment on his face. He smiled widely as the door closed and took us down to the food hall. He didn't need to say anything; the look on his face when we stopped said it all. He had been rummaging around in someone's thoughts.

We got out, me blushing, and moved silently towards the loud buzzing hum of the residents gathered to eat. Quiet spread outward from the closest tables as one by one they turned to stare. I frowned, highly confused. There hadn't been this kind of reaction the first time I walked through the doors.

"What are they staring at?" I whispered.

"You," Daniel muttered, leading me to food.

"Why?"

"You're casting a little glow, and that bite on my shoulder is showing. They think you've claimed me as your private feeder."

"Why am I glowing? And why can't I see it?"

"That would be a question for Fiona, not me."

I let go of him and grabbed a tray. Loading it down with fruit, I bypassed the eggs and piled high the bacon. Adding a tall glass of milk, I looked for an empty table. Finding none, I made my way to Nicole and Graham at their wave.

"You look happy," Nicole smiled. "Anything we should know?"

"No idea," I shrugged. "Any news on the gossip wheel today?"

"Nothing major," Graham shook his head. "A few people on the upper floors said they felt like they were drowning in pain, but it passed quickly."

"Interesting," I filed that away for later. A hand touched the back of my neck and I tilted my head back. Daniel brought his head down and brushed my lips with his. I opened mine and he dropped in my pill, making it look to everyone else like it was a kiss. He pulled away, and I took a giant swallow of my milk. Serenity winked at me and took a seat.

Graham heaved an exaggerated sigh. "Well, there goes my shot at anything."

I laughed. "You really think a relationship needs to be strictly between two people? 'Cause monogamy is a genetic quirk inherited by few and forced on the rest of society."

“What do you mean?” he frowned as the others set into their food.

“We need to replicate in order to survive, yes? By having more than one partner we diversify the gene pool. It helps weed out recessive genetic diseases.”

“So you’re taking it as *carte blanche* to be a slut?”

My arm snapped out before I could stop it and drilled him in the jaw. “Suddenly, I’m not hungry anymore,” I bit out between clenched teeth. “Daniel, stay and eat. You need to keep your strength up. I’ll see you guys later.”

“Your gloves,” he reached into his pocket and handed them to me. Slipping them on, I let my anger and disgust simmer as I walked away.

Hermes was waiting when I arrived, his smile gone. “Gym?”

“Sure,” I shrugged, not really caring. A shiver went up my spine and my mouth started moving.

“The children here need a proper education, *midoros*.” *My son.*

“That one is too human, *Metaria*.” *Mother*. “And he is bull-headed. About the best we could do is take him out and beat him.”

“How have you been?”

“Surviving. Maggie and I are happy.”

“No kids?”

He shook his head. “All Daevas.”

“I’m sorry. I wish I knew why they happen.”

“It’s okay. We had a few years with them. It’s better than nothing, and far better than what Hades and Seph have had to deal with.”

Fiona frowned. “What have they gone through?”

“All theirs have died in their arms within moments of being born.”

Pain stabbed us in the chest. “They didn’t say anything.”

“They have trouble talking about it. But it’s part of the reason she’s sick,” he touched our shoulder. “Every time they lose one it takes a little piece of her with it.”

“My poor baby. No wonder she looked so frail.”

"We all stopped trying a long time ago. It hurt less if the memories aren't fresh and being repeated every few years."

"Still. No parent should ever have to bury their child."

"Though many do," he opened the doors. "Say hi to Arty for me."

"We will," she inclined our head and stepped out. We stood alone in silence for a minute. "I apologise, Amelia. I broke my word in always asking permission before taking control of your body."

"It's okay. It's *our* body, not just mine," I shrugged. "It's ours to share any time you wish. And I have a warning every time you surface."

"A warning?" she repeated.

"It feels like an ice cube is going up my spine every time you make yourself known."

"Interesting," she scratched our nose. "Though I find it more interesting that you weren't seeing the life forces of everyone in the hall."

"I have a denial complex, and I forgot I had that ability now."

"Very useful," she laughed. "I could never turn it off in my previous life."

"Maybe you were just too connected to the worlds around you. Isolation can have its benefits."

"It seems it can," she agreed.

"Out of curiosity, why do you speak to the gods in that old language?"

"Habit. It's a part of the language I was born speaking, and the language I taught them when they were created. It's a reassurance to myself, and to them, that I really am back."

I was about to say something when a high-pitched squeal came from our left and we were tackled by a golden blur.

17

"HI!" a golden-haired beauty with luminescent green eyes grinned as she sat on our stomach.

"Hi Artemis," we grinned. "Mind getting off us before our lungs explode?"

"'Course," she was chipper as she bounced up. She didn't seem the slightest bit fazed about our use of plurals as she extended a hand to us. Taking it, she hauled us to our feet with ease.

"You've been well?" Fiona asked, following the willowy goddess past all manner of sporting equipment. She looked to be around five foot seven, which meant she had been near semi-mature trees in the past day.

"Mostly," she nodded. "Humans have been killing my forests at an exponentially increasing rate, but I turned some against the logging industry."

"Good. These humans have changed so much since I left."

"You've been gone for ten thousand years, don't forget that part," Arty chuckled.

"It's been ten thousand years?" Fiona frowned, bemused.

Arty stopped and looked at us. "No one told you?"

She shook our head. "I haven't been back long. Maybe they forgot."

"Or maybe they didn't want you to feel guilty for leaving."

"Possibly."

"Where did you go? Why did you leave us?" Arty turned from happy to sad/angry so fast it made my head spin.

"I didn't think you would notice," Fiona sat. "You were busy with Atlantis, and I had been trapped in a physical form for too long. I needed a break from it all, and you were already hundreds of millions of years old."

"You were still our *Metaria*, our *gisareh*. We still needed you. Atlantis blew up in our faces after you left, and Rylynne had to rip the city out of time because we couldn't figure out how to completely destroy it."

"What did they do to deserve destruction?" Fiona was using her ultra-calm voice.

"You remember how advanced they were technologically?"

"Very well. They had bio-neural circuitry and a sustainable climate control system that didn't damage the environment," Fiona nodded.

"They developed a serum that they believed would make them gods. Their test subjects were turned into mindless supplicants that answered only to the person who turned them," Artemis took a seat. "When they finalised their serum they planned to unleash it on the entire city, whether willing or not."

"Aspirations of deification is nothing new. Why not just destroy the formulas and erase their memories?" she asked.

"We did, the first time. And the second. The last time they killed the queen and high council in preparation, so they would have no opposition."

"What were their average lifespans at the end?"

"Women were reaching eight hundred, men five."

"And the men were the instigators of their cockamamie plan?"

"A couple women were in on it, but it was overwhelmingly men, yes."

"How was the social structure? Were people happy?"

"Most were," Arty shrugged. "They had jobs based on their personality traits, all except the queen who inherited her position. The council were all elected; most were elderly and unable to do physical labour. The priests and priestesses were hybrids of hybrids who didn't fit anywhere else."

"So why kill them all? Why not just the unstable ones?"

"It was spreading. The idea of immeasurable power and immortality was jumping from person to person like a sickness. It was only a matter of time before people would be lining up for the injection," the goddess shook her head. "Enough of the past. Where did you go?"

"*Vrai Morte.*"

Artemis smacked her forehead and started laughing. "Of course you would go there! The one place none of us looked because it was too damned obvious."

Fiona chuckled. “Sometimes the best place to rest is the one least likely to be checked. How Hades missed me, though, is a good question.”

Arty sobered instantly. “Someone broke out the Malachai. He was busy dealing with that TARFU situation.”

“TARFU?” Fiona asked, and I smiled to myself.

“Totally and royally fucked up,” I chuckled aloud.

“Hi Amelia,” Artemis giggled.

“Hi Arty,” I grinned widely.

“Hope you don’t mind not being included in this chat.”

“Not at all. You have a lot to catch up on. Though I have no clue what a Malachai is.”

“They are Laksinki-Hellhound hybrids. We nicknamed them the Dogs of War.”

“Why was Hades dealing with them? Why not Ares?”

“The Malachai can only be controlled by the Seraphym, and those bastards are extremely rare. They also hate Ares for creating Hellhounds in the first place.”

“Being rare would explain why I don’t know Seraphym either.”

“Nephylem-demigod hybrids. And before you ask, you get a Nephylem when you cross an angel with a vampire. Though mixing a Nephylem with a human won’t give you a Creator.”

I frowned. “Why not? Creators are half-human, quarter-vampire, and quarter-angel.”

“It’s a magic thing. The gifts need to be passed from both sides to make a Creator. If all the power comes from only one side, nature won’t balance the way it needs to.”

“Well, that’s annoying. Back to the Malachai. Why did Hades have to find Seraphym to deal with them? Why not let them run around?”

Artemis just about choked. “Malachai are wanton destruction. Every time they kill, it feeds their power, and it’s cumulative. If they were to kill one of us, they could destroy the galaxy.”

“If they’re that powerful, why do they submit to the Seraphym?”

“Because the Seraphym can’t be killed. They are more energy than matter, and exist in a state of flux. Malachai rely on their prey being more matter than energy, therefore grounded, to kill."

"Neat?" I shrugged. "Anyways, I interrupted your conversation. Please continue."

"All righty, where were we?" Artemis pondered.

"Hades, Malachai; destruction of Atlantis," Fiona supplied.

"Ah, yes. Once they were gone the Egyptians crafted their own pantheon based on us, and it kept us charged. Did you know that worship by humans adds to our power? I lost a giant chunk of my forests. The Sahara turned into a desert. I lost so many of my precious trees. It was a slow creep. I didn't realise it was happening until it was too late. And I'm rambling. It's gotten harder for me to remember things, now that my forests are being destroyed."

"Did you ever find anyone?" Fiona changed the subject.

"No. Athena, Hestia and I are the only ones who didn't. We saw what was happening to the others and made a promise to each other that it wouldn't happen to us. Tisiphone had Rylynne already, otherwise she would have done it as well."

"What happened to Rylynne? How could she be killed?"

"She was seen using magic in public. A little girl was standing in traffic in her pyjamas, as though she had sleep-walked into the street. A direct teleport would have been too obvious so she used her telekinesis to save her. It was caught on a security camera and mercenaries came for her a few weeks later. She was living as a human, and didn't want to expose us more than she already had. She only managed to get one call out for help, but we couldn't track it back until it was too late. Tis arrived while Ry was escaping, but she was too late. Rylynne was shot to shreds in front of her."

"Did she get vengeance?"

"She left a crater where their facility used to stand. It took her a decade to step outside of her house after that, and her cloak is her only companion. It's the only thing of Rylynne's she has left."

"What happened to everything else? Her magic should have lived on after her death."

"We don't know. If we could find a way into her corner of time we might be able to get some answers," Arty shrugged.

"She never told anyone how to get in?" Fiona smiled a sly smile.

"She told you, didn't she? That sneaky bitch," she laughed.

"I helped her build it, of course I know how to get in," Fiona grinned. "Psyche and Eros are the only ones who can, though. You need to be born on this earth, not made from it, to breach the barriers."

"Safeguard against intrusions?"

"Yes and no. We meant it to keep out any powers from other parts of the universe, not you guys. By the time we realised our mistake it was too late to fix it."

"Do Psyche and Eros know they can get in?"

"Not to my knowledge. Rylynne may have told them after I left," Fiona shook our head. "And I shall leave it at that. I can feel a dragon approaching."

"Which is my cue to finish my lesson plan for the day. Need to teach these new guys how to take a lickin' and keep on tickin' now that Ares is cooling his heels," she got up, kissed our cheek, and loped away.

Daniel poked his head out of the elevator as we stood. "Persephone would like to speak to you and your sister."

"On our way," we nodded. My knees ached with every step until we were in the gilded cage with Serenity, Daniel, and Hermes. "Which floor?"

"Eighteen," Serenity tucked my right hand through her arm. The doors opened and she led me into a violently red and purple amphitheater.

"Don't blame me for the colours," the goddess's voice echoed up to and around us. "The protective wardings in here tinted the paint and we're too lazy to try to fix it."

"Or just too busy," Serenity called down to her. "Why, exactly, does this room have extra wardings on top of everything else?"

"This is our control area for testing powers and their ultimate capabilities. On occasion things get explosive. It also keeps things from bleeding through to other floors. All three of you, step on the landing at the top. Easier than walking all those stairs."

We did as she said and the landing rolled smoothly from the top down to the platform where she stood. When it clicked into place, we stepped off and made our way to the glowing goddess.

"Feeling better?" I smiled.

"So much fucking better. I feel whole again," she opened her eyes and chairs appeared beside her. "Sit."

We did as she bid and she twirled to her seat. She lounged, relaxed for a moment, then sat up straight and tossed something small at me. It landed on my chest and I got flashes of images from it. I pried it off as it started to burn.

"What the hell was that?" I rubbed the spot gently.

"Psychometry, still in its baby version. With training you'll be able to touch an object and see its entire past."

"What else did you give me last night?" I placed the bauble on the arm of my chair.

"Aura reading, emotional manipulation, and hyper-linking," she shifted a little.

"I've never heard of hyper-linking," I frowned.

"To the world, it doesn't exist. Eros and Psyche are the only ones who wield it, and they use it to fuse two souls that are meant to be together."

"Soulmates."

"Yes."

"How do they determine that? It can't be arbitrary."

"Souls all have a unique frequency, a vibrancy if you will. When two start to 'speak' on the same wavelength, they go in and clean their slates of their useless baggage to make it easier to bond the souls. Sometimes four or five will hit the same pitch at the same time, but it works no matter how many there are. It can get a little complicated, but it works out."

"Inactive?"

"Very, unless trained. You'll likely never use it."

"Good. How about emotional manipulation? Is it inward or outward?"

"Outward. I gave you nothing that could cause you harm."

"How does it work?"

"Touch someone and you can make them feel anything you want."

"Now THAT sounds dangerous," I grinned.

"Oh, it can be. Thankfully, though, you have to consciously call on it for it to work. Be careful, though. It can't fix everyone's problems and can be just as addicting as your bite. If you try to sustain a feeling in someone for more than five minutes, give or take, you'll run the risk of draining your energy reserves and you'll have to feed before you're scheduled to."

"Shit," I whistled.

"Yes," she nodded. "In case no one ever told you, the power behind your gifts is your life force. You have an advantage over other creatures, in that you can replenish yourself by feeding. Everyone else needs to rest, or for it to be given to them by someone else."

"It's possible for people to gift energy?" I frowned.

"It's a shifter ability, mostly. Since they're bodyguards, they needed a way to keep their charges alive until help arrived if things got hairy. A few humans have been gifted the ability over the millennia, but their lines have died out."

"Does that happen often? Lines disappearing?"

"It's the same phenomena as Daevas. We don't know why, but it happens. Our best guess with the humans is that their genes mutate and try to fight the abilities, and wind up killing them after a few generations."

"Why didn't it happen with our family, then? Why did we fall outside the norm?"

"Because of me," she smiled sweetly.

18

"Why because of you?" I asked, honestly curious.

"My gifts, what I was made from, is that thin line between life and death. Every other deity is one or the other. Because I straddle the line, how my abilities react to fusion with humans is much less deadly. You know that Psyche was human?"

"I know that mythology says she was human, if she really existed. She was a Greek princess, right?" I searched my surface memories for the story. "Something about pissing off Aphrodite?" I knew she existed, I just couldn't remember her mythology.

"She was actually Atlantean; 'Dite's highest priestess. She was a number of generations descended from a lesser Creator, the one that Colby killed. Her mother was the queen, but there were three others ahead of her for the throne. Long story short, I froze the calendar of her life. She hasn't aged in half a billion years."

"Froze the calendar of her life?" Serenity repeated, apparently as puzzled as I was.

"The way you experience life. If you think of it from a genetics point of view, as you age your telomeres get shorter every time they replicate as your life comes closer to its natural end. I put hers in a state of non-degrading replication. Until I will otherwise, or die, she will remain twenty-three for the rest of time."

"What about her brain? Shouldn't she have developed dementia a few million years ago?"

"Nope. Hers regenerates any damage on its own thanks to her heritage."

"So if you were to do to one of us what you did to her?"

"You, or a human at any rate, would be insane within a century, a century and a half at most. Human brains, though elastic, can only take so much sensory input and storage before the pathways collapse in on themselves."

"Why don't you do it to us, then?" I asked, thinking of an out-clause for our pre-determined deaths.

"I already interfered with the lives of your family," Persephone shook her head. "To do so again could rip a hole in the fabric of the current reality."

I sat back and sighed. "Back on track?"

"Sure. You got a taste of aura reading last night. It is also passive, unless you are in emotional distress. The worse you are, the stronger the emotions you're feeling, the stronger and brighter the auras will appear to you. Everyone has their base colour, and streaks or blocks will appear in it to indicate their health and how they feel."

"Shall we get training, then?"

"Not these things, not today."

"Why did you want me here, then?" I frowned.

"You and Serenity, as Creators as well as sisters, have two halves of a very powerful gift. Combined you can reverse the flow of time. Within reason, I think," she added.

My mouth fell open and Serenity froze in her chair.

"You are the living link to the future, and Serenity is a living record of the past. If I'm correct, which I most likely am, the two of you can create a time displacement field that will allow you to step into any point in the past where your ancestors were together. Why don't we test my theory?"

Serenity shook her head. "We risk altering the past, which could destroy the present."

"Paradoxes and their risks," I nodded.

"Hm," the goddess frowned. "I've never had to worry about paradoxes. This is something Rylynne would have been better with, her domain being time and all. Why don't we work on something simpler, then?"

"Why not," I shrugged.

"What's your hunting like? When you're going after the enemy rather than food?"

"Total blackout after the first few kills."

"Interesting," she steepled her fingers. "Did you ever accept your vampire side, or do you fight her when she rises?"

"I accept that it is a part of me, but no, I have not made peace with it. I don't like it, or how it makes me feel when it comes to play."

"Ah," she smiled. "Right there."

"Right where?"

"You refer to that part of you as 'it'."

"So? It's a violent, blood-thirsty monster."

"*She* isn't," Persephone stressed the pronoun. "*She* is a living thing, a living part of what makes you who you are. *She* revels in bloodshed and mayhem because your human half has been trained to believe they are bad. She is the outlet for your natural urges."

"I don't have natural urges. Nothing about me or my existence is natural," I retorted.

"*Au contraire*," she shook her head. "Stand up and step into the orange circle over there."

I stood as she asked and hobbled to the fluorescent orange circle on the floor. "What now?"

"Close your eyes and breathe. You may feel an intense itching along your spine."

I closed my eyes and wheezed through several breaths before the itching started. After a moment it turned into a tingling, then stopped.

"Open," she ordered.

I blinked slowly. "What now?"

"Look left and right."

I did, and took a step back. To my left was my twin with wings, and to my right was the red-eyed demon I couldn't look in the mirror, let alone full in the face.

"She makes you uncomfortable, doesn't she?" Persephone's voice was hard.

"It does," I nodded.

"She, Amelia. She is what you would have been had both your parents been pure vampire. Though likely not with red irises as they are a rare mutation in the vampire population. You need to make peace with her, as a sentient being."

"Why?"

"Because you, and your power, will be fractured until you do. If she wanted to, she could make you feed anytime she felt like it. That makes you easier to attack, and injure, and I fucking feel it," she snapped. "By cutting her out, you are cutting yourself off from important senses that can keep you safe."

"How do I make peace with…her?" I almost choked on the word.

"Talk to her. Treat her like a person. We will be back in fifteen minutes. Work your shit out, or I'll do it for you."

A black curtain of something fell around me and my parts, sealing us together.

"Ground rules for you two," the me to my left smiled. "No yelling, no hitting, no being mean. I don't want to piss her off more than neccssary."

"Agreed," the vampire giggled. "Now, Amelia, I am not an evil creature. I'm a survivalist. Yes, on occasion I enjoy killing. No, it is not my driving force in life."

"Then why do I blackout every time you go on a killing spree?"

"It's a defence mechanism of your human brain. It doesn't believe that it's okay to like what I do, sometimes enjoy it, so it blocks it out to keep you from doing it willingly. I make you feed when you need to, not when I want to, because you don't deal with it very well. It's understandable, after everything we've been through, but cutting men out of the potential food supply? Daniel was a very rare treat for me, and you didn't use his full potential as a feeder. I could have gotten a lot more out of that bite."

"That was all him," I shrugged, then paused. "Are you responsible for that fantasy that popped into my head?"

"Nope," she smiled. "That was all you. I did share it with him, though. I hoped it would change his mind so I could do a double feed, but his will is too strong."

"Double feed?" I repeated.

She sighed. "You really don't know much about our bite, do you?"

"Aside from being addicting, apparently not," I shook my head.

"One bite from a vampire of any kind causes instant arousal so that we can feed at the moment of peak euphoria."

"When our food orgasms," the angel supplied.

"Ah."

"Indeed. It also makes it more fun, less clinical and clean. It's part of why vampires are an addiction. Yes, some of us feed on fear and anger, but it isn't as filling as the good emotions. Moving on a bit, we still have the three bites, ever though we aren't a purebred. Do you know what they are?"

"No," I shook my head again.

"Feed, turn, kill. You need to will both the turn and kill bites as our fangs have chambers inside that store the things that do both. Killing by bite is the release of a neurotoxin that mimics botulism. To turn someone, you must maintain the bite for at least thirty seconds for the virus to reach sufficient levels in their bloodstream. You must not suck out any blood during that time as it will bring the virus out with it."

"How do you know all this?"

"We were born with the knowledge. It was written into our genes."

"And you're okay with all this?" I rounded on the angel.

"I find the two of you highly amusing," her smile became a grin.

"Are we okay now?" the vampire asked.

"Probably not, but I'll promise to work on it?"

"Good enough for me," she nodded.

"How often do you want to feed, if I'm holding you back?"

"Every four days, give or take. Sometimes I hibernate," she shrugged.

"I can do every six."

"Deal."

"Out of curiosity, do you guys know what Fiona does when she isn't making her presence known?"

"She sleeps, studies your memories, plays with us, teaches us things about how we were in her original universe. The fun stuff."

"She isn't bored to tears?"

"Not in the slightest. She likes watching. And not in a creepy way."

"There's a way that watching isn't creepy?"

They laughed at me.

"Think of her as the mother we lost," the angel shrugged.

"It will also help her take over our life when we die," the vampire added.

"So people won't know we're gone?" I asked.

"Yes. Don't ask us why, though. The future can still change."

"She can see it?"

"Just the big things right now," the angel nodded. "She has unfettered access to all Creator abilities, not just the ones that have broken through. However, when she has control of our body she can only use what you can. Thinking about it can give you a headache."

"Thinking simply, my body's limitations prevent her from being all-powerful all of the time?"

"Yes," they nodded. "But we'll overcome them in time. Just like everything else."

"We're like cockroaches; we'll always survive," I snorted.

"Eventually we'll also thrive," Fangy inclined her head. "We just need to get through the last of your scholastic and tactical education. After that we can go anywhere, do anything, by anyone we want."

"Six more months. Just need to get to our birthday, then we can leave."

"Why six months? Can't we delete unnecessary programmes from our curriculum?" the vampire's nose twitched.

"Based on the North American standard education system, classes should end near the final week of June," I shrugged. "I'm guessing these guys follow that system."

"All programmes are necessary," Wings added. "What if we decide to attend a human university? Tactical training isn't on the entrance requirements. We need the scholastics."

"But they're boring!" Fangy whined.

"Dyonisus might blow something up, would that amuse you?"

"Probably, yeah. But that's useful stuff."

"I think our time might almost be up," I looked at my watch. A watch I didn't remember putting on in the first place. "We good?"

"We will be," they nodded as the darkness lifted.

"Put us back together," I looked at Persephone.

"You've worked things out?"

"Within reason," we nodded.

"Good. Stand together, this will only take a moment," she waved us into the orange circle.

Fangy and Wings moved into place on either side of me, and their outlines began to blur. Their faded outlines touched my hands and dissipated between blinks.

"Learn anything?" the goddess raised an eyebrow at me.

"I'm nuttier than a fruit cake and should quit while I'm ahead?" I joked.

"Don't joke. I'm pushing you, probably more than I should, because you need to grow up a hell of a lot in a very short amount of time. Prometheus had a billion years on me, and no blood-bond to the All Mother, which allowed his potential to grow exponentially. His main tool has always been fear, terror. You know that better than anyone," she was in my face, angry – so angry. "You will have to face him, soon, and you can't feel the slightest quibble of uncertainty because he will use it against you. Deal with what he did to you, and move on."

"Seph?" Serenity piped up. "Even I don't know what happened. I know the events leading up to it, and the aftermath, but nothing about the month he had her."

"You've seen the scars? The physical damage he did?"

"She spent six months in physiotherapy," my sister nodded. "Daily physiotherapy."

"That's foreplay for him. The more damage you can take, the happier he is," the goddess returned to her seat. "Only three mortals have every survived being in his 'tender' care. Two of them killed themselves after."

"What happened to the third?" I asked, assuming I didn't count as mortal.

"She's been comatose for the last year."

19

"She's human? Or a shifter?" I asked, curious.

"Very human. We transferred her to one of our long-term care facilities once she was mostly physically healed," the goddess shrugged.

"Do you know why she survived?"

"Our best guess is that she entered a deep meditation that simulated death, so he discarded her."

"How old is she?"

"She just turned fifteen. Right in his target age range."

"Where was she from? What was she raised as?"

"Tibetan Buddhist, from Gyantse. She was the oldest of four children."

"Her parents let you take her?"

"When you appear to them in full deific glory with the promise of peace of mind? Yeah, they let us take her. We also had Demetre fix the soil they were trying to grow food in so it would actually produce enough food to keep their family fed."

"Where is she now? I want to see her," I reclaimed my chair.

"The Muses have her. They've made her as comfortable as they can. I'll arrange a time for you to visit, but you'll have to abide by their rules at all times," Persephone reclined. "Maybe helping her will help you. Who knows. Anyways, it's lunch time. Don't worry about most of your classes, either. I've already spoken with the others and they agreed to just download the information straight into your brain."

"Does the download hurt?"

"Not in the slightest. Hermes does it with your history lessons every day. He finds it easier since everyone has to use the elevator anyway," she shrugged.

"Why aren't all classes done like that?"

"Children need schedules, routines, to keep with lives balanced. Without structure, they develop behavioural problems. If we eliminated the class structure, we take away something they'll need in the outside world."

"Then why do it for me?"

"You're already fucked up. There's not much we can do to make that worse."

"Gee, thanks for the vote of confidence."

"What? Most of your life will be spent helping people around the world, not sitting in a boring nine-to-five. Except for a few, most of the residents here can pass for human and will be easy to reintegrate. The rest we can set up in companies like the one you're heir to so they can survive on the outside. But you, and your sister, have a higher calling. You two were born to bring this planet back to life while humans are effectively killing it. Before that can happen, however, you need to kick the pneumonia and learn to control your gifts."

"And to do that I need food. You said something about lunch?" I heaved myself to my feet and hobbled to the platform lift. Serenity and Daniel followed as I lost myself in my thoughts. Hermes was silent when we arrived, and kept his quips to himself as he brought us back to the food hall.

"Grab a seat, we'll bring you food," Daniel whispered in my ear as he slipped a pill in my half-clenched hand. "Not many people should have arrived yet."

I nodded and did as he said while they branched off. He was right; not many people were there. I chose a table in the far corner so that I could people watch. Pale shimmers popped in and out of sight around people trickling in. It was disconcerting, and distracting, to see how strangers felt. Serenity and Daniel arriving barely registered until she touched my cheek.

"What's wrong?" she asked, taking a seat beside me and placing a plate in front of me. A sandwich, of course.

"I don't want to do this," I picked at the crust, a tear rolling down my cheek. "I don't want to be special, or necessary. I want a normal, boring, human life where none of this bullshit exists."

"That's normal. Do you think I wanted to hold Mom in my arms while she died? To know I would die within six months of her and come back a homicidal monster? None of us want the lot we're dealt in life, Amelia. We roll with what we get, or we die," she placed her hands over mine. "What else is wrong? Wait, eat first. Tell me after."

"Okay," I nodded, not sure if I could actually tell her. I hadn't told a soul in the two years since it had happened.

The hum in the hall was subdued, scared even, compared to this morning. It was like they knew something was wrong. I washed my antibiotics down with hot coffee, then slowly ate my food. When I was done my plate and cup disappeared, and I returned to watching the other orphans.

"How secret are secrets here?" I shifted my eyes to Daniel.

"Depends on where the conversation took place," he shrugged.

"Any idea what everyone here knows?"

"No idea," he shook his head. "But Nicole is approaching."

"And she's unusually well tapped-in to the rumour mill," I nodded.

She paused at our table and looked at me, fear and dread equal parts in her cascading eyes. "Graham suffered a psychotic break in the gym after you hit him. People are scared of what you'll do to them if they speak out of place. You should never have come here. You're upsetting our balance."

She was gone again before I could open my mouth.

'Fiona?' I thought, calling up the ancient.

'Yes?' her mental voice sounded sleepy.

'Any idea how us punching Graham could cause a psychotic break?'

'It wouldn't.'

'Thanks.'

'Anytime. Oh, Amelia?'

'Yes?'

'Don't be afraid to tell someone the truth. When you do, start with Jeremy.'

She faded away before I could think anything else at her.

"Fiona says we didn't cause Graham's break," I glanced between Daniel and Serenity.

"Changing the minds of people here may be a tad difficult," she shook her head. "Some of those looks are treading into dangerously hostile territory."

"They won't risk Sanctuary being revoked. They'll posture, but they won't act," Daniel shrugged. "They're cowards."

"Most people are. Shall we go before things get ugly? I'm tasting ozone," I struggled to my feet before taking Daniel's offered arm. It was highly unpleasant walking past all the confrontational stares. Once we were out if felt like a giant weight was lifted from my shoulders.

"That was…unpleasant, to say the least," Serenity picked her nails. "Where to now?"

"I have to tell you something, where no prying ears can hear," I spoke at the elevator.

"James?"

"Can hear it from you after. I don't know if I could say it with more than you there."

"Your room?"

"Sure. You don't mind not being included in this, do you Daniel?" I asked my 'bodyguard.'

"I already know the gist, I don't need the details," he inclined his head as the doors opened. "I must speak with the Caretakers even still."

"Thirty-six, please, Hermes," I managed half a smile at the god.

"Coming right up. The Muses said to tell you that you can see their guest after dinner."

"Thanks. Do you really drop information into everyone's heads?"

He chuckled. "It's easier than a real class, since everyone goes through me anyways. Here you are."

He opened the door and Serenity and I stepped out. He and Daniel were gone a moment later. We walked silently to my room, and maintained the quiet as we entered and took seats. I sat in one of the comfy chairs, while she settled on the couch.

I sucked in a deep breath and started. "Do you remember the night Jeremy died?"

"Vaguely," she nodded. "That was the night you disappeared for a month. He was in pieces on the carpet."

"An ambush was waiting for me when I got home. He arrived when they were dragging me out the side door, and they murdered him when he tried to save me," I picked at my gloves, not looking at her. Thinking about it made me feel dirty. "They took me to a bunker in the mountains, and Prometheus was waiting. He kept me chained in a dungeon while he beat me, tortured me…raped me. If I fought too much, he would have his minions hold me down, or he'd smash my head into the wall until I just stopped moving. He kept trying to make me beg for mercy, but I couldn't. He would have killed me if I had. He got tired of me when I stopped healing, I was so hungry, and he threw me away like garbage when I no longer amused him. Hunters found me in the woods, normal hunters, not the bad kind. They were horrified by me; I could see it in their eyes. They didn't know how I could still be alive with my guts hanging out. I kept asking them 'call my sister', but they didn't. They called an ambulance, but I passed out before it got there. They next time I came to you and James were there."

I closed my mouth before my voice could break and looked up. Serenity was green. She stood slowly, then sprinted for the bathroom. I could hear her retching, but I didn't go to her, I couldn't. I couldn't put the genie of that memory back in its bottle. It was like living it all over again; I could still feel the blades slicing through my flesh, the fists breaking my bones. I took a deep breath, closed my eyes, held it. I let it out with a big cough and the phantom sensations faded. I opened my eyes again when she touched my knee. She was crouching in front of me, tears in her red and gold eyes.

"I'm so sorry, honey. I should have been there when you got home."

"It was date night, you couldn't have known," I wrapped my arms around her shaking shoulders.

"Fuck date night. I should have been there. At least you told me," she hugged my legs. "Will you allow me to take the memory from you? So you'll never have to relive it again."

Fiona's shiver ran up my spine, and Serenity jerked away as though she felt it.

"Sorry for startling you. I was unaware the sensation could be shared," she relaxed our body.

"It's all right, I just wasn't expecting it. What's up?"

"I cannot allow you to take these memories from her, not yet. I can use it as fuel to destroy the monster I created, without draining Amelia's life energy."

"Memories can be used as fuel?"

"For me, yes. What Prometheus did to your sister ignites a rage inside me that this world is not prepared to see. I could implode the galaxy with it if he weren't my target."

"That's ten levels of frightening."

"It should be. If it weren't for my love for my other children, I would do it. Though I may rethink Ares. He is too much like Prometheus, in a bad way."

"Ares may be an asshole, but he doesn't harm children outside of the training room. He just has rage issues," Serenity shrugged.

"Maybe not, but he already has a strike against his life," Fiona nodded. "Rylynne existed because he assaulted Tisiphone. It may have been a case of mistaken identity, but he could have stopped the moment he realised she wasn't Alecto."

"Certain personality types don't stop for anything. Is there anything you or Amelia need right now?"

"Just some time to ourselves before we go see the girl. Go, see James. Tell him what Amelia told you, if you wish," Fiona patted her shoulder. "She'll be okay."

"Yell if you need anything," Serenity stood stiffly and left.

Fiona was silent for a long moment as she departed. "I hope you don't mind that I intruded."

"Not at all. I don't want her to know the specifics of what he did. A glossed overview is good enough. She already feels guilty for being out with James that night."

"And you don't want her to suffer unnecessarily."

"Yes."

"Admirable."

"If you say so. Out of curiosity, how were you able to get past the door?"

"When I sealed it with ice, I left a crack as an access hatch. Your willpower kept the memories in, but I wrote in a back door while you were doing other things."

"So you know."

"I know everything, and it saddens me. The world is not a pretty place, and I should never have let that evil live after what he and his brethren did."

"The landscapes are great; it's just the people that suck."

She chuckled. "True enough."

"Can you teach me some of your old language? It's so soft and lyrical. Soothing."

"If you wish, I can teach you a few sentences."

"I do wish."

"Aye dies moren chshara."

"I love…"

"My family. Our words had a weird way of conjugating and pluralising. We didn't have contractions."

"Neat. Was it easy to learn?"

"Like any language, if you weren't a native speaker it could be complicated."

"Tell me something else."

"Sec gisareh, mar tomos, dama nie gorro ma sesava."

"Gisareh," I repeated the word. Artemis had used it earlier.

"The guide, your heart, will never steer you wrong. Artemis always confused me with her true guide. She didn't listen to her heart enough."

"She's still a little girl in a lot of ways. She didn't lose a lot of her innocence."

"And that's a good thing. She can still hope for the best."

"Until her naivety gets the better of her. She'll have to grow up sometime, whether she wants to or not."

"And that is something I hope never happens. Unlike Apollo, her twin in so many ways, she is renewed in body, mind, and spirit as her element cycles through its many lives."

"Lucky her."

"Lucky indeed."

"Were they all innocent when they were first made?" I was thinking of Ares.

"They had rough edges, but they had no inclinations towards violence. They picked things like that up over millions of years of planetary shifting."

"What do you think happened to change them so much?"

"Life."

20

"That seems like a cop-out of an answer," our nose twitched.

"Why? From the moment you're born your experiences change you. When you die, you have nothing in common with the person you started as."

"Still. There are people who grow up in violence, who know nothing but, and yet they do not involve themselves in it."

"There are some people, and creatures, who are innately good, yes, but my children were neutral. They have freedom to choose how they fall, as good and evil are purely human concepts. Violence, as distasteful as it is, is sometimes necessary. Like destroying the monstrosity I unleashed on this world. The knowledge of when to put the swords down and speak in peace is also something I never got to teach some of them."

"But if good and evil are human concepts, why do you refer to Prometheus as evil? Isn't that hypocritical?"

"Yes and no. I believe in good and evil, but I was raised to believe in them. They are concepts constructed by human minds to create cohesive societies."

"How different are humans in this universe compared to yours?"

"Mentally, remarkably similar. Physically, there are many differences. Most humans had three eyes, some four. A few billion had three sets of teeth in their mouths. Interbreeding with species from other planets produced some interesting results. Angels and vampires evolved from very early humans, trillions of years before my parents were born. They were already thousands of years old when they met. Unlike you, my mother was the half-vampire and my father the half-angel."

"Wait," I paused. "Female vampires can reproduce?"

"Oh yes. It doesn't happen often, but vampire babies do exist. They mature faster than humans, or even half-breeds, and they have perfect control over their hunger. Ma'at, the Egyptian 'goddess', was actually a purebred vampire. She was born not long before I went on vacation."

"Ma'at? She wasn't linked to any of the existing gods?"

"She was one of the ones who was not. Ma'at was one of Colby's line of vampires, through both her mother and father," Fiona paused. "Dinner should be soon. Would you like to change your clothes?"

I frowned. "How is it almost dinner time? We've barely been here half an hour."

"I manipulated your perception of time. Our short conversation has actually taken several hours. Daniel is waiting outside for us."

"Why did you fuck with my head?" I snapped, suddenly angry.

"To protect you."

"From what?"

"Yourself."

"Why would I need to be protected from myself? It's not like I'm going to take a flying leap off the balcony."

"You did it once before. Only it was a cliff, not a balcony."

I froze, confused. "I did what now?"

"You don't remember?" she raised one of our eyebrows.

"Remember what?"

"The first time I ever surfaced, it was because you threw yourself off a cliff. You couldn't have been more than fifteen."

"How did we survive? And why don't I remember?" My flash of anger was smothered and replaced by perturbment.

She giggled, then cackled. "You keep forgetting what your grandfather was. Angels have *wings*, Amelia. It was the first time we flew. As for why you don't remember, I honestly don't know."

"Another mystery, then," I sighed, setting our feet on the floor and flinching as our knees popped. "Shall we eat?"

"We shall," she brought us out of the chair. "I feel like a steak tonight, and your memories of potato salad are tantalising."

"Done. Anything else?"

"A good beer."

"That might be a little harder. I don't know what the rules on alcohol are here."

"We'll find out then, won't we?"

I nodded and walked to the door. It opened at our approach and Daniel stood there, as Fiona had said, waiting for us to emerge.

"Are you all right?" he asked as we closed the door.

"Been better," I shrugged.

"I can't imagine how painful that must have been for you."

"I would rather have teeth pulled out without anaesthetic than do that again."

"Understandable," he nodded. "Food, then infirmary. We are expected in the next hour."

"Okay. Eat quickly then."

The elevator doors opened and I paused. Hermes wasn't our driver for the evening. Colby, Blair, and an Unseelie sidhe stood inside. Fiona perked up and grinned.

"Callasulashin, it's been a very long time," she placed our hand against something I couldn't see. "How are the sidhe doing? Has the in-fighting stopped?"

"It comes and goes," he/she/it spoke with a voice that didn't help with identifying gender in any way. "The Caretakers told me you had returned. I didn't expect your new body to look so much like your old one."

"Quirk of nature, and maybe a little gene manipulation aeons ago," Fiona shrugged. "Amelia, my hostess, has run across the sidhe before, it seems."

"My sister asked them to help us, once. They turned their backs and left us to die," I barely managed to keep my tone polite through clenched teeth.

Confusion flitted across the face of the obsidian sidhe. "Why have you not destroyed the consciousness of the body? Surely it must be straining to house you both."

"This is her body, Calla, and she is a Creator. I speak through her mouth, with her permission, because she is a person and I have no right to end her short life."

"When did you develop a conscience?"

"When did you lose yours?" Fiona countered, crossing our arms over our chest and turning our back on it. When the doors opened again, Fiona stalked out; Daniel, Colby and Blair following us. When we were halfway down the hall two hands on our shoulders brought us to a stop. Fiona turned to face the trio, and they all took a step back. "What now?"

"We've been thinking," Colby started.

"Discussing, really," Blair continued.

"All ears here," Fiona tapped our foot.

"Tensions among the student population have been rising since Amelia arrived. They know she's a Creator, but they don't understand what that means, or that you're back. Most of them don't even know who you are. We're thinking of an introduction," Colby glanced around furtively. "Amelia took down Ares with her own power, and they should know that."

"So that they don't attack her for being that much different?"

"Fear of her might remove their fear of losing Sanctuary. Fear of you may calm them down."

"Small minds have a way of lashing out," Fiona shrugged.

"But they are still children. Give them a reason to back off. Make it flashy. Introduce yourself to the little world we have here," Blair motioned towards the food hall.

"I just want a bloody beer," Fiona sighed.

"Perfect starting point. Some of the students will try to stop you as our age of majority is eighteen," Colby nodded. "They know Amelia is seventeen."

"Essentially I get to start a fight."

"Without the consequence of losing Sanctuary," Blair added.

"Fine, I'll do it. And I'll try to not blow anything up."

"Easy one there. I can't control fire yet," I piped up. "Can we go? I need to eat, soon."

"But we can drain them of their life energy," Fiona reminded me. "By the way, what's your alcohol tolerance?"

"Very high."

"Good. Let's go eat. Do you mind playing second fiddle?"

"I don't mind at all."

Fiona smiled, and it felt evil. She turned on our heels and strode confidently to the open doors; walking through as though she owned the place. The hostile glares started immediately, but she ignored them and grabbed a tray. She seemed to feel none of the pain that every breath, every step, sent stabbing through me. She filled our plate and came to the end of the buffet. Bottles of beer sat behind the coffee, tea, milk, and juice. Fiona reached for one of the slender-necked bottles, and as though on cue, a feline-esque hand gripped our wrist.

"You're underage, Hartley," the girl growled.

"Remove your paw, leopard," Fiona smiled. I felt her spark, as though she came to life inside/beside me. Fiona removed our hand from our tray and straightened to our full height.

"No beer, Hartley. You may think you're royalty because of thc special treatment you're getting, but you're not. Being a Creator doesn't mean you're above the rules of Sanctuary."

Fiona laughed. It was deep, full, and terrifying. The leopard let us go and took a swift step back. When she opened our mouth I could feel the fully extended fangs, and the rippling of our eyes turning to pools of silver. Seconds later I felt our back open up and heard our clothes rip. She turned and faced the room at large, moving our wings just enough to take us off the floor.

"Children," the rolling harmony of three voices speaking as one came out. "Amelia isn't here right now. She is my host body. My very powerful, very dangerous host. She bested one of my children without my help." She closed out eyes and breathed deeply for dramatic effect. "Such power in the hands of an untrained. Now, for introductions. My name is Fiona Amina Seratie Morovica. If any of you know the origins of your species, you might recognise me by my other name. I am the All Mother. From me all life came, and to me it shall return. I survived the destruction of the last universe and the birth of this one. I walked the space between the stars of my birthplace for trillions of years before it became this place. I see all. I hear all. I know all. Now let me have a fucking beer in peace."

She set us back on the floor and tucked our wings in. She took in the looks of shock and horror, giggling inside our head. A piece of cutlery fell out of someone's hand and hit the floor. The dead silence broken, the room erupted into pandemonium. Fiona grabbed a beer and took a swig, watching as the screaming adolescents ran for the elevator. It took a few minutes for the room to clear out, but once the last person was gone Blair, Colby, and Daniel all had a good laugh. Our wings evaporated, fangs retracted, and eyes returned to normal.

"That was fun," she grinned. "When can I do it again?"

"Do you want to go species by species, or tell everyone at once?" Colby was still chuckling.

"Oh, I think everyone at once," she took a long drink.

"Give us two months," Blair came over and grabbed his own bottle of beer.

"Done. Shall we eat now?"

"We shall," Daniel grabbed our tray and brought it to a table nearby.

Sitting, Fiona dug in while the others got their own food. She was halfway through the food when Serenity and James arrived. They looked around the empty, messy hall, confused. Two vacant seats appeared at our table and Fiona waved them over.

"What the hell happened in here?" James asked as they sat.

Daniel held his hand out to my sister. "Better to show than tell."

She stripped off one of her gloves and took his hand gingerly. A moment later she started laughing until tears welled up in her eyes. Releasing Daniel's hand, she grabbed one of James's; he soon smiled, then laughed until he choked.

"I'm sorry we missed that," Serenity chuckled.

"You can see the next one live," Fiona giggled. "All members of all species at the same time."

"When?" James asked, recovering.

"Two months," Colby finished his meal.

"Where? Not in public, I hope," Serenity inquired.

"Hades might loan us one of his halls," Blair thought about it for a moment. "They expand as needed for events."

"What if they don't want to accept that she's back and try to attack Amelia?"

"If all goes to plan, I'll have Prometheus's head on a spike by then," Fiona shrugged.

"And if your schedule gets blown off track?"

"I'll deal with it. Now go get some food. I need you strong."

21

Once everyone had food, Daniel handed Fiona my antibiotics. She washed it down with a grimace.

"I don't understand how Amelia can swallow those vile things without some form of liquid," Fiona sat back, our plate clean.

"Dry swallowing? Some people can't do it at all," Serenity shrugged.

"Why would anyone want to do it?"

"Amelia doesn't care, most of the time. The only thing she really likes drinking is coffee."

'And tequila,' I thought, slightly snidely.

"Hm," Fiona nodded, to both of us.

She waited until everyone was done eating before speaking again. She weighed her words, testing them almost.

"Since we're all assembled, what do I really need to do? Amelia is my perfect host for a reason. Why? Why now?"

Blair and Colby exchanged a look I couldn't decipher. Neither could Fiona, apparently. She frowned at them and they leaned away from us.

"You have learned much about schooling your features in the last ten thousand years. Speak, my children. Before I dig it out of you."

They sighed and relaxed an iota. "We really don't know. The undergrounds have been hotbeds for rumours, but nothing has been substantiated. Every lead we follow turns into a dead end, and we have to start over."

Our nose twitched. "How many so far?"

"Five hundred and seventy-three," Blair paused. "Seventy-four, sorry."

Fiona smiled. "Don't you remember how to *see*?"

"As with Stuart?" Colby raised an eyebrow.

"Indeed."

"We don't think to use that sight anymore. You were the only one we knew who could hide things in a way that would force us to use it."

"It was a gift carried by one of the lesser Creators, and I know he had children. Search again, and look through the obvious."

"Of course, *Metaria*," Blair nodded. "I do have one question."

"Ask it."

"If you can access all gifts when Amelia is in control, how can you not see the cause of your return?"

"My sight is being blocked," she shrugged. "Whoever, or whatever, is doing this is using an eddy to hide their actions. Until the distortion is fixed I will not be able to see clearly."

"I wish Rylynne were still here," Colby sighed. "She could see through anything."

"I know, *midoros*. If I can, I'll try to reach out to a version of her from the past. Not being bound by paradoxes can be very useful, especially for her."

"The Muses are expecting you," Blair changed the subject abruptly.

"They are," Fiona nodded, looking at our small group. "Shall we?"

"Indeed," they spoke as one.

Rising in unison, we moved as a comfortable unit. The sidhe was still in the elevator and silently brought us to the medical floor. The sterile place was quiet. Only two beds were in use, their occupants asleep. Fiona took the lead and marched us into the bright room. The Muses looked up from their tasks and smiled.

"*Metaria*," the ringing harmony of their voices held notes of happiness.

"How did you know?" Fiona smiled.

"Your presence is different from Amelia's," the redhead, Melpomene, left her microscope and came over to us. Giving Fiona a quick hug, she took our arm. "Amelia walks with her shoulders hunched, as though expecting to be attacked. You move with a force that says you will destroy the world."

"Should I rectify that?"

"Only if you're outside of Sanctuary. Humans fear strong women more than they fear the unknown."

"Good to know. Now, unless I am mistaken, Amelia has an appointment to keep."

"Indeed she does. Daniel can come with you, but everyone else must remain here. The facility we have her in will only accept two visitors at a time, and they must be brought in by one of us."

"Safeguard against attack?"

"Yes. Some of our patients are still being hunted. If only the nine of us know how to get there then there is less risk to their recovery."

"Daniel?" Fiona looked back at him. He nodded and touched our shoulder; the Muse pulling us out of Sanctuary and into a dim hall a blink later. Fiona retreated, like ice down my spine, and I hunched over as my lungs protested their use.

"I do have a few rules for you, Amelia," Melpomene stepped away as Daniel slid an arm around my ribs to hold me upright.

"Go ahead," I wheezed.

"If I touch your hand, you must stop. I will be monitoring her vitals at all times, so if anything goes wrong I can pull you out. We don't know how fragile she is, mentally. If you push too hard, she could break completely if she hasn't already. And whatever you do, don't use any abilities while inside her mind. Her brain isn't wired to handle any of our powers."

"To recap; stop when told, be gentle, and don't do anything freaky?" I straightened.

"Exactly. She's through the door behind me, and we won't be disturbed, but I would like Daniel to stand guard inside."

"Talk to him about that, not me."

"It's done," he nodded. "Inside to protect Amelia and the girl in case something unexpected happens?"

"Yes," she turned and opened a pale blue door. Lights came on inside as she led us in and pointed to a padded chair beside the bed.

The girl was pretty, beneath the purple and yellow bruises. Her thin nose was braced, likely broken, and stitches ran from her forehead to her ear on her left side. Her cinnamon-colours skin looked dry, even from a distance.

"Why do her wounds look fresh? I thought Seph said she's been here for a year."

"Every time we heal her, they reappear. We've taken to just patching her back together when everything reopens."

"Some of mine did that. We could never figure out why."

"Hm," Melpomene frowned, seeming to store that information away.

Daniel helped me perch on the edge of the chair and stepped away as I reached for her hand. It was cool to the touch, but I could feel her heart beating steadily. I closed my eyes and removed one of my gloves before taking her hand. For a moment it felt like I was falling, then my feet hit solid ground. I opened my eyes and frowned. I was standing in a field of lilies; a gentle breeze whispering through the flowers. I looked around the clearing for a moment before spotting her. She was sitting with her back to me; her long black hair in a simple braid. I blinked, and she was suddenly standing in front of me.

"Why are you here?" her voice was high and clear.

"To speak with you. I've been told that we have something in common."

"How did you get here?" she was highly suspicious.

"I'm a memory reader. I can slip into anyone's head just by touching them."

"Are you demon, deity, or other?"

"Define other," I smiled. She was quick.

"Mortal."

"I am neither demon, nor deity; but I may not be mortal either."

"Anything not demon or deity is mortal," she huffed.

I sighed. "I am a Creator, a renewer of the earth. Our lives extend so long as there is work to be done. Demons and deities are creations of my species, meant to take over our duties when we need to rest. We can shed our mortal shell, but our energy cannot truly die."

I don't know how I knew most of that, but it felt true in my bones. The girl frowned at me, looked me over.

"How old are you?"

"Seventeen."

"Do you know why I'm trapped here?"

It was my turn to frown. "You aren't trapped. Your body is safe; you're in the care of the Muses."

"The Muses?"

"Goddesses. Mythology says they inspired artists, but they are healers. Among other things."

"Do you trust them?"

"I don't trust anyone except my sister, but they have proven that they mean no harm."

"Did they put me here?"

I scratched the back of my head. "What's your name?"

"Padma."

"Padma. What is the last thing you remember before you woke up here?"

Terror flitted across her face for a brief moment before she shook her head. "I don't know. I don't want to know."

"I'm sorry to push this, to push you, but burying the memories will do nothing but hurt you. It's been two years, and I finally told someone. I still feel dirty, worthless. Like it was my fault that I was taken. But you don't have to. Telling me, showing me, will make it easier for you to heal."

"And how will it do that?" her voice was shaking.

"I can eat your pain, because I share it. I've been able to do it since I was a little girl. It won't hurt you, I promise. You'll keep your memories, but you won't be affected by them anymore."

"Won't you be harmed by it?"

"Yes and no," I shrugged. "I'm starting to understand that pain and suffering are my lot in life. If I don't fight it, I can learn from it."

"How do I know you aren't lying?"

"I cannot lie right now. A person's mind can lie to itself while alone, but not when it is connected to someone else's."

"If you can't lie, tell me how I got here."

"You entered a deep meditation that simulated death, so you were discarded. At least, that's what I was told. You created this place as a safe haven for yourself."

"Why don't I remember doing that?"

"It's tied to the memories you're trying to repress."

"So I can't leave."

"Not until they're either buried deep, or you let me help you."

"Those are my only options?"

"If you ever want to see your family again, yes."

She sighed. "Can I think about it?"

"Of course you can. I'll be back tomorrow."

"Thank you…" she paused, looking intently at me.

"Amelia. My name is Amelia."

She smiled and nodded. "See you tomorrow, Amelia."

I inclined my head before closing my eyes and concentrating on my own body, on breathing deeply. It took a moment, but I could feel my aching body again. Melpomene's smile was curious when I opened my eyes and let go of Padma's hand.

"I gave her a choice," I put my glove back on. "She said she'd let me know tomorrow morning."

"But she's okay?"

"If she accepts my offer, she'll be able to go home to her family. She built herself a sanctuary to escape the pain, and it won't let her out until there's no pain to fear."

"So she's caught in a loop."

"Basically, yes. When would be a good time to come back?"

Melpomene paused for a moment. "Just after lunch, I think."

"Sounds good," I nodded, suddenly exhausted. "Shall we?"

"We shall," she took my hand as Daniel touched my shoulder. We were back at Sanctuary, standing, in a breath. The infirmary was quiet, dim.

"How long have we been gone?"

"Three hours, give or take," Daniel wrapped an arm around my ribs as my knees trembled.

"Damn. No wonder I feel drained."

"Do you need to feed again?"

I thought about it as he led us to the elevator. "I hate to say it, but I might need to, yes."

The doors opened, and Hermes stood there, grinning. "Did you miss me?"

“I’ll take you over a sidhe any day,” I flashed him a small smile.

“Thirty-six?”

“Yes, please.”

“Done,” he chuckled. There was a slight rocking as he brought us skyward, but it wasn’t a hell-ride. I was ready to fall asleep when the doors finally opened.

“Not a word of this to anyone,” Daniel hissed as he leaned over and folded my knees over his free arm.

“Word of what?” Hermes chuckled as Daniel carried me down the hall.

Sleep sucked me under before we reached my door. Flashes of images taunted me, but I couldn’t hold on to one long enough to dream.

22

A warm hand on my cheek broke through the darkness and startled me awake. It took a moment for the blurry outline to turn into Daniel, but when it did his face was obviously concerned.

"What time is it?" I asked, my throat dry.

"Six-thirty," he removed his hand.

"Why so early?"

"You were screaming in your sleep."

I sat up and stretched. "I didn't dream last night, so I don't know why I was screaming. But I feel better."

"Feel better in what way?"

"My joints don't hurt as much and my lungs feel better."

He frowned. "You should feel worse, not better. You didn't feed last night."

"But I feel okay."

"Amelia, you *need* to feed. I can't risk you losing control and eating one of the other residents."

"I fed off you too recently. And I really shouldn't have to do it again so soon."

"You used up a lot of energy yesterday; you need to replenish. I have more than enough to spare, and I don't have to worry about bite addiction, remember?"

"Doesn't change the fact that I don't want to."

"I know. But I will force feed you if I have to."

"Just for the record, I'd hate you for the rest of your life if you did that."

"Which would only make it easier to maintain my objectivity. Better that you hate me than anything else."

"It's easier for me to ditch tails I hate."

"Then don't hate me and eat, Amelia. You have a lot to do today."

"Fine," I sighed. "Where would you prefer."

"Shoulder is fine, if you can get close to the original spot."

"Then strip," I threw off the covers and crossed my legs. Daniel pulled his black t-shirt off and sat in front of me, bitten shoulder closer. I stroked the punctures, my mouth watering. "Why do I suddenly crave your blood?"

"You've had it twice already, and there is power in it. Not god level, not by a long shot, but enough to make me preferable to a human," he took a deep breath and nodded. "Do it. Fast."

My fangs dropped and I aimed for the holes. He tensed as I tore into his flesh, and relaxed again as blood flowed freely. A sliver of my control came undone and I felt a core of lust looping between us. It was travelling to him, then back to me with his blood. He shuddered before pulling me into his lap; breaking my bite as he did so.

"Damn it, Amelia," he was panting. "I thought I made myself clear."

"I didn't do it on purpose," I licked my fangs. "I think that was one of the abilities that Persephone pulled to the surface."

"Why lust, for fucks sake? Why not rage? Or terror?"

"I don't fucking know! It's not like I consciously chose to do it."

"Some part of you did. Are you aiming to be traumatised more? Is that it?"

Peace and rage slid over me. "Let me go."

"Not until I'm sure you won't do it again."

"Let me go, now."

"No."

"Fine. Your funeral," I bit into his throat, willing it to hurt. He winced, but didn't let go.

I was just starting to think 'kill' when Fiona surfaced. She pushed me out of the driver's seat and let go of his neck.

"It is all right, my dragon. You can let us go now," she forced our fangs away.

He relaxed his grip and Fiona stood, moving to the closet and stripping on the way. She picked things at random, dressed, and returned to the grand room. Finding a chair to her liking, she sat and studied Daniel as he approached, slowly.

"Why are you resisting my attempts, half-hearted though they may be, to get you in bed with Amelia? And don't say you'll lose your objectivity or traumatise her."

"My duties as her guardian –"

"Say nothing about it. Since I'm the one who wrote the rules of being a guardian, I would know."

"Why would you, of all people, try to get her to sleep with anyone knowing her history?" Daniel sat on the chair opposite us.

"Because sex, in its purest form, is not about power and control. It is sharing, and healing, and leaves a little bit of happiness afterwards. If it's good."

"But not love."

"It can be an expression of love, but you are correct. Sex is not love."

"Why me then? Why not someone else? Someone closer to her age?"

Fiona chuckled. "Have you seen the candidates her age? They are inexperienced beanpoles who wouldn't do anything but take their own pleasure and walk away."

"But they're malleable. They can be taught."

"I don't trust them. I trust you to do what is right for Amelia, and yourself."

"I don't trust myself, not with this."

"Why?"

Daniel glanced at the door. "James."

"What about him?"

"He was supposed to protect Serenity, not fall in love with her."

"And you're worried you'll fall in love with Amelia."

"Yes."

"Well, stop worrying. Serenity and James are soul mates. They were always meant to find each other, fall in love. They were bonded in their first lives, and separated by death before he was converted."

"And Amelia?"

"She doesn't have one. She'll fall in love, most likely marry, and have her daughters. But she will never have what they have."

He sighed. "That's depressing."

"Some people never find their other parts," Fiona shrugged. "Her soul will find its other part, or parts, in another life."

"Just not this one."

"Correct. Now, I do believe you have a guardianship bond to complete."

"The oath of protection? Amelia said no."

"But I say yes. We are two souls in one body," she reminded him. "Bond to me, and it will encompass her by association. That way, if she dies, you will not and you won't destroy your morals later."

"Does it actually work like that?"

She laughed. "I created it, of course it does. Now hand me a knife."

"What about Amelia? Won't she try to resist?"

Fiona shook our head. "I have her well in hand. She won't interrupt."

'Like hell,' I snapped at her.

'It's all right, Amelia. I know what I'm doing.'

'Just because you know what you're doing doesn't mean I accept it.'

'You don't have to. Now shush.'

Daniel held out a small dagger, blade in his hand. Fiona took it gingerly and dug the point into our left palm. Blood welled up and she handed it back. He did the same, then knelt before us. Fiona smiled.

"Dragon."

"All Mother."

"Do you accept the duties of being the eternal protector?"

"I do."

"Do you swear to always do what is in my best interests, even if I say otherwise?"

"I do."

"Do you swear to keep my vessel safe at any cost?"

"I do."

"Good. Take my hand. Blood to blood."

He did as she said, and I felt a shock go up our arm. The whole thing reminded me of a twisted marriage ceremony.

"Do you accept me as your guardian, from now until Death's Time?"

"I do," Fiona nodded.

"Do you accept the mark of the protected?"

"I do."

The shock turned into a burning on our left shoulder. A bright white light flared between our palms, then faded as Fiona pulled away. She let go of whatever she had holding me and I reached up to rub our shoulder.

"What the hell was that?" I tried to scratch.

"It's the symbol that my kind can use to protect our charges in the world at large without being visible."

"So…"

"Think of it as a way for me to always be with you, without being obvious."

"I'm still confused."

"I am a shapeshifter. I can become the mark, and only materialise if there is a clear and present danger."

"Ah. That seems a little intrusive."

"It can be, but it also connects me directly to your visual cortex. I can see if there is any actual danger."

"Still intrusive."

"Deal with it."

I snorted. "Where are your horns? Shouldn't they be sticking out the top of your head?"

"I can feel them. They are choosing to remain hidden."

"Your horns can think for themselves?" I raised an eyebrow.

"They can," he nodded. "It should be time for breakfast, give or take a few minutes."

"What about Fiona's show yesterday? Won't they be afraid of me?"

"That's the point," his half-smile appeared. "The more they fear you, the less likely they are to act. Fiona effectively made you their dominant."

"In my experience, dominant isn't always a good thing."

"Here it is. The protectors, Caretakers and deities are all dominant to the residents. We are respected, feared, for our power. No one takes us on because they are afraid of what we can do."

"And you think it will be the same for me."

"Fiona made it clear that she created those who created their species'. There's no greater fear than pissing off the one who can destroy them all."

"But I can't destroy them. I can kill individuals, but not the species."

"They don't know that. And we won't tell them."

"Not on purpose, at any rate."

"Shall we?"

"As soon as I find my gloves. I don't remember taking them off."

"I took them off while you were sleeping. They're on the bedside table."

"Thank you," I stood and went to retrieve the leather pieces. Pulling them on quickly, I turned and nodded to Daniel. He nodded in return and opened the door.

It was a short walk to the open elevator. Hermes was waiting, as usual. He grinned after a moment and rocketed us down to the subbasement. The landing was a little rough and he giggled.

"Do we still feign involvement? Or are you strictly business now?" I paused half way down the hall.

Daniel frowned for a moment, calculating. "These bites are highly visible. It would be wise to continue the ruse until you are completely healed."

"And after that?"

"One step at a time."

"I really hate answers like that."

He chuckled. "Maybe if I use them enough, Fiona will lay off."

"Good luck with that," I muttered as her evil laugh rang through my head and he dropped an arm around my shoulders and led us to the hall of hostile teenagers. I pasted a stiff smile on my face as we entered. There was a collective intake of breath as everyone stared, terrified.

"I'm not going to eat any of you," I looked around, then grinned. "Not today."

Daniel squeezed my shoulder gently as a few people choked. We resumed our path to food, collected trays and breakfast, before moving to an empty table at the back of the room. He hid my pill in the cutlery bundle again. Taking it, I chased it with a fork of eggs. And promptly gagged.

"Everything okay?" Daniel glanced around quickly.

I held up a finger before reaching into my mouth. Something sharp was stuck in my gums, and it was hurting more with every passing second. Digging it out, I held a tiny shard of glass in my fingers. I pressed my tongue against the deceptively small gash as blood poured out.

"What the hell?"

"Someone isn't as afraid of you as we hoped," he frowned. "Don't touch your food again; there could be more in there. And don't leave the shard here. It has your blood on it, and if there's a rat here they'll give it to someone on the outside."

"What should we do, then?"

"We step up our schedule. Hermes can inform the Caretakers while we talk to the Muses. After that, you get to train with Persephone until your head feels like it's going to explode."

"Shall we?"

"Quickly. Before anyone wises up."

23

'Fiona?'

'What do you need?'

'Can you ask Fangy if I can borrow her speed? I don't know how to access it without killing everyone in here.'

'Can do. Stand up; your leg will twitch when she's ready.'

"Prepare to run," I murmured. "I hope you're fast without a warm up."

"I can teleport, of course I'm fast."

"Meet me at the elevator," I stood. Clenching my fist around the shard, I felt a short ripple in my thigh.

It was exhilarating, the rush of running so fast no one could see me move. There was perfect clarity; no objects moved quickly enough to obstruct my path. I was in the elevator in seconds, Daniel keeping pace easily. His hand shot out faster than lightning and caught something before it hit the floor.

"Infirmary, please, Hermes," Daniel cupped his hand and brought it up to mine. "After that, let the Caretakers know Amelia's food was tainted."

"Tainted how?" Hermes frowned.

"Glass particulates. Substantial enough to penetrate veins or arteries."

"How did you not see it?"

"It was transmuted after she ate it."

The god whistled. "Not many here can do that. We'll get this sorted shortly."

"I hope so," I grimaced, slowly opening my hand. "I don't want to eat glass or needles for the rest of my stay here."

Hermes sucked in a sharp breath at the blood in my hand. "Did you leave any behind?"

"Not that I know of," I shook my head.

"Good. Your blood can be used by people with the know-how to tap into the ether. Especially since it holds a touch of Fiona's essence."

"Tapping into the ether would be bad?"

"Very," Hermes nodded. "If you can tap into it, you can travel through it and bypass all our security."

"Shit."

"Yes. Go get patched up, I'll talk to the others."

"Thanks."

"Not a problem."

A shrill "Don't touch whatever's in your hand!" came from the bright, sterile room.

"It's just a piece of glass," I tried to assure her. "Just need a little super glue."

"No need for that barbaric stuff. Come sit," she led us to a bed. Perching on it, she clucked her tongue at me. "How the hell did you get glass in your hand?"

"I pulled it out of my mouth, first," I tongued the oozing cut.

"I'm going to assume you didn't mean to eat it."

"Of course I didn't mean to eat it. If I wanted to publicly commit suicide, there are much easier ways to do it."

"Very true. Hold still, please. This is liable to hurt," Melpomene placed one hand under, the other above, my extended appendage. The shard came free and blood rushed from the tiny wound. Her eyes flashed white for a brief moment before heat seared both my mouth and my hand. It stopped abruptly and she exhaled.

"All better?" I raised an eyebrow.

"All better. Including, oddly enough, your lungs. Any idea how that would happen?"

"No idea. I felt like crap yesterday, woke up fine today."

"Very weird. Another great mystery we'll probably never solve."

"We need to step up Amelia's schedule. Is there any way she can see the girl now instead of this afternoon?" Daniel let go of my hand and wiped the blood away with the hem of his shirt. "After she's done she needs to prep for Prometheus, and we're running out of time. A resident here is working against our cause."

"I'll get one of the others to cover my work. Give me a few and I'll take you to her," Melpomene nodded. She popped over to one of her sisters, gestured, spoke quietly. They nodded before she walked back over, pausing to write something along the way. "Ready?"

“As I’ll ever be,” I held a hand out when she was close enough. She took it and Daniel placed his on top of the pile. She jerked us through space to their special medical ward. Instead of dumping us in the hall, she brought us straight into the room.

“I hope this goes quickly. For your sake and hers.”

“Me, too,” I let go of her hand and removed my damaged glove. Sitting, I touched Padma and immediately felt the swirling, sucking sensation of falling into memory.

“You’re back,” the high, clear voice was behind me. “Has it been a day already?”

“Almost. My schedule has been accelerated, but you are my top priority. Have you made your decision?”

“I want to go home,” she nodded. “I want to see my family again.”

“Take my hand. I can protect you when the mountains come down.”

“Will it hurt?”

“Only if you let go. You may feel like you’re being pulled into darkness, but don’t give in. Stay with me and you’ll be able to go home.”

She grabbed my arm instead of my hand and pressed herself against my back. I used the physical contact to access her connection to the mountains.

“Close your eyes and take a very deep breath. I’m going to open a small door to control the flow of memory.”

She nodded and her chest expanded. I split the mountains in front of us, just a tiny crack. Emotions poured through, and I inhaled them. Some of it I turned into fuel, but the majority was added to the memories I refused to dwell on. The schism widened and the stream turned into a flood. I was about to lose control of the intake when Fangy surfaced. My canines descended and suddenly I had no need to breathe as I inhaled. Wings added herself to the mix as the entire range came down. I drank deep until I felt like exploding, then drank some more. Padma shuddered as the last of it dissipated.

“Is it over?” her voice was small.

“The memories will never hurt you again,” the growling harmony was starting to fade. “You will always bear the memories of what happened, but they will never cripple you again."

"So I can wake up now?"

"Yes. Do you want me to pull you up, or can you do it on your own?"

"I think I can do it."

"Okay. See you on the other side."

I pulled out of her head and slid back into my own. Her eyes were fluttering open when I looked up and pulled my glove back on. The hole in it had disappeared. Padma was trying to sit up while I reoriented myself in the room.

"We tried to pull you out," Melpomene tossed a glare at me as she placed pillows behind Padma's back. "Her vitals tanked and you didn't respond."

"Someone must have been locking us in," I shrugged.

"Did it work?"

"She's awake, isn't she? Ask her."

The goddess huffed before manually checking Padma's pulse. "My name is Melpomene, one of the Muses. I will be your healer today. Can you tell me your name?"

"Padma," she squeaked, looking at Daniel. "Amelia said I would be able to see my family again."

"As soon as we're sure there will be no side-effects to what she did, we'll take you home. This may hurt, so please take a deep breath," Melpomene placed a hand on her forehead.

Padma inhaled, then flinched as her wounds and scars disappeared.

"Feel better?" I asked, slowly getting to my feet.

"Much," she nodded. "Will I ever see you again?"

"If you're lucky, no," I shook my head for emphasis. Then I had a thought. "Melpomene?"

"Yes?" she looked away from Padma.

"Can you link an object?"

"Link how?"

"Imbue it with power so I can tell if the wearer is in trouble."

"Old parlour trick," she nodded. "Give me something and I can do it right now."

I took stock of everything Fiona had put on. Choosing a small ear cuff, I held it out. Melpomene took it, muttered something, then placed it on Padma's ear. As soon as it was secure, it morphed until it covered her entire ear in a sturdy, yet intricate scroll design.

"You'll always be able to find her, now. You'll just have to concentrate."

"Thank you," I inclined my head to her. "Stay safe, Padma."

"I'll try," she nodded.

"Daniel, please touch Amelia. I'm going to drop you in the infirmary," Melpomene straightened. His hand found my shoulder and she threw her hand out at us, as though air was supposed to throw us backwards. Instead we fell through the void and landed in Sanctuary.

My knees hit the floor and I dry-heaved. A bucket appeared in front of me and I grabbed onto it for dear life; finally ejecting what little I had eaten.

"Is she okay?" one of the Muses asked, unperturbed by our sudden appearance.

"I'll be fine," I raised a hand. "I didn't know it was possible to throw someone from one place to another."

"We don't usually do it. I take it the girl is awake?"

"Awake and talking," I nodded, wiping my mouth and standing up. "Anything else you need me to do?"

A few of the goddesses looked at each other. "Maybe have a look in on Graham? We can't pinpoint the source of his psychosis, and we can't fix it without knowing the source."

I grimaced. I didn't particularly care for Graham. "Where is he?"

"Door to your left. We have him strapped down so he won't hurt himself."

"Locked?"

"Unnecessary. Protective barrier that allows us out but keeps him in."

"Neat."

"If you say so."

I flashed a small smile. "I'll be back shortly."

Daniel moved to follow, but I shook my head at him.

"I'll be fine. Stay, have a break."

He gave a short nod and stayed put while I strode through the shimmering door. I blinked slowly at the scene in the sterile room. Graham was strapped to a secure gurney; his odd eyes wide with hatred as froth spewed from his mouth.

"Stupid bitch," he snarled. "You did this to me you freak."

I sighed and stripped off one of my gloves. "Bite me and I'll hurt you," I warned him, sitting on the edge of the stretcher. Placing my fingers on his throat, I fell into his head and sucked in a deep breath.

Graham and a giant black wolf were fighting. Graham was too determined to stay in control, while the wolf was struggling for freedom. They paused in their war when I appeared, both confused by the interruption. The canine reacted first; breaking off and lunging for me before Graham could subdue it. Sharp teeth pierced my wrist, but it didn't hurt. Instead, I could hear the animal's voice in my head.

'I want out,' it growled. *'I am half-blood, not quarter. I need to run.'*

'I don't know how to help you,' I shook my head. *'I might be able to find someone who can, but you have to let me go.'*

It let go, but licked the wounds until an odd sensation ran up my arm and stabbed into the back of my neck. Forcing myself out of his head, I put my glove back on and rubbed the aching point in my neck. Leaving the secure room, I waved away Daniel's look of concern.

"He's at war with his wolf, and someone lied about his paternity. He's a halfer, not a quarter," I informed the Muse who had pointed his room out. "The wolf wants to run, but he has no idea how to let it out."

"Thanks for the help," she nodded. "We can sort him out now that we know. Go and rest. Seph is expecting you at eleven."

"Thanks," I flashed a small smile before turning for the elevator. Daniel held his arm out to me, and I took it gratefully. Something passed over his eyes, but he hid it as he led me to Hermes's Delivery Service from Hell.

"Could you please keep the nasty nicknames to a minimum?" the god sighed as he shut the doors behind us. "I don't know how much more I can take."

"I'm just teasing," I stuck my tongue out at him. "Besides, your ego needs deflating every once in a while. And I've been fairly good."

He chuckled darkly. "If you've been good then I'm the pope."

"Eh, the pope is overrated. He's too much of a mouthpiece," I shrugged. "Usually you're faster at dropping us off than this."

"Where are you going? You have too many contradicting thoughts in your head for me to tell."

"Thirty-six, please."

"Aaaand we're off!" the compartment rocketed skyward. He was laughing maniacally when we came to a jarring halt. He shoved us out with a quick "Have fun kiddies!"

Daniel and I exchanged a very confused glance before a spark ignited.

24

The orange in his irises brightened, and he looked like he wanted to fight the warmth that was spreading through the both of us. Instead he shuddered, relaxed, gave in.

"I'm going to break someone's head when this is over," he growled, pulling me into his chest. "And then I'm probably going to do it again."

I was about to ask 'Do what?' when he fisted one hand in my hair and his lips crashed against min. He kissed me as though I were the last bit of food in the world; ravenous yet gentle. Winding his free arm around my ribs, he exerted just a tiny bit of his strength and lifted my feet from the floor. I wrapped my arms around his shoulders and my legs around his lean waist as he moved to my suite. The door was open and he walked right in without breaking contact with my lips. Pinning me to the wall just inside, he finally came up for air.

"We shouldn't do this," he panted, moving his hands to my hips.

"Do we really care right now?" I gasped, rubbing against the bulge in his pants.

He groaned and thrust against me. "Quit teasing or I'll cut those damn clothes off."

"Now who's teasing?" I laughed, arching against him.

He growled before easily breaking my hold. Turning, he threw me to the bed and began stripping his weapons. I kicked my shoes off without looking away; he kept one small knife as he peeled his shirt off. Stalking towards me, his eyes were the only point of expression in his otherwise determined countenance. When he was close enough, he grabbed the neck of my shirt and made a tiny slice. He ripped it the rest of the way before pulling the rags off. Dropping the blade, he moved to my pants; pulling them off easily.

"Don't speak," he muttered, lightly brushing his hands up my legs. "Your skin is so soft."

I didn't move a muscle as his hands caressed higher. He skimmed past my underwear to trace his fingers over my stomach. In a lightning-fast move, he was at my lips again and pressing me into the soft bed. Not sure what to do with my hands,

I ran them down the rippling muscles of his back. He flexed involuntarily, as though it tickled.

He pulled away again, breathing heavily. “If you say stop, I’ll stop. No questions asked.”

“If you stop now, I’ll gut you on the floor,” I panted, digging my nails into his lower back.

He chuckled at that and ground his hips against mine. It felt good. Almost too good. He moved down a little, started nipping at my neck as he brought his thigh up between my legs. He shifted slightly, in rhythmic circles, until my brain wanted to shut off.

“Pants,” I moaned. “Why are you wearing pants?”

He reached down and fumbled one-handed with his belt. I brought my hands down to help. Once it was open I wrenched the button and zipper away.

“Impatient much?” he teased my earlobe before straightening. Smiling down at me, he grabbed the discarded knife and made three quick slices. My bra fell open and he tore my destroyed underwear away. He dropped everything on the floor and took a moment to play with by nipples before coming back over me and reclaiming my lips. With a free hand he reached between us and positioned himself, pausing only to stroke me. I shuddered at the soft touch and he slid in.

It was an odd sensation, being filled, stretched. He held still, waited for me to adjust to his rather impressive size. Wrapping my legs around his hips, I clenched around him and he gasped; the sound not going much further than my mouth.

“Please don’t do that again,” he groaned. “You’ll finish me before we get started.”

“So get started,” I rocked against him. Daniel slid his hand beneath me and lifted my hips just a bit before he started moving, pulling out slowly. When he was halfway out he thrust back in and stroked nerved I didn’t know existed. If my brain had been on the verge of shutdown before, it leapt willingly over the edge now.

Daniel was laughing quietly in my ear when I finally came back down from the unexpected high. His face slowly came into focus above me, with a hint of a grin pulling at the edges of his swollen lips.

"If I knew you were that easy I would have just used my fingers."

"I didn't know it felt like that," I panted, my body loose and jelly.

"Think you can handle another one?"

"Hit me with your best shot," I grinned.

He twitched his hips, just the tiniest little movement, and my muscles reacted, tightened. An involuntary gasp escaped my lips and he pulled out completely.

"Can you move?"

"I can now," I shivered.

"Good. Hand and knees. Hold the headboard if you have to," he bent over and unlaced his boots. I did as he asked and didn't look back as the bed dipped. I yelped when his hand unexpectedly landed on my ass. His fingers danced up and down my back before he grabbed my hips and pushed back into me.

"Fuck!" I groaned. "Who knew this actually felt good?"

He didn't respond to that. Instead he concentrated on finding a solid rhythm while his fingers toyed with me. My grip on the headboard tightened as my muscles tensed and his pace increased. He pressed his chest against my back, never faltering. His breathing was becoming laboured as his free hand found one of my breasts and he rolled my nipple between his fingers.

"Come with me, Amelia. I don't know how much longer I can last," his voice was rough in my ear. Taking a hand away from the headboard, I buried it in his hair. That slight change of angle was just what I needed to go over again, but this time he joined me in bliss. His whole body jerked as he held me in a vice-like grip. Relaxing, we collapsed on the bed and he rolled us to our sides so his weight wouldn't crush me.

"Was it as good for you as it was for me?" I laughed when I could breathe again.

"Probably better," he nuzzled my ear. "I don't think I want to move right now."

"I'm comfy, what's your excuse?" I ran my fingers up and down his arm.

He moved his hips the tiniest bit, which drew a moan out of me. "It'll shrink in a little bit. Until it does, I'm not going anywhere."

"Is it a dragon thing? Or a shifter thing?"

"No, it's mostly a male thing. The nerves are highly sensitive right now and moving would be excruciating. And I like the smell of me on you. I don't want to wash it off yet."

"Okay," I snuggled into his chest and wiggled my hips. He tightened his arms around me and gave a half-hearted thrust before laying still. "That was fun, but I still don't like sex."

"You probably won't for years," he gently traced circles through the scars on my stomach. "I really should get up. You feel way too good for me to think straight."

"When was the last time you held anyone like this?"

"Never," his tone was distant.

"Were you a virgin?" I froze.

He laughed. "No, but the few females I have been with didn't waste time afterward."

"They did the female equivalent of wham-bam-thank-you-ma'am?"

"I don't know what that is."

I chuckled. "It's when you use someone to get laid and walk away right after."

"Ah. Yes, they did that. It made me feel like a cheap whore."

"I bet. Though that's not something men usually admit."

"I'm not most men," his voice was a dark rumble. "Five more minutes, then you should have a shower. As much as I would like to stay here all day, you need to train."

"I don't want to train. Not today," I sighed.

"We're accelerating your schedule, remember? We need you strong enough to survive killing one of the oldest beings on this planet. I would rather not bury you now."

"Why would you care about me dying? It's not like you really wanted to do this."

"You're too cute, and strong, to give up now. Besides, I may want to do this again soon."

"Really now? Will you need someone else to push you over the edge again?"

"Nope," his arms tightened momentarily. "Why would I fight against doing this?"

"Because I'm a terrible lay?"

"If you were a terrible lay, I would be soft by now, Amelia. You're passionate, when you let yourself go. If you were to go around your entire life with that fervour in every step the entire world would bow down at your feet."

"But I don't want people at my feet."

"Which is exactly why people will follow you. The best leaders are the ones who don't want the job."

I nodded noncommittally. It felt weird to be held, while naked, by someone who wasn't family. But it felt good, too. "Should we get back to the day?"

"Probably. I'll get the shower ready."

How he got up without groaning, I'll probably never know. I definitely did, and I enjoyed watching his muscles ripple with every step. Maybe I enjoyed it a little too much. I stretched, and was about to get up to follow him when he poked his head back into the room.

"Are your legs working, or would you like me to carry you?"

"Let me check," I smiled, sitting up and swinging my legs over the edge of the bed. My knees felt like jelly, but I managed to stand and take a few shaky steps. "Is it normal to be this sore?"

"Sore means I did a good job, just so long as it doesn't hurt," he chuckled before striding over and sweeping me into his arms. He was swift, his movements sure as he carried me into the lavish bathroom. Steam was clouding a corner of the room and he set me down just outside the glass enclosure. I managed to walk in under my own power, and the first thing I noticed was a bench wide enough to lie comfortably on.

"I can think of a few things that could be used for," I giggled as water poured from the ceiling.

"And it probably will be in the near future," Daniel stepped behind me and slid his hands around my waist. "Keep your hands to yourself and we can get clean quickly."

"Ask for no promises and I will give you no lies," I relaxed against him.

"You're cheeky," he chuckled playing his fingers over my abdomen. "But we need to get clean so you can see Persephone."

"Maybe I'm enjoying being dirty right now."

"You can be dirty again later," he leaned away and grabbed something. Brining it under the shower-rain, he rubbed a soft cloth over my exposed flesh.

"Do you enjoy this?" I asked as he scrubbed the one spot on my back I could never reach.

"Enjoy what? Washing you?"

"Yes."

"I made the mess, it's my duty to clean it up. It feels…good to do this."

"Mess?" I repeated, confused. Then it hit me. "No protection."

"I forgot, and I don't exactly carry any around in a building full of people under sixteen," he cleaned everywhere he had touched.

"Sixteen?"

"The age of consent. We don't advertise that fact, and it's kept out of the guidebook to discourage sex among the students. Dyonisus covers sex-ed during the biology part of his classes, so they know what they're in for if they do decide to get frisky."

"Interesting."

"Indeed. So long as I do not hold a position of power over you, what we did was perfectly legal, even by the standards of our world. Though we do try to abide by some of the laws of the country whose airspace we're occupying."

"If we were being held to human rules, law makers might take offence," I laughed. "Six more months until I'm completely legal by their screwed up set of ideals. Unless some countries are more varied about their age of majority laws."

"I don't keep track of all countries, or their laws, just the ones of the countries we're currently hovering over. Which, at the moment, is Canada."

"Since you're bound to Fiona, not me, and you're not a teacher or a coach, we're in the clear?"

"How did you know that?"

"Vague memory of something from human school."

"You're right. According to human law, and some of ours, if I held a position of power over you then your consent would be irrelevant."

"Good thing I didn't agree to the oath then, isn't it?" I turned and grabbed the cloth from his hand.

"Very good," he groaned as I wiped him down. "If you don't stop, we'll never get out of here."

Stepping close, I licked a small trail of water as it cascaded down his muscular chest. It was that moment, that shuddering moment in time, that the intimacy of the moment hit me. Well, steamrolled over me. Something clanged shut in my head and I moved away from him.

"We should get dressed," I dropped the cloth and stepped around him to the door.

He caught my arm before I could go too far. "What's wrong, Amelia?"

"Nothing," I shrugged. "I need to train."

"Bullshit," Daniel growled. "What slammed shut in your head just now?"

"It doesn't matter."

"Yes it does. Everything about you matters."

"Let me get dressed and I might tell you."

He leaned over and kissed me before letting me go. "I'll hold you to that."

I grabbed a towel off the pile on my way by and secured it. Going to the closet, I selected loose, long clothes all in black. Putting them on, I towelled my hair before grabbing shoes and gloves. As soon as they were secure I returned to the main room. Daniel was there, pants on, buckling his belt. He barely glanced at me at he retrieved his shirt and weapons. Finally looked at me when he was rearmed.

"Why the sudden change?" he crossed his arms over his chest, his expression guarded. "Why did you go cold on me?"

"Do you want the long, complicated version? Or the simple one?"

"Why not go halfway between the two?"

I snorted. "I'll try, but I make no promises."

"Trying is better than nothing."

25

"I'm not sure I know where to start," I hugged myself. "I was a virgin when I was taken, and sleeping with anyone afterwards was something I avoided. I'm not used to kindness, or being cared for."

"You've never had intimacy. You're scared of it," his face softened.

"Basically, yes."

"Come here," he held his arms out. Crossing warily, he pulled me to his chest and just held me. "You don't have to fear anything with me, Amelia. I can't do anything to hurt you."

"That's part of the problem. You can't hurt me, but I can hurt you. It's not fair."

"Life's not fair. Now we should probably get going before someone sends a search party."

"They won't send a search party," I laughed. "I'm guessing it was Aphrodite's message that Hermes hit us with."

"It tastes like her brand of power," he chuckled. "But I don't know who she's been talking to. It's not like what goes on in here is publicly broadcast."

"She's a goddess. My guess is that she could feel it."

"Shall we get going?"

"Sounds good. Can we kill Hermes?"

"Not today. We still need him to run messages around."

"Damn. Can we maim him?"

"Again, not today," he let go of me and the door swung open. Leading the way to the elevator, its doors were oddly closed. I pressed the button, but nothing happened.

"Has this ever happened before?" I raised an eyebrow.

"Not that I can recall," he shook his head. "My best guess is that the floor has been sealed because of a breach."

"I thought Arcturus had us sealed off from the outside world."

"If we stopped for a pick-up she would have to let part of the defences down."

"Is there any way to find out?"

"Only if you lock yourself in your room. Make sure the windows are locked and the rest will take care of itself. I'll be back soon."

I did as he said and locked the door behind me. Checking the windows, only one latch needed securing. Suddenly bored, I took to thoroughly searching the room. It didn't take long to find compartments hidden in the walls. One, to my delight, held paper and an array of drawing implements. The little girl in me squealed with glee when I took a pad and some pencils to the couch. I hadn't sketched in years, and it took a few tries to produce something half-decent. Fiona decided to make an appearance mid-sketch.

'Amelia?' the worry was evident in her hushed tone.

'What's wrong?'

'I need an arm. If I take full control I'll no longer be able to see.'

'Take it. Just flip to a new page.'

'Promise.'

She gave a metaphoric, mental nod before ice rushed up my spine. Instead of going to my head, it diverted to my shoulder and down to my hand. Flipping to a new page as I asked, she started drawing. At first it was just lines, but our hand flew across the developing image so fast, shaded so expertly, that it looked like a photograph.

"Is that the present or the future?"

"I can't tell yet," she clenched our jaw. "The images are coming too fast for me to see them clearly."

"I wish I could help, I really do."

"I know. If you were older I'd be able to project all the images onto paper at the same time. Whatever you were doing earlier unleashed a hell of a lot of energy."

"You don't know?"

"I don't," she flipped to a fresh page when the one she was working on was full. "Something was blocking me from your primary functions."

"Well…somehow word got around to Aphrodite of your attempts to get Daniel in my bed…"

She paused for a moment and giggled. "She gave Hermes a jolt to pass along to you, didn't she?"

"She did. And it was fun."

"I hear a 'but' coming."

"As much as I enjoyed it, I didn't like it."

"You probably won't like it for many years to come."

I snorted at that. "Daniel said pretty close to the same thing. I just realised something."

"What?"

"I didn't get a single flash of his memories, even though a lot of our skin was touching."

Fiona froze. "Not even a tiny sliver of an image?"

"Nothing, nada, zip."

"We need to get out of here."

"Can't. The elevator is frozen. Why do we need to leave?"

"A Draconis can sense impending threat, even if they aren't consciously aware of it. Their inner beast shields all thought and memory so their charge can't be found through them."

"You really put a lot of thought into their design, didn't you?"

"I would never trust the safety of my blood to anyone who couldn't protect them. Where is Daniel?"

"He went to find out why we're trapped up here."

"How long has he been gone?"

"Half an hour, maybe?"

"Shit, bloody bugger fuck damn."

"Gahzeunteit."

"Look at this picture, Amelia. What do you see?" she tapped the page.

It took a moment for the image to register. When it finally did, I felt like vomiting. Daniel was on his knees, a battle axe resting against his throat. Behind him there were cages with indistinct figures locked inside.

"This is live," I whispered.

"We're being baited. They want you angry so you'll go in guns blazing."

"Can you bring anything to the surface? Anything I can use? I don't care how much it hurts. Help me save them."

"Give me a moment. Let me dig. I think I can find what you need."

I nodded, frozen in place, as different points along my body began to tingle. When pain erupted near my left kidney Fiona came back.

"I have it," she spoke through clenched teeth. "Prepare to see stars or vomit."

"Do it, fast."

She nodded, and I felt a strange tugging before agony set my nerves on fire. She pulled again, and I fell to the floor. One final haul from her sent blood and bile explosively from our mouth. She was panting as hard as I was, our hands starting to blister against the floor. She forced us to stand and wiped our mouth.

"What did you get us?" I clenched and unclenched our hands.

"For lack of a better term, god bolts," she tore the sweater off. "I need to change."

"Wear what you want," I didn't fight for control. "What are god bolts?"

"Balls or waves of highly concentrated energy that can be modulated based on the wielder's needs. They can stun, kill, disintegrate, or give a tiny shock," she spoke while stripping on the way to the closet. Pulling on a black tank top, she grabbed a pair of black leather pants and highly impractical heels. Throwing the gloves on the floor when she was done dressing, she pulled our hair into a tight tail and strode to the giant windows. "I hope you don't mind taking a back seat. I have untold aeons of battle experience, and I feel like using it."

"Go right ahead. You have a better track record than I do when it comes to winning shit like this."

"Oh I do," she smirked. "If we're injured, I'll direct the damage to you. I will not show them what they want."

She opened the window and forced our wings out before I could object to the last bit. She threw us out head first and barely did anything to slow our descent. Spotting her targets around the twentieth floor, she flared our wings to adjust our angle and flipped us around so we would land on our feet. It was then that I felt the energy building up in our feet.

Fiona let all the air out of our wings and we plummeted; falling like a cannonball aimed at the ground. She released the energy she had been building when we were skimming the tree in the courtyard. It impacted before we did, sending dust and debris into a cloud around us. The shock going through our knees jarred our teeth, but she ignored it. Surprisingly, our shoes survived the landing.

Whoever had managed to break Sanctuary didn't wait for us to go to them. Fiona was dropping fangs when an axe sliced through the air beside us. She grabbed it and used it like a baseball bat on its original owner's head. Without missing a beat, she flapped our wings enough to clear the dust cloud. Manifesting two spheres, she fed them my anger until they were murder balls. She threw them, then created two more as the circle rushed us.

Fiona was having fun, I could feel it. She was thinning their numbers faster than I would have been able to. She actually started dancing, and it distracted me. It was rhythmic, hypnotic, and I barely noticed that she kept lobbing death spheres.

Finally a piercing "No!" broke into my head. The air at out back was moving. Fiona spun so fast I felt like puking and grabbed the man by the throat. Squeezing, she lifted him from the ground and held him at arm's length. Studying his ruddy skin for a moment, she shrugged before digging our fingers into his flesh and tearing his throat out. Blood sprayed our face as he crumpled. Dropping his missing pieces, she turned back to our targets and licked the warm blood from our lips, then our fingers. Someone screamed and Fiona hit the origin of the offending sound with a stun bolt.

Daniel was in front of us, exactly as Fiona had drawn him. A goliath of a man was holding the axe against his neck, and he looked more than ready to use it. As we approached I studied Daniel's face. It took a few seconds to realise his eyes were dark blue. Fiona silently acknowledged the discovery and altered one of the spheres to destroy the powder on his face without harming him. She flicked it at him, and it hit him with enough force to snap his head back.

"So," she finally spoke, though she picked our nails instead of looking around. "Who do I have the pleasure of making into dinner tonight?"

When no one responded she looked up. Daniel was on his side, facing us. His eyes were normal again and he winked. I smiled, Fiona didn't. She pirouetted on the spot and looked at all the bodies on the ground.

"Don't tell me I already killed the dumb fuck who did this."

Finally someone stepped up to the plate. "I don't know who you're calling a dumb fuck. Personally, I thought it was a brilliant plan to break into the most secure house of half-breed leeches in the world," a disembodied male voice spoke.

"For some reason, I don't believe these children were your targets," Fiona rolled our shoulders and dissolved our wings. "You're after a bigger fish."

A rather short man stepped out from behind the goliath. His features were strikingly similar to James's, though he was a good six inches shorter. "You are far too perceptive for your age, Amelia Hartley."

Fiona sniffed the air quickly. "You're human, with a slight taint of demon. Since you're not really one of us, I'm guessing you don't know the histories."

The man paused. "What histories?"

"The demon you used for its parts was most likely created by a god. Have you never thought about who created the gods?"

"The gods were created by the primordial source," he shrugged. "Death and Life were the first personified, into Prometheus and Gaia."

Fiona chuckled, then broke into full-out laughter. "Who told you that steaming pile of bullshit?"

He frowned at us, at her. "My master's word is truth."

"And who, pray tell, is your master?" Fiona tried to control her laughter, though I could feel her suspicion. It felt like she already knew the answer.

"Supreme Lord of Death and the Netherlands, Prometheus Titanus," he drew himself up to speak the over-inflated name.

"You mean Prometheus of the Tiny Dick who I should have reabsorbed as soon as I created him?"

The man frowned again. “Master was not created by a seventeen-year-old girl.”

Fiona sighed. “You still don’t get it, do you? Why don’t we play a game. What am I?”

“You’re a Creator.”

“Very good. Do you know what Creators are?”

“They were the children of Master and Gaia.”

She shook our head and blasted him. I’m not sure what strength she used, but he did a slow crumple to the ground. A moment of stunned silence precipitated all hell breaking loose.

26

The goliath raised his axe and rushed us. Fiona ducked the first swing, but he brought the end back and smashed it into our ribs. As promised, she diverted the pain to me and kept moving. I wish I could say we were winning, but he had an advantage. Why she didn't blast him, I don't know. Just when I thought we were going to lose she wrenched the axe from the brute's hands. She was about to bury it in his chest when she suddenly reversed course and brought the flat of the blade down on his head.

"Does anyone else want a shot?" she held our arms out in open invitation. A few looked like they were going to take her up on it, but reconsidered after looking at all the corpses around us. Instead they threw down their weapons and dropped to their knees. "Aw. I was just starting to have fun."

"Can you stop being disappointed in the state of today's warriors and let us out of here?" Serenity called from inside one of the cages.

"These creatures aren't warriors," Fiona spat, dropping the axe. Stepping on or over bodies, she moved swiftly toward Daniel and the others. She paused to kick their leader on the way by, and I was surprised that he was still breathing. She finally reached the cells and tried to touch them. Pain shot up our arm, but she didn't pull away. Instead, she pressed the invisible wall harder. I was starting to see spots, but still she pressed on. The barrier finally imploded as my part of our brain shut down and darkness sucked me under.

I have no memory of what happened after that, and Fiona didn't share. I just floated in blissful darkness for an eternity. Eventually a field appeared, and I came to rest on a soft hill. The sky was a bright, pale blue, but there was no sun in the sky. It wasn't long after that that Fangy and Wings faded in. They smiled and sat quietly beside me.

"I think I like this place," I finally whispered.

"It's very peaceful," Wings nodded.

"Too bad there's no blood," Fangy sighed. "I'm getting hungry."

"I fed this morning, you shouldn't be hungry."

"Fiona used up most of our energy with those spheres," Wings placed a hand on my knee. "When you wake up you'll need to feed or Fangs will lose control."

"Resulting in the potential slaughter of innocents," I hung my head. "We can't have that, now can we?"

"No, we can't," they shook their heads. "But you should wake up now."

They vanished, taking the field with them. It took a while after that, but I finally managed to swim to the surface and wake up. My body was warm, and on something soft. Wherever I was was dark, but lights slowly came on as I became more awake.

"Are you Amelia or Fiona?" Daniel's voice came from behind me.

"What kind of question is that?" I groaned, trying not to move as my ribs crunched.

"Welcome back," his voice softened.

"How long have I been out?" I coughed, tasting metal.

"Fiona's been breaking ass for over a week, and we had to force her to sleep. That was three days ago."

I sat up, and regretted it. "Ten days?"

He nodded. "I am never going to intentionally piss that woman off."

"Were you with her the whole time?"

"Most of it. My arms had to be popped back into place."

"Can you tell me why it feels like I got the shit kicked out of me?"

"She dismantled Kahlia's network and traced it back to Prometheus's current command centre."

"Kahlia?" I repeated. The name was so familiar.

"James's younger brother. He was supposed to have died a few decades after James was turned, but it seems he made a deal with the devil."

"Did Fiona kill him?"

"She has him chained up with your father," he shrugged. "Are you hungry?"

"I need to feed," I nodded, just before realising I was naked. Pulling the sheet over my chest, I frowned at him. "Did you strip me?"

"Fiona asked me to. She hates wearing clothes."

"We have something in common there. Could you help me to the bathroom? I feel dirty, and would rather not spread germs to whoever I eat."

"Um, Amelia? We aren't at Sanctuary anymore. The Caretakers won't let you back until they've erased everyone's memories of that day. With the thousands of people they have there, it could take a while."

"Where are we then? Where is more safe than Sanctuary?"

"There are two known places safer than Sanctuary. Right now, we're staying with Hades and Persephone."

"We're in Hell?"

"Metaphoric hell, yes. You won't be on Hades's torture list, though."

"I wasn't worried about that. There aren't any feeders here."

"I'm your walking blood bank, remember? Full-service fill station at your command."

"I'm too hungry. If I'm not careful, I'll drain you completely."

"And I can't die. It may take a few hours, but I'll recharge."

"That sounds ten levels of creepy."

"It probably could be," he chuckled. "So, how do you want me?"

"Naked and covered in chocolate?" I grinned.

"Once you're healed, maybe. Until then, keep your hands to yourself."

"What did she do to my body?"

"There are a few cracked ribs, numerous deep bruises, most of the cuts have healed. One or two might scar. You should be right as rain in a few weeks, if you feed a lot."

"A lot as in more than usual?"

"Yes. Likely every day to make your recovery time as short as possible."

"Fuck me," I flopped back on the bed.

"Already have. Quite enjoyed it, too," he quipped. "Now, throat, shoulder, wrist or other? Pick a spot, any spot."

“Oh, give me your shoulder,” I pushed my hair out of my face.

Daniel was over in a flash, weapons oddly missing. He pulled his fitted black shirt off and glanced a kiss off my lips before sitting on the edge of the bed and helping me sit up. Pulling me into his lap, he exhaled and my fangs descended. Biting into him, Fangy drank greedily as I wrapped my legs around his waist. He was shuddering, his skin cooling, as I fed. His hips jerked under me before he fell sideways and his head hit the pillow. My fangs retracted automatically when they no longer felt blood flow.

“See you in a few hours,” I whispered before getting off him to hunt for clothes.

Three bulging suitcases stood by the wall across from the door. I reached for one of them when I was close enough, but a blast of energy left my hand and knocked it over. Cringing, I closed my hand and gingerly touched the zipper with just my index finger and thumb. It was easy to open, and clothes were packed inside in neat rolls. Taking a few stacks out, I located a shirt and pants, but no socks or undergarments. Opening the other cases, I found lacy, racy bras and underwear, and enough shoes to make a fashion show seem undersupplied.

“Someone needs a hobby outside of making me a living doll,” I muttered, grabbing the least offensive articles and putting them on. When I was fully dressed I checked to make sure Daniel was breathing before pulling the blanket over him and going for the door. It opened silently, but no one was on the other side. The walls were shimmering swirls of burnt gold and dark brown, and the hallway extended hundreds of feet in both directions. I was about to go right when the swirls became an arrow that pointed let. A little farther down was another one.

Figuring it knew the place better than I did, I followed the arrows until the pointed to an ornate black door. It swung open when I was close, like the other door, but no one was there. Again.

“The doors and corridors are on a telepathic interface,” Hades spoke from across the room, his back to me. “The arrows will point to whichever direction you want or need to go, whether you know it or not.”

"Useful,"

"Very. It was Seph's idea in case we ever had visitors."

"Speaking of, how is she? I heard that Fiona did a lot of damage to my body while I was out."

"*Metaria* internalised a lot of the damage, but some did bleed over. Seph is resting right now," he turned and clasped his hands behind his back. "Have you fed?"

"Daniel made me drain him, but it wasn't enough. I'll need to do it again when he wakes up in a few hours."

"Is he showing signs of addiction?"

I frowned. "He told me he was immune."

Hades chuckled. "No one is immune. Not even me."

"So he lied to me."

"Draconi were spectacular liars. It's a defence mechanism for them."

"So he could be addicted already?"

"How many times have you fed from him?"

"I don't know. At least five."

"Take it easy on him, then. If he starts getting agitated, come find one of us and we'll feed you."

"Is that safe?"

"Not in the slightest," he grinned. "Feeding on us always runs the risk, especially with you, of us being reabsorbed into the ether. Some of us have lived long enough that we wouldn't mind a change of scenery."

"Quit scaring my granddaughter, you priss," a deep voice that used to read me to sleep came from behind the door to my right.

"Grandpa Sam?" I peeked around the door. And there he stood. All seven feet topped with my dark hair.

"Hi Sweetie. How have you been holding up?"

"It's been a rollercoaster," I shrugged. "Did you hear about Mom?"

"I collected her and your aunt myself," he nodded. "You've come into your gifts?"

"Some of them. There are still hundreds to go, at least."

"Do you have control?"

"Not over most of them," I shook my head.

"Good. Control is overrated."

I laughed at that. “Tell that to the dragon I drained ten minutes ago.”

“There’s still a living Draconis?” he seemed genuinely confused.

“You didn’t know?”

“I heard about the slaughter of the last clan, and the death of the final daughter. I wasn’t informed that there was one still living.”

“He is currently tucked in my bed, recharging.”

“Have you slept with him yet?”

“GRANDPA!” my jaw dropped.

“What? You’re a Creator, and I’m going to presume that he is your oathed guardian. It is natural for you to sleep with him. It’s how they used to be.”

“How do you know I’m a Creator?”

“I’ve known since the moment Serenity was born. Our world stood still, held its breath, until she screamed the first time. Since no sisters in your family have ever had different fathers, you had to be one, too.”

“Why didn’t you ever tell me?”

“Your mother made me promise not to.”

“What else have you promised not to tell me?”

“Nothing, I swear. It’s the only thing I’ve ever kept secret from you.”

“Okay. But you got one thing wrong.”

“What might that be?”

“He isn’t oathed to me. He’s oathed to Fiona.”

“Fiona?” he repeated, confused.

“Ancient, angry. About me high.”

“The All Mother?”

“The All Mother,” I nodded.

“She’s back?”

“When she isn’t hibernating with my other parts. She forgot to teach me how to control energy balls, and I accidentally blasted one of my suitcases.”

“I heard about what happened at the school. By the descriptions, I thought it was you that kept some of my warriors busy.”

"All her," I shook my head. "We didn't have time for her to teach me, and I can't use our wings."

"You can't use your wings? Why not?"

"I didn't know I had any until recently, and I can't bring them out on my own."

"We'll have to fix that, then. Can I get a hug from my favourite granddaughter?"

"Of course," I smiled, stepping around the door and into his open arms.

It felt good to hold him, but without my gloves on I couldn't stop his memories from rushing through my head and knocking me senseless.

27

"She wasn't lying, her control sucks," a disembodied male voice broke through the fog that was holding me down.

"She had been working with Seph, or was about to. We didn't know she hadn't had even the most basic of training," another male spoke.

"I watched her mother teach her control over this one. She did it with both girls from the moment they were born. Something must have happened in the last couple of years to break her," the first male spoke again.

"You should have been with us at Sanctuary a couple weeks ago," the second one laughed. "Seph had to restart her heart, and oh boy. When her walls came down we got a look at everything that's happened since your daughters died. Serenity and Amelia have not been lucky."

"Why weren't they taken straight to Sanctuary the moment Gabi and Josie died?"

"Stuart tried to claim them. Serenity packed Amelia up and ran with her; Blair and Colby couldn't find them for the longest time."

"Stuart's alive? How? I dropped him in an active volcano."

"Our old pal, Prometheus. He's been collecting people for we don't know how long."

"Rylynne?"

"Died in eighty-eight."

"Bullshit. No one collected her soul."

"No one collected her soul? How do you know that?"

"Fiona tasked me with storing your souls if you died so she could remake your bodies when she came back. No one brought me Rylynne's soul."

"You knew *Metaria* was going to leave?"

"I suspected when she gave me the mission, but she never said so in as many words. She was always careful with what she told us, wasn't she?"

"She was," the second male sounded drained. "Amelia should be back with us soon. She can hear us, but she can't feel her body quite yet."

"Sometimes I forget that you're a telepath," Sam? Sam sighed.

"You used to be one, too. Never forget that," Hades shuffled something.

"I gave it up for a reason, you know that. I couldn't handle the screams anymore."

"Children and the murdered are the hardest," Hades agreed. "It's why I take so much pleasure from torturing their murderers."

"Sadist."

"What can I say? Sticks and stones can't break my bones, so knives and blood excite me."

I managed a shudder as he said that.

"Ah, good. Can you feel your toes, Amelia?" Hades's voice was cheery.

"Can't…see," I barely managed to get my mouth to work.

"Give it five to ten minutes. You got a massive download of memories and your brain wasn't designed to hold that much information. It should be clearing itself out, and we found a pair of gloves for you."

"Th…ank…you," I blinked, light and dark beginning to separate. Sensation was slowly returning, but my vision was still swimming. "Why didn't I get a download like that when I touched Daniel earlier?"

"He could have been controlling himself," Hades shrugged, almost in focus. "Do you think you can stand?"

"Give me a minute and I should be able to. The world is coming back into focus," I brought my hands up and cracked my knuckles.

"So, you blasted a suitcase. Did it feel good?" Hades was grinning.

"It was confusing. I thought that gift had to be focused-on to be used."

"For Fiona, maybe. But all of your controls seem to be down, so who knows what needs to be called to work right now."

"Am I allowed to tell her to go fuck herself?"

"She'd probably enjoy it more than you, so probably not wise," Samuel chuckled.

"Well then," I rolled over and got to my feet. "Can we discuss how Prometheus is going to die?"

"I was already working on that," Hades nodded. "He's currently living at the wolves' compound. Elizabeth has all but crowned him their king."

"Graham's grandmother? The one who was supposed to step down when he was old enough?"

"The quarter-blood? Yes, his psychotic bitch of a grandmother. Any of the pack who refuse to bow to Prometheus are being tortured."

"Slight correction there. Graham is half-blood, not quarter," I followed Hades and Samuel to the table by the far wall. On it were maps and dozens of pages of notes. "But Prometheus knows his torture. Poor creatures."

"How do you know he's a halfer?" Hades raised an eyebrow at me.

"His wolf told me. The Muses asked if I could give any insight into his sudden break, so I did the stupid thing and was bitten for my troubles."

They both froze. "Were you in his mind when the wolf bit you?" Samuel looked at me with wide, almost scared eyes.

"Yes…" I drew out the word, confused.

"Fuck."

"Damn it."

They spoke so quickly I couldn't tell who said what.

"Is that a problem?"

They looked at each other before Hades spoke.

"It's the first step in the shifter version of soul bonding. Unlike what Eros and Psyche do, a shifter can force the bond on someone. It's very dangerous, and not many survive to the third step. If you do make it, your life forces become linked and even I cannot separate them."

"Why would he do it, then?"

"Graham may not have known. The inner animals of shifters are drawn to power, and if given half a chance they will try to claim it for themselves."

"Is there any way to reverse it?"

"Kill him before it goes any farther."

"I can't kill an innocent."

"He won't be innocent for long, especially if the bonding is completed and you refuse him. A rejection on that level can result in insanity."

"So that's why Sanctuary's guidebook had soul bonding on the list of major offences."

Hades chuckled. "They actually have that listed? Looks like I need to make a phone call." He strode a short distance away from us and removed a small black phone from his pocket.

Samuel gingerly touched the back of my neck and closed his eyes. After a moment he exhaled and stepped away.

"It's only infecting your arm below the elbow right now. We still have time to fix this before any more damage is done."

"How can you tell that?" I rubbed my arm.

"Targeted psychometry, with an extra or two. Your control *is* down, but I can't see why. Maybe it's just time you relearned how to do everything."

"I don't have time to relearn everything. Prometheus needs to die, soon. If I don't have control, I can't do it."

"Why do you have to do it?"

"Because no one else can. He can only be destroyed by that which created him."

"Fiona knows the mechanics of destroying us. Hell, she completely obliterated Gaia and Prometheus's siblings. She has control. Why not let her do it?"

"She wants to, but I *need* to do this. I need to feel the life draining from his putrid meat suit."

"Ah," Samuel nodded. "If you try taking him on with vengeance in your heart he is the one more likely to triumph. You need to keep your emotions out of it if you're going to succeed."

"How do I keep my emotions out of it when I have so much to be angry about?"

"Anger is fuel. Eat it, play with it, but don't allow it to win. The moment it wins, you lose."

"How do I keep it from winning? From running me over?"

"By knowing why you're angry. If you can find the root of it, you can control it."

"Why *aren't* I angry? My mom and aunt died on my fourteenth birthday, my father works for the creature that destroyed my life. I've been hunted for so long that I can barely remember my childhood. I have been beaten, shot, stabbed, tortured, to name a few things. I'm a multiple murderer, and I don't feel bad about most of the deaths. Oh, and people think I'm either a great saviour, or the worst demonic creature to be cursed to this generation."

"Chase it down. Be specific. Where do all those things come from?"

"Things I can't control," I finally said after a long pause. "I'm angry because I haven't been able to control most of the shit that's gone on in my life."

"You couldn't control those things because they weren't your to control. My daughters were meant to die, for a time. You were hunted because humans are xenophobic and don't understand the world around them, aside from the fact that most fall into the category of 'fucking idiots.' You're a murderer? So are most of us. We kill because we need to, not because we want to, Amelia. Death keeps the world in balance," he scratched his head. "You are neither saviour, nor demon until you choose what path you want to follow outside of your nature's calling.

"I don't want my nature's calling. All I want is a normal, human life."

"Even though you were not born human?"

"I just want a taste of normal, for once in my life. Once this is over, I want to live where I won't be bothered by any of this shit for a while."

"We could probably arrange that. Wherever you go, wherever you live, will need to be heavily warded if you want peace."

"Heavy warding means multiple-source power links. Anyone able to track that sort of activity will be able to find me."

"Not if it's being done by one being at a time. By weaving it into the local flora and fauna we can dampen our energy signatures."

"It also spreads over a wider area."

"Indeed," he nodded. "Shall we get back on task?"

"How does Prometheus die?" I managed half a smile.

"Yes," Hades re-joined us. "Blair and Colby are going to chat with Graham when he wakes up. Apparently the Muses forced him to shift, and it was bloody. They had to sedate him so he could recover."

"Do they know why everyone thought he was a quarter and not a halfer?" I stroked the pages of floor plans and notes.

"His mother is married to a human. It was assumed that he was the father of all her children, so they raised Graham to believe he couldn't shift," Hades shrugged. "The mind is a powerful thing."

"It can be," I muttered, more to myself than to them. "How much information has been retrieved from Stuart and Kahlia?"

"Enough to know their average guard force and where they are most likely to be found," Hades pulled a small stack of pages from beneath my drumming fingers. "Two guards are posted every ten feet in the longer hallways. All exits have four guards; two inside, two out. The torture chamber, I mean library, has eight guards inside at all times. The catacombs beneath the compound have been turned into a prison, and is the second most-guarded area there. The entire place is locked so that only a wolf or someone who has been there before can teleport in."

"Fuck a duck and call it dinner," I whistled. "Would we be able to bypass the lock if we were with someone it recognised?"

"We don't know," Hades shook his head. "If we try, and fail, they'll know we're coming and pack up shop."

"Hm," I chewed on my lower lip for a moment. "Would angels be able to get through? Since they can shift between corporeal and energy, would the lock recognise them? Or would they be ignored since they're technically guides to the dead?"

They both gave me looks of shocked wonder.

"We must be getting really old to have missed that," Samuel finally spoke.

"Speak for yourself, feather-brain," Hades rubbed his face.

"What did you two miss that took less than five minutes for a girl to figure out?" Persephone popped in on the other side of the table.

"Something far too simple," Hades reached over and stroked her face. "Wolves have been dying, and we have been receiving their souls, right?"

"Yes, we have," she nodded. Then it hit her, too. "Angels."

"They can bypass that stupid lock the wolves have to keep everyone out," Hades grinned.

"It's so simple," she giggled. "No one could block an angel, even if they tried."

"And no one thinks to try to block us," Samuel shuffled some papers away from the floor plans. "There are very few beings left who were alive when we last went to war. With the short memories of most creatures, no one is likely to remember that we are also warriors."

"Would you be willing to send some of your people in with Amelia?" Persephone was looking at me as she spoke to my grandfather.

"I'll ask for volunteers, but it is highly unlikely any will say no," he nodded. "She needs training first, though."

"I can get on that right now. You guys get going on basic infiltration and strike while we go blow some shit up," she held her hand out to me. I took it, smiling, and she jumped us back to my bedroom. Daniel was still tucked in and unmoving. "Care to explain why he's recharging?"

"He told me to drain him since Fiona didn't feed while I was out," I shrugged.

"Is he addicted?"

"I don't know. He told me he was immune, but your husband disabused me of that notion."

"Fuck, Rylynne. Why did you have to fuck with his head all those years ago?"

"I'm going to guess that that was more to yourself than to me?"

"Correct. When Daniel was first training with Colby and Blair, Rylynne put his mind in a fog so he could heal and learn. Lying about that may have been one of the things she forced into his head."

"Without her here, we won't know," I shrugged. "Did Aphrodite send that sucker punch that Hermes hit us with?"

"Oh probably. She enjoys getting people in bed. It helps keep her charged."

"Keeps her charged?" I repeated blankly.

"Every time any creature has sex, she gets a power jolt."

"That's just a little creepy."

"It only is if you didn't want it in the first place. She refuses to bypass consent."

"That's good, at least. So, can we get on with training?"

"Sure. After you remove your gloves. I need to see your hands."

"Why my hands?"

"I just need to see them."

Frowning, I pulled off the soft gloves and held my hands out to her. She inspected them, traced the lines before catching them in an iron grip and shoving energy through me.

"What the fuck are you doing?" pain was starting to shoot up my arms.

"Crash course in everything you currently can't control," she spoke through gritted teeth. "It's only temporary, so don't get used to it. It'll last until you kill Prometheus, but be prepared for a long recovery after you go nuclear on his rank ass."

"So long as this doesn't give me permanent brain damage, I don't think I give much of a shit right now," I desperately wanted to wipe away whatever was dripping from my nose.

There was a blurred movement in the edge of my peripheral vision. Daniel was on his feet, and pressing against an invisible bubble around us. What little I saw of his eyes when he passed behind Persephone showed nothing but a blank, animal stare. When he had circled the bubble twice, he punched it. The field reacted and launched him into the wall. The moment he hit the floor he was on his feet again, growling.

Persephone's grip relaxed as red swirls carved their way up my arms. They burned their way over my shoulders, down my collar bones, and up my neck; stopping just below my chin and over my breasts. She let go completely as Daniel came at us again. Throwing her hand out, he froze mid-step.

"Go to him. Touch him. You'll know what to do," she spoke, never taking her eyes off me. "And wipe the blood off your face. The smell of it may have triggered his inner beast into action."

"Are we going to blow anything up after?" I brought part of my shirt up to clean the tacky blood away.

"Just to be sure you have a handle on what I did, yes. But not until he can think like one of us again."

"Sounds good. Let him go and get out of here, I'll be okay with him."

"Are you sure?" she arched a delicate eyebrow at me.

"He can't hurt me," I nodded.

She flashed a small smile before vanishing. The second she was gone he was free, and the force he had been fighting was no longer there to stop him. His orange and yellow eyes were all animal; there was no sign of the kind-hearted man I knew was still in there. He was almost in arm's reach when I took too deep of a breath and one of my recently cracked ribs reached its splinter point. Intelligence came back into his eyes as my knees hit the floor and I held my right hand against the source of the pain.

Daniel was eye-level with me in a blink. As soon as his hand touched mine the animal behind his eyes receded completely. He pulled my hand away and probed the area gently until he found something. Lifting my shirt just enough to expose the area, he turned one finger into a claw and sliced me open.

"Whose side are you on here?" I gasped as he dug around in the hole.

He ignored me until a small smile flashed across his lips. "Yours. And please don't scream in my ear until later."

"Why would I scream –" I didn't get to finish that thought. He pulled something out of my chest and I vomited on him for his efforts. He was chuckling when I passed out.

28

I came to on a soft couch in a room I didn't recognise. My shirt was gone, but a soft blanket had been placed over most of my chest.

"You haven't been out for long," Persephone's voice was distracted and to my right.

"Any idea why I feel like shit this time?" I managed to avoid wincing as I breathed.

"Something we missed. When Fiona took that blow to the ribs, something was embedded into the bone. It broke that rib," she leaned over and looked at my side. "We're still digging parts of it out. It's high tech. Like something out of a sci-fi movie."

"What does it look like?"

"A square spider with too many legs that are extremely flexible."

"Gross."

"But fascinating," she flashed me a small smile. "We might have to send it top-side for more tests, but it seems to be a receiver, not a tracker or wire."

"It's basically a miniature torture device."

She froze. "I hadn't thought about it that way."

"It would make sense, though," Samuel appeared and held a small container open for the goddess. She gingerly dropped the object inside before wiping her hands on her pants. "Kahlia's network was really Prometheus's by proxy. It's doubtful they would make anything without his approval."

"When can we go after the sick fuck?"

"As soon as I'm sure you're ready," my grandfather laughed. "It won't be for a week, at least. The Muses are a little swamped right now, and none can break away for a house call."

"Just stitch me up and slap on a bandage. I'll be ready to go tomorrow."

"Nice try. That would work if we were going in with guns, but they're expecting that. We're going Greek," he grinned. "Battle axes and broad swords, for most of us. The guards are, supposedly, wearing body armour that's only good against bullets. This is one of the few times that it's okay to bring a knife to a gun fight."

"It helps that you guys can't die."

"Doesn't mean that bullets don't sting, though."

"True enough," I sucked in a sharp breath as something long was tugged out of my side.

"Longest one yet," Hades chuckled beside me. "It was a nice catch on the dragon's part, but he did a hatchet job taking it out."

"Speaking of, where is he?" I repeatedly clenched and relaxed my hands.

"Shower, washing off the fountain of blood you drenched him with," Seph laughed. "To his credit, he didn't flinch away in disgust."

"Why would I be disgusted? I inflicted the pain that resulted in such a reaction," the deep, familiar rumble was approaching from behind my head.

"Dragons must have stronger stomach than most males," I tried to shrug. They slight movement shifted Hades's tool and he stabbed a nerve by mistake. The say that it hurt would be a massive understatement.

"Don't move, please. I might nick an artery by accident."

I nodded, but didn't try to speak. A nicked artery was a death sentence, even when surrounded by deities. Most of the time. He waited for my breathing to even out before resuming his search for the macro machine parts. Almost a dozen tugs later he sat up and rolled his shoulders.

"That's the last that I could find," he removed a pair of odd glasses from his face before stripping off his latex gloves.

"Why the gloves? My last blood tests were clean," I frowned at him.

"We can't get infections or diseases, but I don't know about the technology behind that chip. Personally, I don't like being in any sort of pain."

"Pansy," Samuel chuckled.

"Masochist," Hades shot back.

"Uh, guys?" I raised a hand and waved to get their attention.

"Yes?" Samuel raised an amused eyebrow at me.

"Hole in my side oozing vital bodily fluids?"

"Right," Hades flashed a small smile before grabbing something I could see. Seconds later something cold and wet touched my side, stinging more than a little. "Let that dry for five minutes, then go have a bath."

"What is it?" I touched the tacky area gently.

"Well, you sort of stink…"

"Not what she was asking," Persephone laughed. "It's a Muses' blend adhesive bandage in an aerosol can for expediency in battlefield medicine."

"Thank you," I grinned before sitting up.

"You're welcome. Follow the arrows. They'll take you to the bathroom."

I nodded and moved swiftly, or as quickly as I was able, to the small door to my right. Daniel silently tucked my hand into his arm and kicked the door shut behind us.

"You're tense," he finally spoke when we were a few hundred feet from the door.

"Should I not be?"

"Not with me," he shrugged. "A Creator is always supposed to be calm near their guardian."

"You're Fiona's guardian, not mine," I tried to pull my hand away, but he tightened his grip and held me fast.

"What's wrong, Amelia? What's changed since this morning?"

"Those who do not believe that there is truth to be sought are often the most blinded by its illumination," I snarled, finally wrenching my hand away.

"I'm still not functioning at full capacity, so I'm not sure what you mean."

"You lied to me."

"I lie about a lot of things, but I don't remember lying to you."

"Bite addiction. You're not immune."

An oddly adorable frown of confusion contorted his face. "Yes I am."

"No one is immune. Not even the gods," I turned from him and stalked the arrows until they led me to a beige door. It opened, like all the others, without a hand to guide it. Inside was a softly lit bathing hall, with a tub/pool set into the floor. It was full of water that had wispy curls of steam rising from the surface. I had kicked my shoes off and was shimmying my pants down my legs when the air behind me shifted. I extricated one leg and straightened, but didn't have a chance to turn around.

"I didn't lie," Daniel's voice was a low rumble in my ear. "My memory tells me that I am immune, and lying to you would break my promise."

"Since you said that you couldn't suffer from bite addiction before you made that promise, forgive me for not believing you," I stepped away from his warmth and kicked my pants the rest of the way off. Stripping my underwear, I dropped it on my shoes and strode to the pool.

I was already waist-deep in the water when I heard his heavy jeans hit the floor. Not long after the surface rippled as it was disturbed. His arms encircled me, pinned mine to my sides, as he pulled me against him.

"I don't know what to do," his voice was uncertain.

"About what?" I fought to not melt against him. It was hard to resist.

"You," he shivered. "I'm not used to being questioned, goaded. I spent the last four hundred years honing my physical skills, but my mind was in a fog. I don't know how to deal with fresh emotions."

"And what fresh emotions are plaguing you now?" I asked, half afraid of the answer.

He inhaled sharply. "Fear. Affection. Things that distract from my objectivity."

Affection was bad. "I think objectivity went screaming out the window when we fucked."

I could feel his flinch. "Never call what we did 'fucking'," he growled.

"Why not? It's the truth," I stiffened, testing his hold. "We fucked because Aphrodite though you needed a kick to sleep with me. We both know you wouldn't have done it otherwise, and there's no use in denying it."

Daniel relaxed a little, chuckled. "I know what you're doing."

"Speaking the truth? Reminding you that you never saw me as someone compatible in bed?"

"You're compartmentalising, and fighting with yourself. A small, battered part of you still believes in love, but the broken pieces only see lies, deception, and manipulation. It's easier for you to push people away than let them in."

"Love is overrated. It makes terrible options look like the best choice."

"The same could be said of any emotion. How about we indulge in an experiment?"

"What kind of experiment?" I tried, and failed, to keep the suspicion out of my voice.

"For every day that you don't pull away emotionally, I'll let you dig through my head."

"Now why would you do that?"

"A test, for both of us. No one has ever seen every memory in my brain, and it seems like a good trade for you opening your battered heart."

"You've already been in my bed, why do you want in my heart, too? Are you testing how masochistic I am?"

He sighed and rested his forehead on the crown of my skull. "Caring can make you stronger, Amelia. Sure, the people in your heart can be used against you, but fighting to protect them can make you more ruthless. And it's not like the people around you are weak, or human."

The human part struck a nerve, and I flinched. "I need to wash and get back."

"There you go again, closing yourself off. The past can only hurt you if you let it."

"Tell that to the younger version of me. I don't let people in because the last person I loved was murdered in front of me. He was addicted, and he shouldn't have been there."

"Was he human?"

"Of course he was. I couldn't risk being around any of our kind back then."

"I'm not, nor have I ever been, human. So long as I'm not blind-sided again, I won't die on you."

"But you can be blind-sided, which means that I'm safer not giving a shit."

"You can pretend you don't care, but we both know you have a gentle heart."

"My gentle heart can take a flying leap into an alternate dimension and leave me alone."

"Let go. Just for a minute. Please. Relax and be calm."

"Why?"

"Because I want to hold you without worrying that you'll tear my throat out."

"I'm not a fan of hurting people, remember? I don't enjoy murder."

"Don't advertise that," he laughed, lifting me just enough to carry me to one of the benches by the deeper end of the pool. "Fiona killed a lot of people while pretending to be you."

"How many more deaths are now attributed to my hands?" I could feel the fight draining from me. He turned us and sat, pulling me onto his lap so my chin stayed above the water before answering; rubbing his hands up and down my arms.

"Dozens," he finally exhaled. "Maybe hundreds."

"Is it okay to say I hate her right now?"

"It is okay to say whatever you like at almost any time, Amelia. You are currently our world's Queen High Bad Ass."

"Until someone knocks me off that throne," I spoke through clenched teeth. "Looks like I get to be this generation's nightmare demon."

"There's nothing wrong with that," he gave me a quick squeeze before moving his arms to my waist. "It may be better to be loved than feared, but fear works just fine in a pinch."

"Have I ever told you that I hate philosophy?"

He laughed. "Not that I can recall. Shall we get you clean?"

"As quickly as possible," I nodded.

Daniel dunked us so quickly that I didn't have time to take a breath. We were back above the surface before I could inhale, but I sputtered anyways. He chuckled and pressed his lips to that spot just behind my ear. It sent chills down my spine, and I relaxed completely.

"Are you sure you have things to do today?" he murmured against my ear.

"Fairly sure," I nodded, my eyes half-closing.

His fingers danced lightly over my abdomen and he nibbled on the curve between my neck and shoulder. "How about now?"

"Blow shit up," I barely suppressed a moan.

One of his hands skimmed down and pressed me into his solid groin. "And now?"

"Someone might walk in," I bit my lower lip.

"That's half the fun," he chuckled, fingers never still.

"I don't like being watched. It's humiliating," memories broke through the lusty fog and I stiffened.

He brought one hand out of the water and flicked it at the door. A lock snapped into place and he nipped along my shoulder. "Better?"

"A little," I nodded, but I couldn't relax again. "Let's just wash and get out of here. Things need doing."

"Later?" he held me tight.

"Maybe," I shrugged.

He let go without another word and grabbed a bottle of pomegranate body scrub from a dip in the floor around the edge. He poured a generous amount into his palm before massaging it into my grimy flesh. It took a while, but I finally started to feel clean.

For the first time in a long time, I felt like I was more than just a bunch of broken parts. I felt like I could be whole again.

29

Daniel was very thorough. By the time he was done with the scrubs and body polishes I almost felt like a new person. Shampoo and conditioner took a little longer. Mostly because he kept finding bone fragments in the snarls. When he could run a brush through without it catching on anything, he let me rinse out the last of the conditioner.

I wanted to stay in the pool forever, but the day needed tending to. Daniel seemed to sense my reticence; he held me loosely and brushed his lips up and down my neck until I was a puddle of shivering jelly.

"Clothes?" I finally managed to whisper after several attempts.

"Cleaned as soon as they touched the floor. They aren't big on doing laundry around here," he chuckled, releasing me.

"Useful," I smiled, more to myself since he couldn't see it. I floated for a moment before finding my feet and standing. "How about a shirt?"

"Use mine. The one you were wearing wasn't salvageable," he stood behind me and touched the bandage. "The Muses are geniuses."

"Yes they are," I nodded. "No offence, but your shirt is probably four or five sizes too big for me."

"Exactly. You'll look adorable and non-threatening."

"Aren't I always adorable?" I turned and batted my eyelashes at him.

He grinned. "You're always beautiful, even when covered in gore. Adorable takes a little more work."

The smile that had been climbing my face froze.

"Did I say something wrong?" his grin faded a little.

"No," I shook my head. "We should get dressed. Get things done today."

"You're closing down again."

"Let me have my neuroses," I turned away from him and waded to the steps. A swirl of hot air wrapped around my hair and had it dry by the time I reached my small pile of clothes. They smelled fresh, and felt clean as I pulled them on.

"Will your neuroses prevent you from taking my shirt?" he asked, holding it out to me. His pants and boots were on but not yet done up.

I looked him over quickly, salivating just a little at his taut muscles. "Do you have hair anywhere except your head?" I asked, taking the soft black shirt.

He laughed. "Nope. Completely hairless except on top."

"Must be nice."

"It can be. Though you're the same way."

"Thanks to electrolysis," I shrugged. "I don't have time to constantly wax or shave."

He shuddered at the mention of wax. "Shall we?"

"Yes," I nodded before pulling his shirt over my head and doing up two of the upper buttons. It fell to just above my knees, and retained some of his scent. I inhaled deeply when he wasn't looking and felt warm all the way down to my toes.

"What's on the agenda?" he offered me an arm as he opened the door.

"Find Persephone, then see if her crash course in control worked."

"Well, you haven't tossed any energy balls since she ransacked your brain, so I'm going to take that as a good sign."

"Just because I'm not firing them, doesn't mean I can create them at will. I don't know the mechanics of actually creating them."

"Didn't Fiona teach you at Sanctuary?"

"She was too busy redirecting damage and killing people to give me an explanation."

"And then you passed out for almost two weeks so she couldn't explain."

"In a nut shell, yes."

"That sucks."

"Right now, yes it does."

"Did you two have fun?" my grandfather's voice was full of barely-suppressed laughter. It had taken barely any time to return to the room they have been left in.

"He scrubbed the gore and bone fragments out of my hair," I shrugged. "It took a while to get it all out."

"Nothing more…fun?" he waggled his eyebrows.

"Nope. And the thought of telling you if we had is kind of disturbing."

"I live vicariously where I can," he sighed. "Angels only get one lover every thousand years, so we try to make it count when we find someone worth the later heartache."

"Sanctuary doesn't mention that in your section of the library," Daniel patted my hand.

"It's not something we advertise," Samuel shook his head. "Maybe I should rephrase a little. We can only take one non-angelic lover every thousand years. We all lost the taste for each other millions of years ago."

"Was Grandma Morganna worth it?" I asked quietly.

Samuels's face softened. "She was worth it. She's the only mortal I can say that about."

"Okay! Enough of the depressing talk," Persephone broke in cheerfully. "Come with me, Amelia, and we'll see if you can blow things up on command."

"Blow things up?" I repeated. "Isn't that a fire-based thing?"

"Technically…yes. But it all comes down to energy manipulation. Once you know how to manipulate energy in its most basic form, everything else is easy," she nodded. "Coming?"

"Where to, m'lady?" I flashed a small smile and let go of Daniel's arm.

She took my hand and pulled me back out the door. Daniel stayed behind knowing I was safer with the goddess than with him. The hallway was much shorter than I remembered, and there were more doors and branches going other directions.

"Don't give yourself a headache trying to figure out the layout," she laughed. "This place is multi-dimensional and shifts as it sees fit."

"Don't you get lost if it's always changing?"

"I did in the beginning, but once I realised that the lack of a pattern was, itself, a pattern it got easier to figure out."

"Hades' idea?"

"Yes," she giggled. "He knew I liked puzzles. Though, he made this place before we met, so he could have been as much a puzzler as I am."

"You guys don't sit and do the crossword together?"

"Gods no! We come up with battle plans for fun. Sometime we even mock up an apocalypse if we're really bored."

"Do you guys get bored often?" I raised an eyebrow at her.

"Every few decades," she shrugged. "Less now that more assholes are dying."

"He's spending more time torturing people now that the human world is tearing itself apart?"

"Effectively, yes. But we still spend time together, so it's okay," she stopped by a dark red door and punched a code into a pad on the wall. After a moment it swung open on well-oiled hinges. Grid lines appeared on the floor, ceiling and walls, and a holographic woman in a white business suit blinked into existence.

"User: Persephone and Guest," the tinkling artificial voice came from hidden speakers. "How may I serve you today?"

"Training map three-two-five. Novice difficulty. Ten minutes advance prep before beginning of simulation, please Elsie," the goddess let go of my hand.

"Map loading. Difficulty set. Would you like the safeties removed?" Elsie's non-descript face registered no emotion.

"Keep them engaged for round one. We'll see after that."

"Acknowledged."

"What the hell?" I could feel my jaw start to drop.

"Artificial intelligence," Persephone shrugged. "I designed her a couple million years ago so we could hone our skills during dry spells."

"Is it – she – fully cognisant?"

"Oh yes. She even writes herself new layers of code for entertainment when I neglect her. Once a month we let her connect to the outside world so that she can download and process all new information."

"ALL new information?" I repeated. "Even secure government stuff?"

"Especially government stuff. She can bypass any encryption system on this planet without leaving a single trace of the breach."

"What does she do with all of it?"

"Breaks it down into categories, marks things as urgent, interesting, threat. Stuff like that. Sometimes she even preps reports on how badly humans are fucking up this time."

"That must be an interesting read."

"It can be. Her writing style is highly adaptive, and more recently it's been showing Shakespeare and Twain as great influences."

"What about before the internet was created? How did she get her information then?" now I was really curious. Ancient AI. I almost couldn't believe it.

"The lesser fey make great spies. With their photographic memories they could describe a room down to the tiniest speck of dust."

"Neat."

"Very."

"Five minutes before simulation start," the tinkling voice broke in. "Would you like me to reset the timer?"

"Nope, I can work with five minutes Elsie," Persephone shook her head. "We'll be working with your right hand only, for now. Using your left would stress your broken rib and impair healing."

"Okay," I nodded. "How do we do this?"

"Touch my arm. I'll give you a live feed on how to create and control a stun-sphere."

"Just a stunner?"

"Stun is the most useful, and takes the least finesse, except for death orbs. But we don't need those here so keep it simple."

"Understood," I reached over and placed my bare fingers on her upturned wrist.

Instead of falling into her head, or absorbing her memories, it felt like I was connected to her nervous system. Little pulses travelled up and down her arm, and I felt an echo of every one in my body. Her breathing deepened, but her heart rate remained steady; every beat pushing energy through her arteries to her hand. A ghost of a thought sped up the process until crackling power sat pooled in her palm.

"Let go," her voice seemed like it was an age away.

I slid my hand away from her, and as soon as we were no longer in contact I became acutely aware of our surroundings. The room had been filled with crumbling remnants of bullet-riddled buildings, and the acrid stench of smoke mingled with the sweet-sourness of decay. My eyes slowly came back to the goddess beside me, and she winked.

"Seems so real, doesn't it?"

"Yes," I nodded. "Where is this?"

"Afghanistan, near the Pakistani border. One of the harder-hit areas of the current war, that is carefully kept out of the news."

"Of course it's kept out of the news. No one would support the war if they could see this in its entirety."

"Well, some would. Now, take a look at my hand. Describe what you see."

I did as requested and blinked. Slowly. "Blue puddle of fractal sparkles."

"Close enough," she laughed. "You try. Remember how it felt when I did it."

I mirrored her stance, held my arm like hers, and concentrated on the feeling of little sparks travelling to my hand. Pale blue lights slowly came to life in my palm until the size of the pool matched the goddess's.

"Good. Now look at it and think 'sphere'."

I tried, but it ended up as a deformed dome.

"Feed it a little more energy. You could have not given it enough."

My hand wavered and the light fizzled. "I don't have enough to spare. Fiona ran me beyond dry, and I didn't get enough when I drained Daniel."

"Elsie halt simulation. Store in buffer until further notice," she lowered her own hand.

"Yes, Persephone. Preferences saved for expedient recall."

"Why didn't you feed again once Daniel was awake?"

"Bite addiction. He told me he was immune, but he's not. I don't want another Jeremy situation on my conscience."

"So tell one of us. We can feed you quite easily."

"But it's more dangerous for you. If I were to lose control you could cease to exist entirely."

"*Metaria* would remake us when she's able," Persephone shrugged.

"But you wouldn't be you anymore. You'd be a blank slate."

She sighed. "Sometimes a blank slate is a good thing."

30

"I'm sorry if I brought up painful memories," I reached out to touch her but dropped my hand. Immortals often didn't like to be touched.

"It's okay. I've lost so many that they've started blurring together. I remember all of their precious faces, but the pain is no longer as sharp as it once was."

"It was still wrong of me to bring it up."

She flashed half of a sad smile. "You're young. You'll learn with time. Now, let's go get you a good feed."

She turned and led me back out to the hall and down to the war room. Samuel, Daniel and Hades were all bracing themselves against the heavy table, occasionally pointing to something in the hologram floating between them. Red spots floated at certain points, some turning green as they spoke in low voices.

"Guys?" Persephone piped up when we were just inside the door. They startled, their concentration broken.

"Yes, love?" Hades's face softened from its hard lines as he looked at her.

"Amelia needs to feed. She's running close to empty."

"How close to empty?" Daniel frowned.

"If the vampiric side of her were to push it, I'd say the slaughter of a small city," she paused, thinking. "Maybe two small cities."

"I don't go that far off the reservation, and neither does Fangy. We've always kept it under a dozen, even when she's starving," I sighed.

"You weren't bleeding as much energy then," Persephone *tsk*ed. "Now that you know what you are, more energy will be transferred from you to damaged parts of the world. You also need to feed for the All Mother, since she's in your body."

"Damn it," I rubbed my eyes with the heels of my palms. "I don't like feeding on people."

"If animals were a viable source for you, we'd offer. Unfortunately they don't have a certain spark Creators need," she patted me on the shoulder.

"How did the first ones survive, then? It's not like there were humans they could eat millions of years ago."

"They fed on Atlanteans, and their bonded dragon," Samuel crossed his arms over his chest. "Why didn't you feed earlier?"

I shrugged. "Wasn't in the mood, I guess."

"Being 'in the mood' should have no bearing on feeding. You feed or you die, it's that simple. Until you're older, you die, we die."

"I know!" I yelled, anger igniting. "If everyone could quit fucking telling me shit that I already know, maybe I could deal with it!"

Persephone stepped away from me, and the others took a large step back, watching me warily. I could feel the rage pulsing beneath my tongue, but it didn't kick up any bloodlust.

"What? Did I grow a second head?" I snapped.

"Can you point your palms at the floor until you calm down?" Persephone shuffled a little -farther away. "Please?"

"Why? It's not like I could kill you with my bare hands."

"Actually, we've found your trigger," she waved at my hands.

Looking down, two deep red, pulsating orbs sat in my palms. Startled, I shook my hands until they disappeared. "What. The. Fuck?"

"Unless I am greatly mistaken, those were death spheres, and they like it when you're angry."

"And yet, I'm too low on energy to create a simple stunner."

She chuckled. "Two different power sources. An ability called by emotion bypasses its need to tap into its primary power source. Instead it uses the emotion for its power until you either calm down, or let go of whatever brought it up."

"And I can't face Prometheus angry. If I do, he wins."

Hades rubbed his temples. "Fiona needs to do it. She's the only one who can win against him."

"I have enough blood on my hands thanks to her. I don't need any more."

Daniel was in front of me in a flash; his large hands gently cupping my face, forcing me to look him in the eye. "We all have blood on our hands, Amelia. And there will be more before the end comes. If you keep fighting with yourself, you'll schism."

"Take it from us; a schismed Creator can rip apart the fabric of reality," Samuel's voice was faint, as though it were coming from a great distance away.

Calm, not quite thoughts, passed through me every second that Daniel kept his hands on my face. His yellow and orange eyes looked like they were melding into electric pools, and an occasional spark leapt from them.

"What are you doing?" the words felt thick and slow in my mouth.

"My job," his words, on the other hand, were clear and quick. "Calm energy without feeding to shore up your reserves. No risk of bite addiction, and I won't be down for hours."

"Not with an audience."

"I remember," his thumbs stroked my cheeks before he pulled away. "Better?"

"Better," I nodded. "So what were you guys working on?"

"Invasion plans. Samuel is receiving updates as to the state of the wolves' compound and things are changing now that Kahlia is 'missing' and their network is smoking rubble," Hades flicked his fingers at the hologram. It duplicated, and they gave a good before and after shot of the target.

"Guards have been added to the library, as well as the catacombs. Elizabeth is forcing everyone they don't have chained up underground so they can be slaughtered if anyone tries to break in," Samuel pointed to the moving blue dots.

"Is this real-time?" I asked, watching some of the lights stutter.

"Unfortunately," he nodded.

"How many angels have volunteered to help?"

"All of them," my grandfather smiled. "Thirty thousand angels, itching for a fight."

I whistled. "I don't think all of them will fit in the compound if they're corporeal."

Samuel and Hades chuckled as Persephone suppressed a smile beside me.

"What?" I stared at them, slightly confused.

"In combat, multiple angels can combine into a single form," Samuel pulled himself together. "It's where berserkers and the deities with multiple limbs and wings came from."

"Deities like the Hindu pantheon? Kali and Durga?"

"Those would be two of many," he nodded. "All religions trace back to the children of the All Mother, in one way or another. The last time angels went to war, it was over what is now India, China, and the countries of that region. The Lazarus guarding a larger doorway called for reinforcements when her portal merged with that of another world. Creatures stronger than any we had created had managed to get a foothold and were advancing on the humans when we arrived. It took a legion of our berserkers ten years to drive them back to their world."

"Wow. Any side effects come with that victory?"

"Plenty," he nodded. "When you're merged for that long you begin to forget who you are as an individual. It's hard to separate into your original parts and act with a single mind again."

"It's not worth the risk to your soldiers, then."

Samuel snorted. "Taking the compound will be child's play, not a siege. *I* would feel better if the group with you were berserkers."

"Why? So I don't fuck up?"

"No," he scowled. "To watch your back and keep you from being diverted from your task. We can't afford for your attention to be split."

"My attention will be just fine," I shrugged. "It's Fiona you'll have to worry about."

"She has no trouble concentrating on a single task," he glanced back at the hologram. "We need a plan for the wolves once we dispose of Elizabeth."

"Graham is their leader, by their own twisted inheritance laws," I shrugged. "Call the Muses and ask if he's stable enough to shift in front of his entire clan to prove his right to lead."

"Already asked," Hades shook his head. "He needs a crutch to remain human. His wolf was denied for too long, and it refuses to shift back unless forced."

"What would work to pull him back?"

"Someone who isn't afraid to hit him," Daniel pulled out a chair and motioned for me to sit. "With the exception of dragons, the base form of all shifters is human. Getting punched repeatedly in the head gets them so angry that they have to turn back to yell at whoever's hitting them."

"No one likes being punched in the head," I grimaced, though I sat. "In case it's escaped your notice with that thick skull of yours, getting hit hurts."

He chuckled. "Decapitate me and I'll pop right back for more."

"And on that note…what's the plan when we breach?"

"Two teams working in tandem. One will drop straight into the catacombs to secure the civilians, while the other will take you after Prometheus and contain Elizabeth. Our biggest concern is a stray bullet hitting you, since we can't die," Samuel waved a hand over the holograms and they disappeared.

"Hm," I twitched my nose. "Daniel?"

"Yes, Amelia?" his fingers brushed the back of my neck and made me shiver.

"What are your defensive capabilities? You've got a good offence, but bodyguards are usually trained in defence as well."

"Depends on the threat and situation. Is there any way we could mock the breach before to see what would work best?"

"Yes, actually," Persephone brightened. "Elsie could do it if she has the information."

"Elsie?" Daniel repeated. Apparently no one had introduced them.

"My artificial intelligence," Persephone smiled widely. "If you go and start feeding Amelia, I can plug these guys in and have it ready to the tiniest detail in a couple of hours."

"Works for me," he kept stroking my neck, but his voice didn't change.

"Sounds good," I nodded.

Hades, Persephone and Samuel passed an amused look between themselves before teleporting out. Daniel's fingers went from stroking to massaging as he brought his other hand up to my shoulder.

"That feels good, but I should probably be draining you right now," I relaxed in the chair. Whatever else he was doing, it was taking away all my physical pain.

"In a minute," his voice held a husky edge. "Just doing what I can to speed your healing while we wait for the Muses to free up an hour."

"And how are you doing that?"

"Partly by transferring the damage to my body, and partly by sharing my durability with you. It's temporary, but should hold for a few days."

"Thank you," I smiled, though he couldn't see it. 'Thank you' was inadequate.

"My pleasure," his voice was warm as his hands stopped moving. "Ready to bite me yet? Now that I have been disabused of the notion of immunity, I can keep an eye out for symptoms of addiction."

"And tell me if they're showing up?"

"I swear on my life."

"Then let's go get fangy."

He laughed, steering me from the chair to the door. "Yes, let's get fangy. If you're lucky, I may even show you just how flexible dragons can be."

31

"Gods, whatever you did, it makes me feel like I can fly!" I exclaimed as I bounced down the hallway ahead of him.

"Well, you do have wings," he grinned. "One day we're going to have to see how well you'll do in an aerial acrobatics race."

I stopped mid-pirouette. "Those exist?"

"It's part of our world's version of the Olympics. Though ours is held once every five years."

"Does anyone die?"

"One or two always do in the Pit."

"The Pit?"

"Gladiator-style fights in this pit dug into the ground. Whoever wins the most matches without calling for a medic or trying to climb out is the champion to face at the next Gathering."

"That one's not for pansies, essentially."

"Exactly," he opened the door to our room and held it for me. "It's an arena to showcase physical skill and endurance. To use any ability to attack another is an automatic disqualification."

"What if you lose control and accidentally use one?" I stepped past him and pulled his shirt off so as to not ruin it with bloodstains.

"You're still out. The Ring is where you go to pummel someone with your gifts. If you have a beef with someone and it wasn't handled to your satisfaction, you challenge them there," he shut and locked the door before stretching his arms above his head and sitting on the edge of the bed. "How do you want me?"

"Fangy mentioned something about a 'double feed' when Persephone split us to make peace back at Sanctuary," I ducked behind my hair, folding my arms over my exposed stomach.

"Ah," his deep voice held restrained amusement. "She would prefer that to a regular draining, would she?"

"Don't laugh. She would prefer it to what she called my 'clinical and clean' feeding."

Daniel reached over and pulled my arms away from my abdomen. "Everything is up to you, Amelia. If you feel uncomfortable for any reason, at any time, say so and I'll stop if I'm the reason. I'll fix it if I'm not."

"You're not like other males," I watched him through my eyelashes. "Anyone else would have told me to fuck off by now."

He smiled, and dimples appeared that softened his face. "I'll always be whatever you need me to be. No questions asked, most of the time. No judgements."

"You're really too good to be real. You sure Rylynne didn't rewire you to be this way when she played around in your head?"

"What little time I had with my clan beat this into me, I promise you. If any dragon was shown to have no patience or compassion they were struck from the family and put on permanent sentry duty for the rest of the clan."

"Sounds a little harsh."

He shook his head. "'Be kind to all you meet, for you never know the battles they face, or what demons their smiles hide.' It's one of the codes of the Draconi. Kindness, compassion and patience are three of the cornerstones of my kind, no matter which clan we belonged to. To be anything else was a slap in the face of the Dragon Mother and not tolerated."

"Doesn't intolerance go against compassion, though?"

He paused for a moment, thinking it over. "It may seem hypocritical, but within the species, no. A dragon is always punished or rewarded by their actions toward both the clan and outsiders. Failure to be our best as taught by our parents brings shame to the family. And shaming the family is something that should never be done."

"Sounds a lot like the old-school mafia."

He laughed. "Who do you think they learned it from?"

I grinned. "Seriously?"

"Cross my heart. Now, shall we get to it?"

"All this talking…are you sure you're *up* for it?" I winked.

He sputtered. "Why do you think I've been in loose jeans all day? Denim offends my tactile sensibilities, but it does a hell of a job hiding the fact that I get hard every time I catch the faintest tease of your scent."

I barely controlled a giggle. "Is my poor dragon in pain?"

"It's manageable right now," a smile teased his lips again. "Though…if you wanted to help me quiet it for a little while, I wouldn't object in the slightest."

"Well then, what do you suggest?" I closed the distance between us and stood between his knees. He let go of my arms as I dropped to my knees. Running my hands down his chest, I paused when I reached his belt buckle.

"That's a good start. Do what you want, at whatever pace you're comfortable with. Don't worry about me."

I unbuckled his belt before I could think myself out of it, then undid his button and zipper. I resisted opening his pants completely; instead, I stood and undid my own. Pushing my pants and underwear down, I stepped out of them and straddled him. One arm immediately went around my waist, but he didn't touch me otherwise.

"Take a deep breath. I can hear your heart racing its way to a panic attack," he stayed very still beneath me.

I did as he said, breathing deeply until I wasn't light-headed. "It's different without Aphrodite's whammy riding us."

"She does pack a punch," he smiled before sobering. "What she did kept your head from getting in the way of your body."

"Yours, too, if I recall correctly. I'm good now. Where to from here?"

"From here we make sure you don't chafe," he tightened the arm around my waist a little as his free hand undid the snap holding the cups of my bra together. I let it slide off my arms and dropped it on the floor. Laying his lips against the hollow of my throat, his hand slid down my abdomen until it rested on my thigh.

Unsure of what to do with my hands, I rested them on his shoulders. He moved slowly, his lips brushing over my right collar bone, then my left, as his fingers stroked up my thigh and across my pelvis. Barely touching me, his fingers slid lower in gently, circular sweeps. When he finally reached what he was aiming for, I jerked at the foreign sensation.

"Stop?" he brought his head up to look at me.

I shook my head. "Go."

He nodded before his lips traced a scorching path over my neck, with just a hint of teeth involved. I shivered, and his fingers applied a little more pressure. I almost jumped out of his lap when his tongue flicked my right nipple. Chuckling, he did the same to the left before nipping them alternately until the combined sensations were feeding a tightness in my lower abdomen. His hand moved lower, his fingers teasing as his palm continued the circular motion his fingers had abandoned.

Bringing his head up, his lips traced my jaw, starting by my ear. "It would be better, easier on you, if you orgasmed first, but it should be fine. You're more than wet enough to go further, whenever you're ready."

I nodded, not trusting my voice. Sliding my hands down his chest again, I hesitated as I touched his open jeans. Not wanting to stop, but fearing going forward, I took a deep breath to steady my hands and pealed the cloth away. I was glad I couldn't see through his head as my hands touched him. He gasped as I gently stroked what felt like steel encased by silk.

"Ready?" he growled, removing his hand from me.

"As I'll ever be," I responded, my voice a little breathy as I let go of him.

I returned my hands to his shoulders as he used the arm around my waist to lift me a little and pull me closer. Lowering me slowly, he captured my lips and explored my mouth before impaling me. I gasped, tensing around him as I dug my fingers into his shoulders.

"Too much?"

"Just an adjustment," I shook my head. "I'm okay."

"Continue?"

"Yes."

He nodded before recapturing my lips and sliding fully into me. Holding my hip, he rocked me against him until I found the rhythm and could do it alone. Bringing his hand up, he toyed with the nipple he could reach; pinching and rolling it until the tightness that had been building released in a rush that left me clawing his back.

"Ready those lovely fangs of yours," he spoke against my lips as he tensed.

Nodding, I felt them descend as I teased my way down his throat. His arm tightened and I struck; biting into his carotid artery as he jerked under me.

Fangy was right. Feeding at 'the moment of peak euphoria' did feel better. Taste better. It was so much more satisfying – to the point that I didn't have to drain him to feel fully charged. Pulling away, I licked the thin trails of blood from his throat and rested my head on his shoulder.

"Done already?" he played his fingers along my spine.

"Mhm," I smiled.

"Shall we go clean up?"

"Soon," I murmured. "My legs still feel like jelly."

"How are you feeling?"

"Better than I expected. Will it always be like that?"

"Only if your lover isn't a selfish ass."

"Since I don't trust anyone else, that shouldn't be a problem."

"You'll have to trust someone else eventually, Amelia. But if they don't treat you right I'll beat them to a bloody pulp."

"Promise?"

"Promise."

"How much time do you think we've killed?"

"An hour, give or take. We have time for a long bath, for sure."

"Just a bath? No soak in a hot tub?"

"Maybe later," he laughed. "We just need to clean up before they finish doing whatever they're doing."

"Elsie is building a holographic simulation of the wolves' compound. She's very talented for an AI."

"Being an AI she would have to be talented. Who made her?"

"Persephone did, a few million years ago. Boredom spell and all that."

"Interesting. Shall we?"

"Sure," I nodded before letting go of him. Lifting me gingerly from his lap, he set me on my feet and didn't let go until he was sure I could stand. Scooping his shirt from the floor, he buttoned just the lower half over me before he tucked himself back into his pants and secured the zipper. Leaving the button and his belt undone, he stood. I closed a few more buttons and followed him to the door. It opened before Daniel could touch the doorknob, my grandfather on the other side.

My face flaming, I stepped behind Daniel and looked around for a pair of pants. Unfortunately, none were within reach. Peeking around his side, I suppressed a sigh of relief that Samuel's back was to us.

"I hope I'm not interrupting anything," I could hear the laughter in his voice.

"We were just on our way to clean up," Daniel looked over his shoulder at me and flicked his eyes to the floor by the bed. Nodding, I darted over and grabbed my pants; pulling them on quickly before moving up beside him. "A few minutes earlier and you would have been interrupting."

Glancing over his shoulder, he smiled and turned. "Elsie finished faster than expected. Apparently she already had the floor plans for the compound. She just needed to fill in the details."

"We'll wash quickly and be down as soon as we're done," Daniel inclined his head.

"We have angels inbound to run through the plans. Their estimated arrival times are within the next half hour," Samuel grinned before melting away.

"At least he didn't just pop into the room," I let out a breath I didn't know I had been holding.

"No, but he could have been watching without us knowing."

"Ew! Gross! That's my grandfather! Gah, where's mind bleach when you need it?" I pressed my palms against my eyes and tried to force that image out of my head. "Why would you say that?"

Daniel laughed and draped an arm across my shoulders. "Some disturbing things just need to be shared. Besides, you're not the one likely to get splintered by him for sleeping with you."

Dropping my hands, I glared at him. "He wouldn't splinter you. Cut off bits of your anatomy that may be useful, sure. But not kill you."

He cupped himself, eyes wide. "Please don't suggest that to him."

"I won't…today. Shall we? Before someone else comes looking?"

"Yes. The sooner we're done, the less likely anyone else is to come looking," he returned his arm to my shoulders and led me out the door.

32

The bathing hall was much closer to our room than I remembered, but that could have just been because the hallways were shifting. A new table was just inside the door with a hairbrush and elastics on it. Daniel shed his pants and boots as I grabbed a couple to secure my hair into a bun high on my head. Disrobing, my ribs pulled a little as I pulled the shirt over my head. Following him into the water, I relaxed as the warmth seeped into my bones. Ducking beneath the surface, he poked his head out until just his eyes breached the surface. I raised an eyebrow at him and he came up laughing. Water rolled off his well-formed physique and I turned away so I could concentrate.

"Soap?" I asked, glancing at him from the corner of my eye. He was on the bench at the deeper end, his upper chest above the water line.

"Set into the floor over here," he held a hand out to me.

I waded closer and took it. He pulled me easily into his lap, but even sitting on his legs my head was barely above the surface.

"Moments like this make me hate being short," I groused. "Then again, if anyone were to talk in they wouldn't be able to see how disfigured I am."

Daniel wrapped his arms around me, and his left hand traced the scars on my ribs and abdomen. "You aren't disfigured. Your scars show anyone lucky enough to see them that you're a survivor."

"Only you see it that way," I shrugged. "A girl at one of my old schools saw them when I was changing for gym when they were still healing. She screamed for so long I though she's pass out from oxygen deprivation."

"So? She was human, and they are very small-minded creatures. Their ideals of beauty and perfection shift arbitrarily."

"Humans are the dominant species on this planet," I shrugged again. "Find me a planet where my scars would be welcomed and I would gladly live there."

"I can't promise a planet, but our hidden world on this one won't curl their lips in disgust. But if anyone does, I'll eat them."

I laughed. "Why do you say the right things when I need to hear them?"

"Because your laugh and smile warm me in ways I thought impossible. Being near you, especially when you're happy, makes me feel like I'm home."

"Are you sure you actually feel that, and it's not bleed-over from me? Or part of the bond?"

"Fairly positive, yes," he gave me a quick squeeze before releasing me and reaching for the soap.

Cleaning us quickly, though thoroughly, he checked the patch on my ribs before carrying me out. As with earlier, a curl of warm air wrapped around us and dried the water still clinging to our skin. He put me down and we dressed swiftly, Daniel foregoing a shirt. Personally, I approved, but I doubted anyone else would appreciate it.

"Shall we?" he motioned toward the door.

I sighed. "Let's get it over with before I decide sleep is more important than combat training."

He laughed and took my hand as we left to find the others. The hallways had changed again, and only the arrows on the walls kept us from getting lost in the maze. The door opened on our approach, and the sounds of a heated argument spilled out to us. Daniel pulled me to a stop just as someone I didn't recognise was thrown into the wall. Samuel stalked out; face livid, movements controlled rage. He didn't seem to register our presence as he grabbed the man by the throat and dragged him back inside.

"Does anyone ELSE want to insult my granddaughter?" he bellowed.

Daniel and I exchanged a glance before he let go of my hand and entered the room, his hands raised to show no violent intent. I peeked around the door frame to watch without being in the line of potentially thrown people.

"Can't we leave you guys alone for a couple hours without someone lipping off?" Daniel lowered his hands as he reached the group of what could only be angels. Two dozen stood in a rough half circle as Hades and Persephone watched from the wall. Elsie was near them, though her eyes were unfocused; as though she were working on complex calculations.

I ‘felt’ Fiona wake up, and the iciness of her slid up my spine, though she didn’t take over. I could feel her amusement at the scene before us, and the obvious discomfort of the ‘guests’.

“Now,” Daniel continued. “Who said what, and will I have to beat you for it?”

“We don’t answer to *you*, dragon,” one man sneered, his lip curled in disgust.

“If you insulted my charge, you do,” Daniel shrugged, completely calm.

“You aren’t bonded to it, so it’s none of your concern,” the angel turned away from him.

“IT?” Daniel roared, his horns suddenly visible and curling from his skull as leathery wings split his back open and unfurled. His hands slid seamlessly from human to huge, clawed talons. When he spoke again, his voice was several octaves lower and rumbled like thunder. “Say that again, coward. Insult Amelia, I *dare* you.”

The one angel did the slow pivot you do when you know something dangerous is behind you as the others cleared the area around him. Daniel’s wings extended to their maximum, a good fifteen feet on either side; the red and purple swirls fading to flat black.

‘Leucious,’ Fiona named him without breaking our external silence. *‘For an angel, he always did have an unholy gift for being a prick.’*

‘Why didn’t you destroy him, then?’

‘I couldn’t. He looked too much like my little brother, and him I could never harm.’

‘You had a brother?’ I raised an eyebrow at her.

‘I had fourteen brothers and eight sisters,’ she smiled. *‘Mostly twins and triplets.’*

‘That must have been hell around birthdays.’

Her tinkling laugh ran through our head. *‘You have no idea. Shall we go diffuse the situation before our dragon turns him into a crispy critter?’*

‘Sure. How would you like to play this?’

‘Go punch him. Grab him by the hair and strike his left ear as hard as you can. If that trick still works, it should reset some of his issues.’

'How do you know that works at all?'

'Just because I *never hurt him, doesn't mean I never asked Svetanya to do it for me,'* she smiled again, and it wasn't pleasant.

Dropping the smile, I ran my fingers through my hair to get it away from my face and adjusted Daniel's shirt before stepping around the door and into the room. A few angels passed calculating glances over me as I approached before returning their attention to Daniel. Big mistake on their parts. Reaching out when I was close enough, I brushed my hand down his back before ducking under his right wing.

"Leucious," I inclined my head to the asshole.

"You don't scare me, bitch," he hissed, stepping closer, into my limited arm range.

I grinned, and it was fangy and evil. My left hand snapped out and grabbed a handful of sinfully soft hair as I brought my right hand up in a fist. Pushing as much strength into the strike as I could muster, I felt bones crack when I connected with the side of his head. He went limp, and I let go so I wouldn't be dragged to the floor.

Daniel's arms wrapped around my shoulders, his hands normal again. Closing my eyes, I leaned into the warmth of him as his wings cocooned us. His lips teased my ear, his voice so faint I could barely hear him. "Which one of you is in control?"

"Fiona's awake, but riding backseat," I murmured. "You don't have to fight all my battles for me. I'm good to go a few rounds every once in a while."

He laughed and released me. "Would it be chauvinistic to say I like fighting your battles for you?"

"No comment," I chuckled, smiling. His horns faded as I watched, but his wings stayed curled at his back. Clasping my hands in front of me, I looked around the small assembly. "Now that that's out of the way, shall we get on with it?"

Hades pushed away from the wall, a grin stretching his face. "I was enjoying the show, but now that you're here, it's time to have some fun."

"Does Elsie have a simulation ready?"

"She has twenty-five potential scenarios already mapped," he nodded. "All she needs is for you guys to get started. Once it's going, she can adjust based on action and reaction. The safeties are on, but they aren't guaranteed."

"Aren't guaranteed?" I repeated.

"She may glitch. We don't know. She's never constructed anything while actively adjusting a simulation in progress. Seph didn't code her for it," he shrugged. "There's no time to add it to her matrix now."

"So we charge in head-first and hope I don't die by accident?"

"Sounds about right."

"At what point are we starting? After arrival or during transit?"

"Since we don't quite know how to get you in there yet, it'll be from the moment of landing."

"Works for me. Where do you want us?"

"Before we begin, I have a question, Hades," a female angel interrupted us.

"Ask away," the god inclined his head.

"How did *she* –" she stressed the pronoun, "know Leucious's name? None of us except Samuel has ever met her before."

Fiona chose that moment to assert control. She straightened our spine, held our shoulders back and arms loosely at our sides. "Anya, my darling. Amelia is many things, but telepathic is not yet among them. I told her Leucious's name, and how to 'fix' him."

"And who are you?" Anya eyed us suspiciously.

Fiona sighed. "If I had known it would cause this many problems, I wouldn't have erased your memories of my physical form before I left."

"*Metaria? Dur cahr?*" Anya's face was incredulous as she spoke in the Old Language. Fiona didn't offer a translation this time.

"*Kie sav meerah. Moren chshara careno mora*," Fiona smiled, shrugging.

Anya took two steps towards us and backhanded us before anyone thought to stop her. Fiona rocked back on our heels, but otherwise didn't give any indication that it hurt.

Testing our teeth with our tongue, she spat a little blood on the floor when she knew none had been loosened.

"I would ask that you refrain from damaging my host's body," Fiona's tone was mild, but held a thread of warmth, of anger. "Amelia is already not happy with me over the damage I did to her body after Sanctuary's invasion. She does not forgive easily, and I would rather avoid fighting with her."

"That's your problem, not ours. We owe you nothing, not after you abandoned us."

"Oh, for fuck's sake!" Fiona bellowed. "Grow the fuck up. I spent billions of years on this planet, dealing with your petty bullshit. I needed a break. I needed time to recharge and sort out my priorities. None of you were children when I left. You all had the duties I created you for."

Anya and the others looked away, shamefaced. A few shifted uncomfortably on their feet as Daniel's hands found our shoulders and started massaging the tension away. Fiona patted his hand in a motherly way before receding. I slumped immediately, my back sore from being held straight. Thanks to an old injury, standing straight for any amount of time was hard.

"Now that we have that reintroduction out of the way, shall we get to it?" I looked at Hades. Fiona was still seething in our head, but she was controlling the shared urge we had to rip Anya's wings off.

"No," Samuel shook his head. "I do not trust any of these ingrates with your safety or the mission. We will re-evaluate our options for infiltration without them."

"Why not just switch out the team?" I raised an eyebrow at the disgust in his tone.

"They are the best at hostage recovery, miles ahead of the others. They also had the least trouble returning to their individual states from berserker."

"Basically they're the most powerful?"

Samuel nodded. "I could understand Leucious's attitude towards an untrained Creator, he has always been a little broken, but the others, no. Just no. You are not just a Creator, you're my granddaughter and the host of our mother. Your safety is too important to be trusted to these children."

"Just because they're like this, doesn't mean the others will be."

He sighed. "Yes it does, Amelia. All angels not in the command circle share emotions during their down time. Their consciousnesses link while dreaming to share information, but a side effect of it spreads their negativity towards a person or place to the others."

"So? Don't let them fall asleep, and we'll keep Fiona under wraps until we're already in and Prometheus's heart is in my hands."

"I like this one," Leucious groaned from the floor. "She's got spunk."

"Feeling better?" Samuel extended a hand to him and hauled him to his feet when he took it.

"Much. I needed that, and didn't even realise it," he shook himself before smoothing his slightly long, blondish hair back. "Aunt Svet used to do that every time I started acting like a prig. *Metaria* always had trouble raising a hand to me."

"You looked too much like her little brother for her to hurt you herself," I shrugged.

"She's really in there, with you?" his face lit up like a little kid at Christmas.

I nodded, a small smile touching my lips. "Am I still an unfrightening bitch?"

"Nope," Leucious chuckled. "I have a feeling you can be a very scary creature when the right buttons are pushed."

I laughed. "Isn't that true of everyone, though?"

"Good point," he grinned before looking at his brothers and sisters. His smile slipped. "What's up with them?"

"*Metaria* yelled at them while you were down," Samuel glared at them. "Anya needed to be put in her place."

"*Metaria* needed a break? So what? We all do, once in a while," Leucious came and stood with us, a clear divide appearing in the assembled group. "We all get time off every few hundred years; why should we begrudge her some time to herself?"

"We were only thinking of ourselves, again," a tall brunette woman separated herself from the others. "It's hard to not get wrapped up in our own problems. Makes it easy to forget that *Metaria* is a person, too."

"The biggest thing she ever did for herself was create us and our brethren to keep the world in balance and give herself some companions," Samuel nodded. "But no matter our age or experience, we are always the students and she our teacher."

"Speaking of teaching," I interrupted with a sudden thought. "Would she be able to tap into my dormant angelic side and poof like you guys do into the wolves' library? Or would she have to ride one of you guys in?"

"You don't have enough angel in you to do it," Samuel shook his head. "She can activate that part of you, but she'll have to piggyback on one of us until you die. After that she'll have no problem."

"It's one of the unsurfaced abilities?"

"Yes," he nodded. "Everything we can all do came from her. Some of us have been able to evolve, but the majority of us remain as we were made."

"I'm starting to get a headache," I rubbed my temples.

Persephone rubbed her head in time with me. "Go rest. We'll shuffle the deck here and run through a few scenarios without you."

"You don't mind?"

"The sooner you get rid of the headache, the less likely I am to take an axe to my own skull to relieve the pressure," she waved me to the door. "See you in a little while."

"Thanks," I nodded to her as Daniel gently led me away.

33

Daniel closed the door behind us before stopping. “How bad does your head hurt?”

“Feels like someone took a baseball bat to the back of my head.”

“Any light sensitivity or visual disturbances?”

“It’s not a migraine,” I shook my head. “I’ve gotten these headaches on and off since I was hospitalised after my mom died.”

“Traumatic brain injury?”

“Baseball bat upside the head,” I laughed, then groaned. “My neurologist at the time warned of unpredictable side effects that could last the rest of my life. The headaches are one of the residuals.”

“Does anything help?”

“Just rest. Something about shifting from vertical to horizontal releases the pressure build up.”

“How long is it between episodes? Have you been able to chart it?”

“It’s random,” I shook my head. “Sometimes they domino and happen every few hours. Other times I can go months without one. I’ll still get the tremors in my hands, but they’re controllable when they pop up.”

“Let’s get you horizontal, then,” he smiled, offering his arm.

I frowned at him. “No sex.”

“Wasn’t even thinking about it,” he laughed.

I took his proffered arm and allowed him to lead me back through the twisting hallways to our room. When the door opened, the lights were dim and the clothes that had been on the floor were neatly folded and sitting on the suitcases. Letting go of Daniel’s arm, I crawled between the sheets and pulled a pillow over my head as my pulse tried to split my skull apart.

“Go back to the others and help with strategy planning,” I lifted the pillow enough to speak. “I’ll be okay here. Promise.”

He sighed. “If you need anything, shout. Someone will hear you.”

"Will do," I gave him a thumbs up as I let go of the pillow and closed my eyes to help ease the pounding ache.

"Is there anything I can do, *moren medara*?" Fiona's soft voice added to the pain in our head.

"Not really," I fought not to shake our head. "It'll pass, it always does. Thank Hunters for this particular treat. Stupid humans."

"Vicious, cruel humans," she agreed. "You lied to Daniel."

"I know. I'd like to excuse it as a little lie, but it's mine to not share."

"Why didn't you just feed?"

"I fed on him less than an hour ago. It's too soon, even for him."

"There are others here to feed on."

I did shake our head this time. "It's too much like sex, even from the wrist. That's why I always preferred women over men; no messy after-shit."

"Why didn't you speak up with the others around, though?"

"Too many strangers, too much tension with the divide in the angel's ranks. I don't trust them enough to air my failings for their dissection."

"Understandable, but eventually you'll have to be comfortable feeding with people around."

"Like I said, feeding is too much like sex. One or two, maybe, but not a group of witnesses."

"I can do it, if you won't. I got over that particular feeling on my original world."

"You were also born where people accepted what you were."

"And I'll ask you to hold that thought," her 'voice' held a note of confusion. "Well, this hasn't happened in a long time."

"What?"

"A telepath is reaching out, and aiming for you," she shivered her way into control and sat us up. "I can't tell who it is, but only my original creations are able to direct their thoughts to someone without the ability."

"That's a long list of people."

"Not so long as it used to be," she sighed.

"The voice coming in any clearer?"

"Female, familiar. But familiar could be anyone to me. She keeps saying 'Amelia, can you hear me?' over and over."

"Care to share the voice inside our head?"

Fiona let whatever barrier she had up fall, and though the boom was only in our head, I flinched as our eardrums popped.

'Amelia?' Serenity's voice echoed in our head.

"What's the emergency?" I frowned, hoping whoever was boosting her could make it a two-way connection.

'Finally!' relief was thick in her 'voice'. *'We've been trying to reach you for hours.'*

"You and who?"

'Colby is boosting me right now. We tried with Blair earlier, but he couldn't narrow your location beyond a continent.'

"Didn't anyone tell you where I am?"

'Security agreement required I not be told until someone could either bring me in, or return you here.'

"Is this conversation private? Or can someone listen in if they know how?"

'Colby is a little iffy on that, since we're Creators and sisters. We should *be okay, but don't tell me anything that may compromise your plans.'*

"Will do. Why have you been trying to get in contact?"

'Sanctuary has been secured. Three turncoats were found and disposed of. And the Muses wanted me to tell you that the wolf is ready to hunt, whatever that means.'

I smiled. "It means the last piece is locked, and the full moon will be bathed in blood," I used a phrase we had agreed on in case we were ever going to be reckless and vengeful.

'Bring me in,' her 'voice' hardened.

"I'll send someone for you. Make sure Arcturus keeps the doors open."

'Hurry,' her 'voice' faded as I opened our eyes.

"So much for my nap," I flopped back down and covered our eyes.

"At least there will be someone at our back I trust when we go in," she rolled our shoulders slowly. "I'll feed while someone retrieves her. Do we bring in James as well?"

"There's no way to take him in on the initial assault. He'll be more useful at Sanctuary."

"True. Should we send for the wolf as well?"

"No," I shook our head. "Leave him with the Muses until the compound is secure. That way he's fresh for the takeover."

"It also keeps him from trying to complete the bond. Though I don't understand how he could even start it when Daniel's mark is supposed to prevent it."

"I've never met a rule that didn't like to break when I least need it to."

"You are a weird one," Fiona laughed. "Shall we?"

"So long as you're the one doing the walking."

"Done," she rolled us gracefully from under the covers and to our feet. My half of our brain seized with the sudden motion and almost brought us to our knees. She managed to keep us upright, and made a few shaky steps before the pain subsided. "Flying will be faster than walking."

"I don't want to ruin Daniel's shirt."

"I packed others," she shrugged, moving to the suitcases as she removed the comfy shirt.

"So you're the one who packed for a pin-up doll photo session! High heels are not appropriate for every situation."

"They are when the heels are reinforced steel with retractable blades," she picked up a black tank top-ish shirt from the top of the bag. Pulling it on, she secured a handful of buckles around our ribcage before our back opened up and let our wings out. Flexing them carefully, she popped a joint in the right one back into its proper place.

"Did someone get a lucky shot in while you were being Madam Mayhem?"

Fiona shook our head. "Old injury of yours from your forgotten first flight."

"Any way to fix it permanently?"

"Not until you're dead," she shook our head again.

"Hm...do you think any of our kind decided to become chiropractors?"

Hovering, she thought about it for a moment. "I'll ask, once the other matters are taken care of."

I flashed a quick smile across our face before she opened the door and returned to the simulation room to update the others. I nursed the headache, concentrating on not paying attention to reality as Fiona comfortably controlled our meat suit. After a while, my part of our brain shut down, and I floated in the comfortable darkness. Hours passed, blank and meaningless, until the blackness became oppressive and I clawed my way to the surface.

My head hurt, but the pain was no longer internally sourced. My crown throbbed, and the brightness of active holograms burned my eyes. I tried reaching 'in' to Fiona, but she didn't respond. A delicate, long-fingered hand appeared in front of my face and waved; the thumb a little crooked from an old, bad break.

"You alive, bèbe?" Serenity smiled down at me.

"Depends on your definition of alive," I groaned. "Who used the back of my head as a chopping block?"

"Fiona asked Daniel to do it," she helped me sit up, slowly. "She had one of her feelings, but couldn't go dormant without help since you were napping and she wasn't exhausted."

"Should I be expecting her back shortly?"

"Whenever she finds what the ether's trying to tell her."

"And that could take a while," I stood slowly, gingerly. "You up to speed on what's going on?"

"Up to speed and in on the planning. Fiona figured out a way to get us in without killing us first. And I agree with the decision to leave Jamie at Sanctuary."

"We know we can trust him," I nodded. "Since Fiona knows what we're doing, I can get her to fill me in later. Do you know the tentative timeline?"

"We go in when Fiona resurfaces. Daniel will go in with you, since he can apparently become one with that brand on your shoulder. After that, we haven't decided if he'll guard you as a dragon, or become armour."

"He can do what now?"

"You didn't know?" she raised a perfectly arched eyebrow.

"I don't know a lot about his species," I shrugged.

"No, but you are sleeping with someone you barely know."

"Who I sleep with is none of your fucking business, and nothing you have to say will change that. Didn't we already have this fight?"

"Probably, but your problem doesn't seem to have gone away."

"We'll agree to disagree on this. My life is not your problem anymore."

"Your life was never my problem, it's my responsibility. And that has not changed just because you have a dragon wrapped around you."

"Less than five months until my birthday. You have until then to let go of the idea before we go our separate ways."

"I'll still be able to find you."

"I know. Just call before dropping by. I'd hate to kill you by accident."

"You're being hostile, and I don't feel like dealing with it, so I'm going to see where everyone else is. Join me if you want," she shrugged and walked away.

I stayed, surveying the paused holographic wreckage. Simulated bodies had been erased, but there were scorch marks and blood trails on the walls. Bookshelves were cracked and broken; windows shattered. It was a mess, but it looked like we won. Winning is good.

I was standing there, lost in thought, when warm arms wrapped around my shoulders and a feeling of home encompassed me. He didn't say anything, but he didn't need to. Everything would work out. Somehow.

34

"How does your head feel?" Daniel finally broke the silence.

"A little throbby, but not terrible," I shrugged. "Can you give me the cliff notes of the plan before Fiona surfaces so I know what to do if something goes wrong?"

"Of course. Shall we go find some place to sit?"

"If you feel like sitting, sure," I pulled away from him, my skin beginning to itch in anticipation of the coming fight.

"Would you like to hit something?" his voice betrayed a smile.

"How did you know?" I turned to study his handsome face.

"Training, and I know how you feel. Some of the training the Guardians put me through included incursion planning, then waiting for execution so that I would be able to control my actions and reactions once the order was given. You feel shaky, electrified, almost out of control with the need to do something to take the edge off. Light exercise can help, but neither sleeping nor sex will do much good."

"Sleeping I understand, but why not sex? If it's good it should release calming chemicals."

"It's a fight or flight response that firmly clicked into fight. Sex in that state is often just frustrated violent fucking, and doesn't do much good, even with orgasm involved for both parties."

"Good to know," I chuckled. "Shall we find a punching bag, then Oh Wise Master?"

Daniel's smile became a grin and he swept an arm toward the door. "After my lady."

I snorted. "If I'm a lady, the universe has a twisted sense of humour."

He didn't say anything as he followed me out. The mighty morphing navigation arrows pointed us to the right; we followed them until they finally stopped at a brushed steel door. The door didn't open like all the others, and I exchanged a confused glance with Daniel.

"I haven't been down this section before," he shrugged. "Your guess is as good as mine."

I reached out and touched the cool doorknob. It vibrated against my fingertips before the door swung inward.

"Welcome, Creator," Elsie's voice echoed in the dim room. "Persephone programmed your profile for unrestricted access. How can I be of assistance?"

"I need to bleed off some excess energy," I looked around but couldn't spot her.

"Physical or metaphysical?"

"She needs to hit something," Daniel stepped up beside me.

"Ah," the ethereal tinkle whispered around us. "Pre-fight tension. I have two candidates in holding who could be useful to you. Unfortunately we are not equipped with a training area; I'll make a note to rectify that since we will likely have more visitors in the future."

"Two candidates?" I repeated, slightly confused.

"Yes. Stuart Oliver Hamilton, human-vampire hybrid; and Kahlia No-Last-Name-Listed, science experiment. For durability I would suggest the hybrid. Would you like your choice gagged so they can't scream for mercy?" her simulated voice was light and very matter-of-fact.

I glanced at Daniel. He shrugged, a bare lift of his shoulders. "Let's go with the hybrid," I let out a breath I didn't realise I had been holding. "Gagged would be appreciated."

"Lights?"

"Enough to see by, but not bright, please."

"Preferences set. I only ask that you do not kill the subject. Call if you need anything else."

"I will, thanks Elsie," I felt a little ridiculous speaking to a room where the AI didn't have a body.

I could hear things moving around before the lights brightened to a visible level. Stuart, I couldn't think of him as my father with conviction or affection, hung by his wrists in the middle of a non-descript rectangular room. The walls were an uninterrupted shade of dark blue; channels were set into the floor at regular intervals and led to a small drain. I looked at Daniel again.

"Best guess about the function of this room?"

"Torture chamber, most likely. Hades's weapons probably come and go as needed."

"Makes sense. Any suggestions about how to go about this?"

"Walk up to him and hit him as hard as you feel like?" he flashed a small smile.

"Sounds good to me," I grinned, fangs stabbing into my lower lip as I turned. My fingers curled into a fist as I stalked towards my punching bag. Fangy reared her head and her laugh bubbled from my mouth as I drove my fist into Stuart's ribs.

Bones crunched, but I felt no pain as my joints and muscles moved like liquid. I lost myself to the intoxicating release of tension; every strike transferring suppressed rage to my target. Somewhere in my fugue, my brain noticed Stuart's hands were no longer chained above him and he was fighting back. Training took over and I blocked the majority of his blows; fewer of mine landing until he stumbled and I found the opportunity to kick him in the chest. I wanted my foot to go through to the other side of his body, but when he fell and didn't get back up I inhaled deeply until I could control myself again. I couldn't hear past the blood rushing though my veins, and I startled when I looked around to find the room no longer empty.

Hades leaned against the wall by the door, his arms crossed casually over his chest with a smile on his face. Samuel mirrored him on the other side, his smile suppressed as a handful of angels looked back and forth between us; their faces a mix of admiration, shock, and horror.

"I hope you were done with him," I spoke to Hades. "I'm not sure if I killed him or not. And at this moment I don't particularly care."

"He'll live, for now," Hades barked out a short laugh. "You can't die in my domain unless I will it."

"Good to know," a very evil smile stretched my face. "Who did Fiona feed on? I feel fantastic."

Samuel stretched his right arm out; two holes marring the perfection of his skin right above his wrist. "Through me you fed on all of us. You shouldn't need a booster for a while."

"Excellent," Fangy's bassy tones added themselves to my voice as Fiona's spark came awake in my brain.

'Tell Daniel that I will need him as a dragon if we are to succeed,' her voice tinkled through my internal ears.

'Consider it done. How soon to departure?'

'I'll be up in five to light a bonfire under everyone's asses.'

'Sounds like fun.'

'It will be,' her voice faded.

Refocusing on the room in front of me, I found Daniel not far from Hades. He inclined his head but stayed put.

"You guys have five minutes to load up," I addressed the others. "Fiona needs Daniel as a dragon. Adjust strategies accordingly."

"Understood," Samuel nodded before leading the angels out.

Hades waited until they were gone before moving. "Persephone has been working on something for you and your sister. If you'll follow me."

I fell into step behind him, Daniel beside me, as he led us out and down a hallway that didn't fit the colours of the rest of the place. Frosted glass doors broke the red and black walls every so often, but Hades didn't stop by any of them. A set of black double doors finally ended the hall, and Hades shoved them open; the muscles in his back and shoulders straining.

Dim lights cast pools of sinister shadows inside the room, and he led us past recessed chests and cases until we reached a heavy wooden wardrobe. Hades opened it silently before stepping aside. Peering inside, I frowned in confusion at the black clothes.

"Body armour. Built to withstand anything we can throw at it. Impervious to blades, bullets, claws, and god bolts while not compromising flexibility. Human militaries would pay a fortune for even one of these. Any energy thrown at it is absorbed and channelled to the wearer's reserves," he grinned.

"That's…fantastic," I smiled, running my fingers over the silky material. "How long have you guys been working on this?"

"Since your sister was born. Previous generations wouldn't have needed it, but this point in time is very unstable. You need every advantage you can get to stay alive."

"Thank you, really. You guys have done more than I can ever repay."

"Don't die and we'll call it even," his face softened. "Suit up and go kick the ass of that sanctimonious prick."

"I would love to. Will Fiona know where to find everyone to go?"

"She can find us no matter where we are. She'll come to us as soon as you're done in here."

"We'll see you soon, then."

He nodded before fading out. Daniel's fingers deftly undid the catches on my shirt and peeled it off me. Undoing my pants, I paused to take off my shoes before stepping out of them. Daniel gently removed the bodysuit from its resting place and unzipped it before handing it to me. The material flowed like water as I stepped into it. The long sleeves and legs moulded to my muscles as he sealed me in it. Holsters appeared in the places you'd expect to find them; around the thighs, hip level, and shoulder draws. A solid ridge formed down my spine as knife attachments formed.

"I think I like this thing," I chuckled as Daniel helped me back into the high heeled boots.

"It is certainly adaptable," he nodded. "Weapons to fit all this will be back in the command room. Shall we?"

Fiona chose that moment to surface and assert control. "Oh hell yes. Lead on, fair dragon. Let us unleash War and her wrath upon this world and bathe in the entrails of our enemies."

"Works for me," an evil smile split his face as his animal peeked out from his orange and yellow eyes.

35

The hallways seemed to fold in on themselves, shortening the walk to our destination. Fiona's strides were sure and even when we walked through the door where everyone waited. Daniel braided our hair into a tight, intricate mass that wouldn't get in our way as she tested the grips on a number of guns until she found some she liked. I couldn't tell their makes or models, only that they weren't human-issue. The knives were much easier to choose. Heavy-weight throwing blades adhered to our forearms while a butterfly knife slid into our right boot. A wickedly curved blade slid into place between the holsters at hip and thigh, while a serrated hunting blade mirrored it on the other side. A machete completed the arsenal in the sheath down our spine as Daniel attached spare magazines to something on the sheath's exterior. Fiona rolled our shoulders and cracked our neck.

"Everyone ready?" she asked, looking around at her creations.

"Almost," Samuel nodded. "You all know what to do."

The angels smiled before they split into groups of three and four. Their splitting made me realise there were more gathered before us than had originally been selected. Forms blurred, became less cohesive, as they merged. The rush of energy coming off of them made the hair on the back of our neck stand up. Somehow, Fiona fed on the power in the air until it dissipated and the others were multi-limbed brutes. They all had multiple sets of wings and arms, but only a couple had more than one head and set of legs. They were grotesquely beautiful.

"On your command, *Metaria*," their conglomerated voices growled as they hefted their weapons.

"Daniel?" Fiona turned to him.

"Yes?" he inclined his head.

"It's time."

Nodding, he touched our branded shoulder and just disappeared. The mark heated, then returned to normal as Serenity took his place beside us. Her suit matched ours, but she had better toys strapped to her. I was envious of her shotgun, but Fiona needed our hands mostly free. Our weapons were for backup more than anything.

"We are a go. Do your duty," Fiona barked.

Samuel approached as the berserkers roared. Fiona took one of his hands as Serenity held the other. She grasped our hand and completed a circuit. I felt weightless in our body, and closed my 'eyes' to enjoy the sensation. The swirling, sucking sensation I associated with translocating brought me out of the euphoric high as our feet hit solid ground.

The library was a perfect copy of Elsie's simulation, minus the scorch marks and broken shelves. A few torture devices from my old history books sat around the room; their occupants either dead, or nearly there. Daniel came off our shoulder as weapons swung around and aimed for us. His weapons vanished as his skin turned to scales and his shape shifted, stretched, grew. The change took ten seconds from start to finish, and he roared; spraying fire that lit his iridescent black scales from within. Half the room went up in flames as the camouflage-garbed mercenaries opened fire.

The body armour did its job and stopped the high-velocity projectiles from harming us. Fiona smiled when they paused to reload. In a smooth, well-practiced movement, she pulled the machete out and twirled the grip in our palm. Faster than lightning, she launched us across the room and shoved the blade hilt-deep in a faceless creature's chest. The berserkers took that as their cue and let out a battle cry that wobbled the glass in the windows and shook the foundations of the compound.

The creature finally hit the floor. Grabbing the knives on our thighs, Fiona slid behind Prometheus's subpar hired help and sliced the tendons behind their knees on her way to check on the wolves.

I thought we were winning, our group still standing as the last guard was dispatched. The back of my head agreed with Fiona's thought that this was too easy. She was right, and I watched in horror as they got back up in the order they had fallen. All except for the ones that Daniel had flame-broiled.

The carved double doors shuddered against whatever was pounding them from the other side. The hinges gave and they crashed to the floor; squishing a few of the reanimated *things*. Daniel curled around us and growled at the seven foot tall creature from my nightmares as his broad shoulders filled the now-empty door frame. Fiona squared our shoulders and lifted our chin as I shrank away from him and the memories of what he did to me. Just looking at him made my scars itch.

A sick grin split his face and his brown eyes filled with his version of pleasure as he looked at us. He even licked his thin lips, his forked tongue snaking out, as though anticipating the chance to torture me again. Fiona sheathed the blades, ignoring his expression as she remained calm to the point he lost his smile.

"You shouldn't be alive, Amelia," his voice was the same as I remembered. I shuddered, but she stood fast and didn't show it.

"Amelia has nothing to say to you, *midoros*," she cracked our knuckles.

"I am not your son, hybrid whore," he growled.

"I may not have birthed you, but I did pull you to life from this earth for a purpose. Your rebellion resulted in your exile, which you have since violated."

"I do not answer to your authority," he snarled, whipping a glowing red sphere at us.

The suit did as Persephone had designed it to; it absorbed the energy and recycled it into our palms. It took a moment of concentration, but Fiona unleashed our second sight and brilliant, fractal suns came to life inside the hearts of the living. The dead tasted of Prometheus's power, but she couldn't syphon from them. Our eyes found the proto-god, and the blinding bronze and black sun that she *could* eat. She sipped it, slowly at first to enjoy its bouquet, before calling a larger piece of it home to her.

The dead re-engaged; spraying the room with bullets that either didn't penetrate or had limited effect due to healing capabilities. Prometheus stalked towards us through the gunfire and swinging blades. Fiona wanted him to come to us; it allowed her to concentrate on eating away his power.

The rush was addictive, seductive. It whispered sweet nothings to me about immortality, indestructibility, so long as I kept it sated. I rolled around in the ocean of power as Fiona fed death into our hands. She ate away at him until he stumbled, finally falling to his knees a few feet from us. She closed the distance, our hands rising. Prometheus reached for us, but a berserker was there to catch his arm. Another held his left arm away and Fiona slammed the balls of energy into the sides of his head.

Prometheus screamed as she used the physical contact to pull him apart at the atomic level; guiding the energy to destroy him from the inside out as she absorbed the power.

Our wings split our back open, absorbing all light in the room and casting sinister shadows as some of the feathers began to turn black. His head finally caved in and his body crumbled to dust at our feet. Fiona dusted off our hands and exhaled sharply.

"Torch the bodies," she spoke, our voice rich and lazy with power. "He may not have been the only one controlling them."

Daniel puffed a snort before obliging; giving each corpse an individual flame bath instead of flaming the entire room. When he was done he pulled himself back into his human skin, clothes and weapons intact. We were about to start the hunt for Elizabeth when she barrelled through the door; eyes wide and graying hair flying around her oval face as she skidded to a halt. Her blue and brown hazel eyes surveyed the room quickly before she took off back the way she had come.

Fiona bolted after her, Daniel beside us. He caught her around the waist and took her to the floor. Something crunched as her face hit the tile and she seemed to be having trouble breathing when he stood. Fiona leaned over her and grabbed a handful of her coarse hair. Bringing her head up, she smiled at the bloody damage.

Elizabeth's forehead was split just above her right eye; her nose smashed rather unpleasantly into her face. Blood ran freely over the sharp angles and dripped steadily to the floor where it was already beginning to pool. When the rest of our party joined us, Fiona began to drag the werewolf down the long corridor to what the building's schematics said was their assembly hall. Her strides were steady, and more sure-footed than I would have been able to manage in her choice of shoes.

Huge double doors stood charred and damaged, but open in front of us. Fiona waited until we crossed the threshold before she threw Elizabeth across the room. A hank of hair hung from our hand as Elizabeth crashed into the base of a dais that held two thrones. Both were highly polished stone, but that was where the similarities ended. One was a black so shiny it looked like obsidian; its curves delicate and intricate even as it called to me like death's siren. The other one was white, but calling it white was like calling the winner of the Triple Crown a show pony. It glittered in the late-day sun coming through the windows behind it.

Fiona looked around the hall at the huddled, bloody assembly. Suns no longer lit up their torsos, but we could feel their terror at what we might do to them. They were so broken that they expected us to attack them, too. Fiona turned our head a little to the right and Samuel stepped up to us.

"What do you need, *Metaria*?" he asked, voice quiet as a spring breeze.

"Have the wards fallen?"

"Yes. Access is no longer restricted."

"Have someone deliver Graham. The survivors need a new leader."

"I'll see to it," he inclined his head to us before melting away.

Turning to the berserkers, Fiona pointed at two of them before speaking. "You two, stay here. The rest of you, locate the others. Render assistance if necessary. Burn any walking corpses you find, and bring me the necromancer animating them. Prometheus used his power to mask their presence, but I can still feel them."

"It will be done," they growled before stalking back the way we came.

'I feel it too,' her silent voice startled me. *'The seat of darkness has an unnatural pull to it that I haven't felt in a very long time.'*

'Where were you last time you felt this?'

'Atlantis,' her reply was short, clipped even.

I didn't prod her for more information. She only ever really shared as a distraction or if the information was pertinent to the situation. That information wasn't pertinent since Atlantis no longer existed.

Our berserker guards took up watch by Elizabeth as Fiona approached the huddled wolves. One woman stood up, defiance brightening her blue and green eyes as two dirty, bruised children trembled behind her. Blood darkened the left side of her shirt, and her knuckles looked painfully shredded.

"What's your name?" Fiona asked, stopping a respectful distance from her.

"Tell me why you're here, first," the woman snarled, a little wolf peeking out.

"I'm here to restore order and balance, now that I've corrected a mistake I made a few billion years ago," Fiona shrugged.

"I'm Lysithia Anne Durand-Collins, regent-presumptive if the bitch is dead," her shoulders dropped a little as she relaxed. "You mean us no harm?"

"I will bring no harm to those who did not aid Prometheus," Fiona nodded. "By chance, do you know any of the wolves living at Sanctuary?"

"There are three, that I'm aware of. One is my eldest child, Graham."

"Well, I hope you miss that bastard," I snapped, forcing Fiona into the passenger seat. "Because you can keep his half-breed ass when he gets here."

Lysithia took a swift step back, confusion twisting her face. Daniel's hand found the back of my neck, though I couldn't tell why. Serenity moved around me, hands away from her weapons to show the wolves she had no ill intent.

"There's a lot to catch you up on," Serenity extended her hand to Lysithia. "The quickest answer I can give you for the questions running through your eyes is that our world is really fucking complicated."

36

"Really fucking complicated?" Lysithia laughed. "Like anything could be more complicated than shapeshifter politics."

"My sister is the vessel for the being that created the gods; her bound guardian is a dragon; I died three years ago, but somehow managed to get pregnant in the last month. No elder sister is the last thousand years of our family has been fertile," Serenity dropped her hand. "Complicated enough for you?"

"Wait a second. Back up," I frowned. "You're pregnant? And you came on this suicide run anyways?"

'Suicide my ass,' Fiona growled at me.

"According to Melpomene, yes. She's just as confused about it as I am, since she's been doing my physicals for most of my life."

I rubbed my temples, a headache beginning to beat a tattoo inside my skull. "Call Persephone when you're done here. She may be able to help with this."

"I believe Mom would have called it a 'shit-uation'," Serenity sighed. "My life doesn't fit with kids. I banked on never having any, since it should have been impossible."

"How about we finish this conversation later?" Daniel broke in. "I can feel two groups coming from different directions."

"Friends or target practice?" I shrugged away from his hand and touched the guns on my hips.

"The hallway are friends. The ones riding the void are too jumbled to tell either way."

"Civilians, find cover," I barked, drawing the mini hand-canons. Their safeties clicked off and I covered half the room while Daniel stood at my back.

Our friends in the corridor arrived first; assessing the situation quickly and blocking their survivors from entering. A nearly-blinding flash seared my retinas as the others dropped in. We all relaxed in a synchronised exhale. Fiona chose that moment to kick me back into the side seat.

"Shall we begin?" she arched an eyebrow as she holstered the pistols.

"Any time you're ready," Samuel nodded, a hand on Graham's trembling shoulder.

"Name yourself, for those assembled," Fiona curled our voice around the room.

"Graham Nikolai Collins, son of Lysithia Anne Durand-Collins," his voice was sure and even.

"What is your status as it pertains to this pack?"

"Rightful heir, displaced due to the incorrect assignation of quarter-blood status."

"What is your true status? How wolf are you?"

"Half-blood, and eligible to inherit," he snarled, his fingers curling.

"Prove it, here, before your brethren," Fiona swept our arms around the room, putting on quite the show.

Graham snarled, his bones reshaping in front of everyone. His clothes tore as his coal black wolf exploded from his human shell. He took two steps before howling; the long, mournful note slowly joined by others from human throats. His howl faded from the harmony and became a growl as he stalked towards us. I was concerned, but Fiona stood her ground. She seemed to know the limitations of our reflexes better than I did.

She brought one hand up, palm out to indicate non-aggression. Graham snarled before pressing his nose to our palm. His rough tongue shot out and touched our wrist before his fur and form pulled back into his human shape. He stood before us nude, a fierce smile on his face.

'Impressive,' I thought to Fiona. *'I was expecting to hit him.'*

'Someone has given him a measure of control,' she agreed. *'He needed to show strength and control to take the pack without a bloodbath.'*

'Will this work if his father is unknown? Some won't accept him without proof of pedigree.'

'Only Lysithia could say,' she mentally shrugged. *'She is happily married, I doubt she wants to remember.'*

I was about to respond when Graham took our hand and his flood of thoughts and memories bowled me over. It was too much for me to see clearly, but Fiona showed no outward sign of my strain. He led her up the stairs of the dais, and I had a bad feeling as he lowered her onto the black throne. He knelt in front of her until she flicked our fingers at him. He was just about to straighten when I saw Elizabeth's hand shift. Fiona had a gun out and was pulling the trigger before anyone else could react to the threat. A small red hole appeared in her forehead as the back of her head exploded in a mess of blood, and brains, and bone.

The seat beneath us pulsed, happily to my senses, as Fiona finally laid our fingers on it. A sharp edge split our skin and it absorbed our blood as it flowed freely. She jerked our hand away from the stone and watched as our flesh sealed without a scar. She holstered the gun while surveying the room.

'This seat needs to be destroyed,' she mentally shuddered. *'Somehow it survived what Rylynne did to Atlantis. If Elizabeth sat in it for any length of time...'*

'How bad is it?'

'This was called the Throne of Corruption. It was created by melding black diamonds and obsidian on the atomic level.'

'Let me guess, it seemed innocuous at first?'

'Exactly. The first dozen monarchs where unaffected by it. After that, it was a creeping seduction to instability. One of my bloodlings figured out what was going on, and we crafted a new seat for the queen. This one was kept in the dungeons for torture after that.'

'Scary shit.'

'For the wolves to have gotten their hands on it, yes.'

'What do we do?'

'Replicate it with safe materials and switch them,' she glanced around the room quickly and smiled at the shocked stillness. No one had moved a muscle since she pulled the gun.

'What if someone else sits in it before then?'

'Hephaestos can make an identical copy in twelve hours, unless he's gotten rusty. If the information I pulled from Graham when you discovered his problem is correct, only one person per generation may sit on the black throne. It is always either the ruler or their consort if they have one.'

'Then why did he sit you here? We aren't wolf, and I don't like him.'

'It's most likely his wolf peeking through. He may not be consciously aware of what he's done.'

'I don't want to set foot here again if I can help it.'

'Once we're done here, I have no intention of coming back.'

I 'nodded' at her and shut my mental mouth. She crossed our legs, and still no one moved. A sigh escaped her and she shook our head.

"Anyone have anything to say?" our voice rang through the room. People startled and turned wide eyes to her. "No objections?"

Lysithia finally stepped forward, face kept carefully away from us. "By our own laws of succession, I acknowledge my son as the new Lykaoro of our pack. Lykaora Elizabeth is to be struck from the history for crimes against our people."

Still, no one moved. It was like sitting in a room of life-like statues. Finally, Fiona stood, brushing non-existent dust from our body armour.

"Sistra?" she arched an eyebrow at Serenity.

"Yes?" she startled, the tension lines on her forehead smoothing away.

"I believe our presence is no longer necessary."

"Agreed," she nodded, moving swiftly to stand by our grandfather.

Daniel took up his post at our right hand as we stepped off the dais. The angels at the door let the wolves through, but kept a badly bruised human within a protective circle. The only thing I could tell about him, for sure, was that his hair was brown. Everything else was hidden by dirt and bruises.

"What do we do with him?" one of the berserkers asked, voice deep yet high.

"Take him to the Muses. When he's well enough, I'll see about whether he was compliant in this adventure or not," Fiona inclined our head. They nodded in return before fading away.

"Where to now?" Samuel asked as our group of six formed a circle.

"I don't know about anyone else, but I have some toys to return to Hades and Persephone," I piped up, mildly surprised that Fiona let me speak.

"Works for me," Serenity nodded.

"A shower would be nice," Daniel added.

"Hi-ho, hi-ho, it's off to Hell we go," Samuel chuckled. "Please keep all limbs tucked against your body and prepare for a bumpy ride. Don't forget your souvenir t-shirt at the gift shop when you leave."

I would have laughed, but the sucking sensation of being dragged from one dimension, through another, and back to my original one threatened all the food I hadn't eaten in the last week. Gray dotted my vision as my feet hit the floor, then slid off it. Daniel, ever reliable Daniel, caught me as Persephone came around a corner.

"Food in the kitchen. Follow the arrows. I keep forgetting she's part human," the goddess dismissed us. "Oh, and stay away from the main bathing hall for now. The Muses had to bring a special…guest to us after an incident at Sanctuary. Hades is with them now."

"Thanks for the warning," Daniel lifted me easily and followed her directions.

Everything was blurry, but the hallways obviously collapsed on themselves ahead of us as we rounded a corner. The navigation arrows dead-ended at a plain bronze door which swung open before we could reach it. A snout poked out and snuffled at the air before the rest of it followed.

"Laos Niké?" I asked, not quite trusting my vision.

The lightning streaks on her wolverine skull wrinkled with her version of a smile. "Ame my girl! Get your tiny butt in here and eat something," her growl of a voice was light. "You should be taking better care of her, dragon. I don't like how skinny she looks."

Daniel shrugged but didn't respond verbally. He followed her tiny form into a chef's wet dream of a kitchen and set me on a high-backed chair near the breakfast bar long enough to seat an army. A plate appeared in front of me, and was swiftly loaded with sweets and bacon.

"I remember what you like, my girl," Laos Niké chuckled. "You always loved bacon with your sweets when you were toddling around."

The bacon was that perfect point between crispy and chewy, and went a long way to easing my stomach's cramping. Reaching for a heavily frosted chocolate cupcake, I licked the frosting off slowly; the sugar giving me a quick jolt of energy as the flavours caressed my tongue.

"What are you doing here?" I asked as soon as I could see straight. "Not that it isn't great to see you."

"The Underworld is attached to one of the portals under my control. Hades and Persephone keep a room for me here," she 'smiled.'

"How many portals do you watch? I can't remember if you ever told me."

"You never needed to know before. I guard three, partially because they're in one location. The council representative of the Lazari always stands at my post; only the strongest of us can keep the fabric of reality from being torn apart by the pull of so many transecting dimensions. When our leader nears the end of their life, all Lazari who have not been through the trial before are brought to the cave and tested. The one who keeps hell from breaking loose with the least difficulty is then groomed for my seat and eventual succession to my position."

"Interesting. This isn't your way of telling me you're dying, though, is it?"

"Oh no, my dear. I have another four thousand years in me, barring accidents involving sharp objects and my neck. My species, however, is another problem entirely. No new Lazari have been born in a thousand years, and none already existing are strong enough to take over for me in an emergency."

37

"My brain is immediately jumping to the conclusion that the Lazari haven't reproduced since my ancestors were brought back from the dead. Tell me if I'm wrong," I pushed the plate away and frowned at Laos Niké.

"Correlation, yes. Causation, undetermined. According to species records, the last one was born the day before Persephone became tied to your mortal line," she nodded. "We were dying as a species, even before I was born, but now we are becoming extinct."

"Do you think Fiona can help? Or did her vanishing cause it?"

"We don't know, but we would like to ask someday soon. If you can arrange it."

"She's in my head, somewhere. I haven't felt her since we left the wolves' hall. Daniel?" I turned to him.

"Dig into your head and see if I can't find her?" he flashed a quick smile.

"If you could, please."

"This may be uncomfortable if any roadblocks pop up. Please try not to shield as I would rather not deal with brain damage."

I chuckled as his hand found the back of my neck and flashes of his memories skittered through my mind. His fingers twitched every so often, and the flow of images slowed before he pulled his hand away.

"We may have a problem," he frowned at me.

"We just dealt with a problem. Can't the next one wait a few days?" I bounced my forehead off the cool countertop.

"If only life worked that way," he sighed. "Fiona's locked in a grudge match with what's left of Prometheus. You weren't strong enough to take him apart completely."

I sat bolt straight and stared at him with wide eyes. "There's a piece of that bastard inside me? How? Get him out, get him out, GET HIM OUT!"

Daniel's hands on my wrists calmed some of my panic as my mind registered the blood on my fingertips. Warm trickles ran down my neck where I had apparently clawed myself. Laos Niké was staring at me, the confusion on her face clear even with her animal structure.

"I think it would be best if you bathed, then slept," Daniel slowly released his hold on me. "We will sort out what needs to be done after your body and mind have had a chance to recharge."

"I need to talk to Hephaestos first. Fiona had a task for him. It's an emergency that needs to be dealt with."

"Where does it sit on the emergency scale? Sudden natural disaster to end the world as we know it?"

"The Throne of Corruption survived Atlantis. It needs to be taken out of play immediately."

Laos Niké cursed a blue streak that made even me blush. "I'll see that it's taken care of. Listen to your dragon, and let me worry about this."

"Why? I mean, I thought you weren't around back then," I frowned at her.

"That artefact could not be destroyed by any power of this earth, so it was stored in one of my portals with a few other objects. Someone stole from me, and I didn't even know it," she growled. "I need to put it back and make sure nothing else is missing."

"You'll call me before going after anyone?"

"Promise, Ame."

Her form shimmered and faded; an angry, hissing growl the last part of her to leave.

"Interesting friend you have there," Daniel quirked an eyebrow at me.

"She was basically my nanny," I shrugged. "Any time my mom had to leave, she came over and spoiled us rotten."

"I was talking more about the fact that she's the head of her species. Council members rarely, if ever, speak with those not of their species unless it's an emergency."

"Huh," I shrugged. "She's always been warm and friendly with us."

"Shall we go, then? I would greatly enjoy peeling that bodysuit from you."

"Just for a bath, I hope," I smiled. "Where should I leave my weapons?"

"As much as I would relish anything else, I promise to behave unless invited. As for your weapons, keep them close to hand until they say otherwise."

"Just in case?"

"Just in case," he nodded. "We never know when a show of force may be necessary."

"Aren't deities and a living, breathing dragon show enough?"

"No one truly fears the gods anymore. It's been too long since they have had to enforce our laws."

"And not all species are as long-lived as yours and Laos Niké's," I slid off the seat and moved toward the door. "Any idea where the secondary bathing areas are?"

"I would say follow the arrows," he chuckled. "It's the only sure way to not get lost down here."

The door swung open ahead of us, and the arrows pointed us back the way we came, at least until we reached a new branch of hallways. They sent us left until we reached a blue fogged glass door. It slid into the wall so we could enter a no less beautiful bathroom. Steam curled up from the pool's surface as Daniel unzipped the back of my suit. It loosened immediately, then slid off with little help from me. The only effort I had to put into undressing involved my shoes and underwear.

"You never know how much your feet hurt until you take your shoes off," I smiled a little, pressing my aching feet against the cool tile floor.

"Having a massage therapist also helps," he chuckled.

"Mm, that reminds me. Are any people from our world chiropractors? I need an adjustment in one of my wings."

"I'm sure there's at least one out there. I'll ask around. And you're delaying getting in the water."

"I am?"

"You are," he placed a warm hand on my shoulder. "Need me too throw you in?"

"Might be a good idea since I don't know why I'm stalling."

He scooped me up easily and strode down the steps into the pool. Instead of dropping me like I expected, he placed me carefully on the stairs with my head above the surface. The water was hot against my skin, hotter than it should have been. Sweat rolled down my face as I waited to feel comfortable with the temperature.

Daniel was completely scrubbed and clean by the time I could move without my vision running in streamers. It was like my body and mind were no longer connected as my fingers brushed lightly down his back. He shivered and goose bumps erupted everywhere I touched. Touching him was like an electric charge shooting up my hand, and I wasn't sure if I wanted to stop or keep going. My body kept going, even as my mind tried to tell it to stop.

"Amelia?" he caught my wrist in one of his hands as my nails explored the dips in his abdomen. His eyes flashed green for the briefest moment. "Tell me no."

A small, evil smile stretched my lips as my other hand came up and gripped his hard shaft. "Make me."

He growled low in his throat and grabbed my other wrist with his free hand. Pulling my arms behind my back, he closed the distance between us so we were touching from chest to thigh. I tried to pull my arms free, but his grip tightened and a chuckle escaped his lips.

"Struggle all you want. I enjoy it," he whispered, dipping his head down to rub his cheek against mine. "Fight me. It'll make it better."

"Adrenaline is the spice of life?"

"Adrenaline, and a little bit of fear," he nipped my jaw before releasing my wrists and turning me around so he was pressed against my back. He cupped my breasts; rolling my nipples between his fingers until they were hard, aching points. He bit my shoulder, hard, before shoving me away.

My foot caught on the bottom of the pool, and I went under. Instead of calming me down, the water stroked my skin's need for touch. Heightened it. I was practically shaking with the need to be touched when I resurfaced. Daniel sliced through the water, his horns visible and swirling red and black. A clawed hand caught me by the throat and tossed me easily onto the floor outside the pool. The landing knocked the breath from me, left me too stunned to aim the kick I threw at him. He caught my ankle easily and used it to flip me onto my stomach.

"Open those wings for me," he growled, dragging me back towards him. "I want to see the shadows dance on the walls."

I wasn't sure if it hurt or felt good as the rough floor scraped my skin. My feet and lower legs hitting the water shocked a little sanity back into me. It didn't last long as claws caressed my hips and lower back, with the occasional stroke up my spine.

"Come on, Amelia," Daniel's voice rumbled from deep in his chest. "Show me those wings."

"You know I don't control them," I gasped, my skin hot and aching.

"I can feel them," he traced a line up my side. "Just beneath the surface. They want to come out again."

I arched, lifting my hips from the floor as a claw dug lightly into my shoulder blade. A trickle of blood eased into the valley of my spine and I lost all rational thought as he closed the distance between us and slid into me.

"Stop thinking like a human, Amelia," he punctuated every word with a hard thrust. "Lose control for me."

A choked scream escaped me as I let go. His thoughts rushed through my head and swept away the shields I kept between my mind and the world. Sensations were sharper, colours brighter, emotions stronger. My back ruptured; wings pulling free in a wash of blood. They pulled in all the light from the room, casting sinister shadows against the walls that moved before we did.

He stopped, his body wedded to mine, and stroked my spine between the wings with fingers instead of claws. My fangs descended, pricking my lower lip as I panted, struggling to breathe. A moan slid past my bleeding lips as he pulled out of me. The small splashes he made as he exited the pool sounded like a hurricane to my ears. Daniel picked me up easily and set me on my feet while my mind struggled with maelstrom that was the world without my filters. His fingers tunnelled through my hair; held me still as his lips caressed mine, gathering the blood before it could be wasted.

He kissed me, eating at my mouth without a care for the razor sharp fangs. My nails scraped his chest, every touch more intense as I let go of my humanity and human ideals of life. His hands left my hair, travelling down my body until they cupped my ass. Lifting me, I wrapped my legs around him automatically. His steps were steady as the whispered creak of leather glanced off my ears. Eyes closed, I was a creature of pure need; not caring when my back met cool tile that bent my wings. Impaling me, he drove a cry from my throat that tore my lips from his.

"That's it Amelia," his voice was a low, deep rumble against my neck. It sent chills down my spine, and I dug my fingers into his shoulders to keep from falling into a hole of pleasure I doubted I could crawl out of. He found a rhythm that kept me on the edge of orgasm, but wasn't quite enough to push me over the ledge.

Fangs nipped my shoulder, barely puncturing the skin before moving to a new spot. The tingles of near-pain added to the ecstasy of him hard inside me. It was just enough, and I sank my teeth into his throat as I came apart; my eyes turning silver as they flew open. His fangs punctured my shoulder and stayed there as he thrust one last time and shuddered against me.

The door crashed open, but I couldn't find it in me to care. Daniel and I were like a completed circuit that I didn't want to break. The present and pleasure kept running through me from where we touched. Hands tried to pry us apart, but they either weren't strong enough, or willing to hurt us.

A blast of energy hit my legs, and the pain finally forced me to release his neck. Tears streamed down my face and he let go, carefully putting me on the floor before he turned and let out a very dragonesque bellow. His wings were the same swirling red and black as his horns as they extended to create a shield. I couldn't see past him to who interrupted us, and at that moment I didn't care if they died.

38

My leg was charred, burnt almost to the bone where most of the blast had landed. My other leg was blistered, but most of the skin was intact. If I could have stood through the pain, I would have been beside Daniel, but I was finding it had enough to stay conscious. My wings folded down, covering me as more people disturbed the air in the shrinking room. Voices were a cacophony of muddled noise that sent shards of pain through my head.

Fangy and Wings asserted their presences slowly, each taking half of our body without a fight. My right wing turned completely black as my right iris slid to pure red. My left side matched it; the wing losing its black feathers as the iris turned violet. Together they forced our body to stand, to walk. Each step pulled energy from the air around us until they brought a light, flowing dress into existence around us. It seemed to float in a pool of their utter serenity. Fangy reached out and touched Daniel's arm; pulling all emotion from him until he was calm. He blinked slowly, his horns fading. Clothes appeared on his body and he took our hand.

"What would you have of me?" his voice was quiet, barely above a whisper, but the six people in the room reacted to it. They all jerked as though slapped.

"Home," the ringing, musical bass tore our throat. Our shell was never meant to make that sound. "We would like a home."

"Whatever you need," he nodded.

"Stop," the high, wispy voice breathed through the room. "You have no idea what you've just done."

Wings arched an eyebrow at Svetanyasieemay's translucent form. "We know more than you think, Dragon Mother. The All Mother taught us everything we needed to know, including what we were to do should we not be strong enough to completely destroy Prometheus. We are doing nothing more than what she asked."

"And what, precisely, did she ask?" a red-headed woman who favoured Tisiphone asked. "Verbatim, it's important."

"'Do whatever is necessary to ground yourselves in reality. Your human half must accept all that you are together. You will know when it is time'," Fangy squeezed Daniel's hand. "He is our grounding rod. Our human half holds no fear of him. We trust him. Fiona accepts all that he is, and all that we can make of him."

"Why is your human half not speaking for herself?" Persephone rubbed her leg where ours hurt the most.

"She is in too much pain, but we speak with her voice. We could not be here if she did not let us go."

"What exactly did she let go of?" Serenity frowned at us.

"Sistra," we smiled. "She let go of everything. She is free. She will be happy now, we promise."

Serenity growled at us, clearly not happy with the only answer she was getting out of us. Hades and Blair exchanged a glance, shrugged, and stayed silent.

"Ready?" Daniel asked, his wings stretching until one covered ours.

"Whenever you are," we nodded.

The room faded away around us. It was almost gone when the unknown woman's voice broke through the fog and sent us on our way.

"You have royally fucked up the timeline, and I can't fix it. Whatever happens now is on your heads."

The darkness seemed to stretch on forever as we drifted through the dead space between dimensions. Daniel's heartbeat was slow and steady as he held out head to his chest; his wings a dome over our heads as ours cocooned his back. We stayed silent as he directed us without the usual pulling sensation of translocation.

The world came back as a dark room encased in glass. Lights twinkled all around and far below as he released us to turn on the lights. The room was massive, taking up the entire floor of the skyscraper in a city I didn't recognise. There was a small kitchen to our right, and a massive bed sunk into the floor to the left. It was sparsely furnished aside from that, but cozy just the same.

"What is this place?" I/we asked, turning in circles to take in the view.

"Home," Daniel smiled, leaning against the breakfast bar with his arms crossed over his chest. "As the sole Draconis and longest living member of the shapeshifter council, I control all assets that once belonged to the different clans of my species. With the interest that's been building since it was all brought to one bank, I have enough to last more lifetimes than I care to calculate. If you never want to talk to your sister about your inheritance, you don't have to."

"And you're okay with that?"

He nodded. "What's mine is yours, so long as you don't kill me."

I/we laughed. "You make us happy, and happiness is something we had all but forgotten. We are confusing ourselves, though. We aren't sure if we should refer to us as separates or as a whole."

"Speak as a whole, your voices will tell me the separates," he responded after a moment.

"We – I will," we smiled. It felt good, the loss of our human voice. Our human brain had one last question, however, before it went to sleep. "Why did people go ape-shit when we bit each other?"

Daniel seemed startled by the question. "Can you not access all memories?"

We shook our head. "Last human question. That part of our mind is blocked because it is too fragile to survive the massive influx of thoughts and information. We do not have the experience to pick and choose what to share."

"I only know what Fiona told me. Though ordered may be more correct," he shrugged. "She said to make sure you were safe by any means necessary; up to and including binding your life to mine. For a dragon to do that, they acknowledge that no other will ever measure up, or be more important to them. It's different from the oath of protection in that it leaves no external marks, and can only be seen by those whose lives are to span centuries."

"Simplified, that means…" I prompted.

"Turn off your human and feel. Extend those fearsome senses and find the answer within yourself."

Fangy smiled and closed our eyes, pushing away one sense to heighten the others. Sound picked up first, became clearer as we concentrated on just the room we were in. We ignored our heartbeat, or tried to, until I realised that ignoring ours silenced his.

"One heartbeat?" I opened our eyes.

"One lifeline," he nodded. "Welcome to your out-clause."

We smiled, and the last of our humanity went to sleep content. It felt odd, to only be two instead of three in our shared mind. The immediate sharing of knowledge, without the human interference was refreshing; a much-needed change of pace after the last few years. And the unfettered access to so many of our abilities – ye gods it felt good!

"What's on your agenda for the evening?" we asked, melting our wings back into our flesh.

"Sleep," he shrugged. "I need to recharge after what we did with the wolves."

"I thought you couldn't truly sleep now that you're an oathed dragon," we frowned.

"That only applies so long as my charge isn't bound to me in return. Your case is a little different, though, seeing as how Fiona is my protectee and you're the one I bit. The short of it is that you can now call any ability of mine that you don't already control to help you should I not be there."

"So you'll still be protecting us even if you aren't there?"

"Exactly," he smiled. "Care to come to bed? I promise to keep my hands in polite locations."

"And if we don't mind a little impoliteness?" we quirked an eyebrow at him.

"My hands are yours to command," he laughed, willing away his clothes as his leathery wings finally vanished. "Do you have anything you would like to do tomorrow?"

We thought about it for a moment. "We need clothes. And ID."

"I'll call about ID, and have you added to my accounts so you can buy whatever you want for here. Groceries I usually have delivered, and they bill monthly. We'll need to check you in with building security at some point, so if you want to wander on your own you can get back in."

"Sounds like a plan," we smiled, taking his hand as he strode toward the bed. Stepping on it was like setting foot on a cloud; solid, yet soft and springy. "What's this made of?"

"Gel foam," he chuckled. "High-density to support humanoid weight, but malleable to conform to natural curves. Humans are finally prototyping a less advanced version."

"Is it comfy?"

"The best sleep I've ever had."

"Is there any magic worked into it to prevent dream-walking?"

"To prevent others from getting in, yes, but not to keep any latent abilities of the sleeper from slipping out."

We let go of the energy holding our dress together and relaxed completely against his warm chest. Breathing deeply, we savoured his natural scent as he pulled us down and wrapped his arms around us. We draped a leg over his hip and slid quickly into the comforting darkness of sleep.

Sounds thundered through the void, chasing flashes of images we couldn't hold on to. The feeling we kept with us was one of impending doom, of coming pain and misfortune for many. It felt near, yet not connected to us. It faded away as time seemed to accelerate and soft light pierced our eyelids.

39

The new day felt like a new beginning as we stretched and inhaled the heavenly scent of coffee and bacon. A soft robe sat on the ledge by our head, and we pulled the red fabric over us as we exited the empty bed. Daniel was leaning against the kitchen island, a paper open in front of him with everything we were smelling spread out beside him.

"Good morning," he glanced over his shoulder and smiled. "Sleep well?"

"Mostly," we nodded, fixing a cup of coffee. We sipped it slowly as Daniel slid the colour comics over. "It's Sunday?"

"According to the paper, Sunday January 25th, 2009. Who knew you would be the resident with the shortest stay in Sanctuary's history?"

"Everything happens for a reason, or so people keep telling me."

"Either it happens for a reason, or someone orchestrated everything so what they wanted would come to pass," he shrugged. "We have an appointment with security in an hour to clear you for the building. Since ID will take a few days, they'll take a picture to keep on file until we can fill in the rest."

"Sounds good," we flashed a small smile before devouring half the plate of bacon. "What name should go on the paperwork?"

"I was going to go with your real one, but change your age. Anyone looking for you will be searching for a seventeen-year-old travelling with her sister, not a twenty-three-year-old living with her lover."

"Makes sense, but what if word has spread that we have an oathed dragon guarding us?"

"The Caretakers were careful to erase my face from the memories of everyone who has ever set foot in their domain. No one knows what I look like, and I can hide my eyes to keep from being recognised that way. Your eyes, however, will be a little trickier since they're now red and purple with thin bands of blue and silver. No one has eyes like yours, and no contact lens will be able to hide the vibrancy of them."

"We can change our eyes to something human," we shrugged. "It takes a little concentration, and only holds so long as we aren't in pain. Our human half couldn't control enough of what we are to take advantage of the natural camouflage. What colour would you like?"

"What's easiest for you to remember?"

"Our human blue. We've looked at it for so long, and it fits with our colouring."

"Then blue it is. I have one question for you, though."

"Ask away."

"Where were you born? The Caretakers didn't have it in your file, and I need to know whether or not we need to edit the government's archives."

We smiled, just a small lifting at the corners of our lips. "Greece, on the outskirts of Heraklion. Josephine owned a lingerie boutique there. Her grandmother thought the island of Crete would be an idyllic place to grow our family's roots, and our furies could be hidden easily there."

"The island does have many places for creatures of myth to hide. It was a good choice, but unfortunately, it means that new identification will take a little longer to get. It takes around a week for the archives to be edited and all traces of the access to be erased."

"So that means…?" we prompted him to continue.

"Driver's licence and provincial ID can be had, but medical card, passport, and birth certificate will have to wait."

"Basically we avoid illness and attempting to leave the country until further notice. Works for us," we smiled.

"Don't forget to speak in the singular. Referring to yourselves in the plural in public can result in a quick trip to a psychiatric facility," he pushed away the paper and finished his coffee. Rinsing his cup, he set it by the sink and studied us. "While in the city I have to avoid using too much power if I don't want our kind of police to investigate. Translocation doesn't trace to a specific person, thankfully, but everything else holds a flavour of the user that can be followed. I can manifest essentials for today, but if we want to stay hidden everything needs to be procured the human way."

"Works for me," we shrugged, forcing ourselves to use the singular. "Since when have our kind had police?"

"They only operate where the human population exceeds ten thousand. We need police to clean up when someone goes rogue and risks exposing us all. Hera and Demetre hand-pick each member of every unit, and have since Atlantis fell and we could no longer live openly. Most members of our world go their whole lives never learning about the men, women, and others who protect their secrets."

"If they protect our kind, why did they never stop the Hunters from coming after *us*? Where were they when we needed help, when we were exposed?" we hissed, baring fangs. "Why haven't they wiped out all Hunters?"

"I don't know, I really don't. They can't go after Hunters directly because the Council has a very delicate truce with our leaders, but they should have stepped in the first time you were attacked in public. The only reason they wouldn't have is if they were dealing with a crisis elsewhere."

Our fangs receded and we frowned. "Is there any way to check? See if there were events that coordinate with attacks against us?"

"Suck up to Hera or Demetre," he nodded. "Only they can grant access to those files."

"Remind me to do that later. Right now, I believe we have an appointment with security."

"We do. Black on black, and runners or heels?"

"Whatever you feel like," we flashed a small smile. "So long as it covers the scars. Our human mind had a thing about keeping them hidden."

Daniel snorted, the corners of his mouth twitching upward. "If I were anyone else, I would abuse that *carte blanche*. But since we're going out among humans, simple is safer."

"Jeans, long sleeved shirt and runners?"

"Blends quite well," he nodded, snapping his fingers. Clothes appeared in front of us and we dropped the robe to pull them on.

"Hair up or down?"

"Down. You have a distinctive scar running down the back left side of your neck."

"Good to know," we closed our eyes and sent a sliver of power into our irises so they would hold as blue. When we were sure they would stay, we opened our eyes and took a shocked step back. Daniel's eyes were a shade of rich cerulean that was disconcerting after the orange and yellow we were used to.

"Ready?" he held a hand out to us, two leather coats draped over his other arm.

"Lead on, fair dragon. A new life is calling," we took his hand, relishing the warmth of it against our skin. "I am ready to dance in the rain again."

Epilogue

5 months later

"Happy birthday, Amelia," Daniel's lips brushed the back of my hand as we sat by the window overlooking the harbour. His jeans rode low on his hips, the button undone as water dripped from his freshly washed hair.

"Thank you," I smiled. "*Tempus fugit.*"

"Time flies indeed. Do you need to hunt tonight?"

"Bars are closed tonight," I shook my head. "I can make it until Thursday."

"What about –"

"No," I cut him off. "I fed from you too recently. I can't have you suffering from bite addiction."

"We've been managing the few symptoms that have popped up so far."

"I know, but I love you too much to destroy who you are so I can stay balanced."

He paused as I realised the three words that had fallen from my mouth.

"I love you, too," he finally replied, a slight smile on his lips. His fingers brushed my cheek as the world around me exploded into white lights.

I lost myself in the light; the constraints of physical form seeming to fall away.

<u>Daniel</u>

I sat, shocked into immobility, as blood poured from Amelia's nose and her pupils became pinpoints hidden by the violet rings. She fell backwards, seemingly in slow motion, as Fiona made herself heard for the first time in months.

"I'm losing the fight. I don't know how much longer I can keep him from bleeding through. Do what you can, but prepare for the worst."

Amelia's head hit the cushions, the purple and black ones she had loved so much; her body convulsing as her fangs descended and her wings forced themselves free. Agony echoed through our bond as the scars on her torso opened from the inside. Her right shoulder popped out of place with a sickening snap that jolted my mind from its fog.

My cell phone flew to my hand just as a call came in. I didn't bother checking the caller ID before answering. Only a handful of beings had the number anyways. "Condition Black, I repeat, Condition Black," training had the words flowing as my free hand held her intestines in place. "Prometheus is rising."

Bonus Scene

There's something to be said for being able to forget things. It can dull the edges of painful memories; ease the hurt as time passes. Unfortunately, it only works if you actually can forget things. Four hundred years ago was the worst day of my life, and I can still remember every tiny detail.

It was late spring, in the last decade of the sixteenth century. Queen Lizzie was ageing, fast, and refused to name an heir. Partly because she was worried for our forest, and our home. One of her private missions in life had been to keep my species from going extinct. You see, I'm a shapeshifter; now the last of the Draconi. Dragons, for those who don't know Latin.

Since a time we have long forgotten, there has been a faction of humans intent on the destruction of all supernaturals. Their affiliation didn't matter; if they weren't human they were dead, or targets. We took one in by mistake. She had been beaten, badly, and was able to fool our elders as to her allegiance. She was with us for a week after she healed when she found out our only weakness. Looking back now, we were stupid. Careless.

The Draconi used to be the most powerful guardians to exist. We were created to protect the All Mother's bloodlings, and the fledgling gods. We had untold abilities, and we were trained in how to use them, how to fight, from the moment we could hold a single form on our own. For most of us, that happened between the ages of three and four. Until we reached that point an Elder of the clan, someone who was at least six hundred years old, had to flex some of their massive will over the constantly shapeshifting youngling. Without the stability of a frozen form, the youngest can neither sleep nor eat.

The flip side to this early vulnerability, unfortunately, is that we cannot die of old age. Time can ravage our bodies, worry at the edges of our minds, but it cannot end us. When an Elder reaches a thousand years or greater, and they can feel the degradation advancing, they ask to have their life ended before madness sets in. In order to bypass our invulnerability, a mixture of lodestone, belladonna, and crushed sapphires and pearls must be blown into our eyes. We don't know why it works, just that it does. It turns our naturally orange and yellow eyes a dusky blue, depending on our age.

The human was with us when one of our Elders decided it was her time. The preparations had been made, and she smiled as the ceremonial dagger was driven into her ancient heart. It wasn't long after that that the Hunters came. We were still in mourning, unprepared for the attack. Too slow to respond. My mother came out of our home, my sister in one arm, a sword in her free hand. She told me to take Tatisesavana and hide; she would find us when it was safe. I did what she told me – she was my mother, and I was only twenty-three. I hadn't done more than scratch the surface of my training. I cradled my sister in my arms and ran for the waterfalls. They had a cave you could only reach if you could fly.

She started flipping between dragon and toddler the moment we passed beyond sight of home. I was able to keep a hold of her, but I couldn't block out the screams. To this day, I can still hear the echoes. We were in the cave for days, and I thought they had forgotten to look for us. She was hungry, and I was nowhere near old enough to freeze her to one shape. It was just after dawn when we arrived home, and I immediately regretted the decision to return.

Our family was dead. All of them. Their bloody, hacked up bodies had been left where they fell. Blue-tinted orange and yellow eyes stared sightlessly up at the lightening sky. Tati was crying, trying to get me to put her down so she could go to our mother. I didn't want to let her go, but she bit me and clawed her way over the messy ground until she could cuddle under the limp arm. Because it was just an arm now.

I fell to my knees and prayed. Not to a god, but to the First Dragon. Svetanyasieemay. I wanted to bargain with her, for even one life to be returned. Sometimes she answers, sometimes she doesn't. I felt a slight pressure on my right shoulder, but when I looked up I broke down in tears. The ancient spirit was crying and shaking her head.

"I can't fix this," her faint voice echoed through the trees. "I'll go find someone who can take you and your sister in."

She vanished in a puff of jasmine, and I waited for her to return. I got the funerals pyres ready, and waited. Tati was growing weaker as the days passed, and still the Old One hadn't returned. I was near-delirious from sleep deprivation when two vampires appeared. They took my sister, held her gently, and spoke in a language I didn't understand. Their tone was soothing, and they created a door between two trees; one dragged me through it into a bright room. The other one handed my sister to a very short woman, running his hand over her little head as she stayed human.

Sleep sucked me under the moment I knew we were safe. I don't know how long I was down, but when I came to, there was a sad hush to the room. Three women stood around a crib to my left, their shoulders shaking.

“I'm sorry,” one of the vampires spoke in a language I knew. “She only has a few minutes left. We didn't arrive soon enough.”

I leapt from the bed and rushed to my sister. She was struggling to breathe as I lifted her into my arms. Her little yellow and orange eyes were terrified as she reached up and touched my face.

“L...love...you...Da...Danny,” she stuttered before going limp, the light fading.

I hit the floor, her fragile body cradled to my chest. A fog crept into the edges of my consciousness, dulling the sharp pain. I rocked in place, just holding her, until the numbness took over and one of the women pried my sister away.

I remember muttering something about funeral arrangements, but whether they answered continues to elude me. The next months existed, but I am unable to recall a single distinct detail of them. They happened, but not to me. Time switched from dim to hyper-real in the blink of an eye, and not a moment too soon. A battle axe was aiming to cleave my head from my shoulders.

I ducked and rolled, my muscles reacting automatically. Air whistled at the speed of the weapon swinging by.

“What in high hell do you think you're doing?” I yelled, confused.

“Testing your limits. You agreed to this a few weeks ago,” one of the vampires spoke from near the wall.

"I don't remember that," I stood slowly. "What exactly did I agree to?"

"Us training you to be a guardian, since that's what you were doing before. Part of that is testing what abilities you have, as well as how much damage you can take before you fall," the other vampire spoke from behind me. "So far, we can't kill you. We cut off your head twice, but a new body appears instantly."

"Draconi are invulnerable, until a special powder is blown into our eyes," I shrugged. "We fall into one of four magic groups; air, water, fire, and spirit. Only the Original had all four. My clan was air."

They chuckled. It was deep and ominous. "Oh the things you'll learn here. You are a very special young dragon."

"Says who? You?"

"Us, and your future. In four hundred years, you'll understand why we're doing this. And until then, you'll just have to learn all your elements. Danielseraphnietzurgatezranasoph, Creators are coming."

"Creators?" I repeated, confused. Again. Then it clicked. "Bloodlings of the All Mother. Does that mean the All Mother herself will return?"

"We don't know," the dark-haired one shook his head. "Our source of information doesn't share everything."

"Then what use it he?" I snapped.

"She. She is a goddess, and we don't know how old she is. We know when she was born, but she can step outside of time and view the known universe. She steps back to the moment she left, and we never know how long she's been gone," the light-haired one snapped back. "She shares what she feels is important."

"Does the destruction of a species not count as important?" I screamed. "My clan was the last of the Draconi. When I die, we become extinct."

"It needed to happen, and I'm sorry," a soft female voice came from my right.

I turned, and took a quick step back. A tall woman, with blood red hair and tangerine eyes had materialised from nowhere. The look on her face was one of deep sadness.

"Why did it have to happen? And who the hell are you?"

“I am Rylynne. I was the first deity born in this world, and my talent lies in the control of time. I wanted to save your sister; she was supposed to live, but circumstances outside of my control took her away. In four hundred years, two Creators will be born. One was supposed to be your charge, the other your sister's. With her passing, another has been chosen to guard one of the girls. You need to be ready; you'll have your work cut out for you with the younger one.”

“You can see so far ahead so clearly? How? How can you guarantee that she'll even exist?”

“Her existence was cemented six hundred years ago when her ancestor made a deal with Persephone. She and her sister were blurs in the mist until that pact happened. I have already stepped into that time; I cannot do that if it will not happen.”

“What about the All Mother? Will she return to train them?”

“I cannot tell you.”

“Why not?”

“Because too much information in the mind of a single person makes them a target, and easy to track. I can cloak every aspect of my being, you can't. Information is safe with me, as I am able to know all.”

“That's a bullshit answer if I've ever heard one.”

“I know, but it's the best I can give you until the time is right. Take my hand, please,” she held out her right hand.

“Why? Are you going to take my memories from me?”

“No, I'm going to give you a gift. You have all gifts but earth. One day, you'll need it.”

I tentatively touched her outstretched hand, and pain shot up my arm. The flesh scaled, hardened, then returned to normal.

“Train,” her voice started ringing, fading. “The Caretakers will awaken you when it is time. Master your gifts, accumulate knowledge. Prepare yourself for the future.”

It felt like my conscious mind slipped into a deep hibernation. My body trained, read, expanded control over things that I should never have been able to touch. Life passed by, and I moved through it like a revenant. Until one day. I snapped out of it with two simple words whispered in my ear.

"It's time," the words were there, then gone. "Sleep. We will find you soon."

I slept, deeply. I awoke to movement by the door, and was on my feet in a moment. The Caretakers stood there, their stances obviously full of worry. Though to what, I wasn't yet privy to.

"We have an assignment for you," Blair handed me a thin file.

"There has been a glitch in the delivery," Colby added. "We are tracking her now. Meet us in the atrium."

They vanished, and I strapped weapons to various points along my body, looking over the notes. It was essentially a psychological report, a warning of sorts. Fully armed, I followed them the slow way. Hermes had the elevator waiting for me, and he seemed to be bouncing with excitement. It was a very smooth ride, for the mischief god. He let me out with a very uncharacteristic pat on the back.

The Caretakers were pacing, mumbling to each other in the All Mother's tongue. It stopped abruptly, and they turned to the door; becoming immobile as it flew open. I followed their gazes, and frowned at the golden goddess and the small, pale pixie in her arms. Their approach reached into my bones and made them ache with the need to bow down in supplication. A moment later, James the vampire doctor strode through the door.

"She needs help, fast," he spoke to the Guardians as they hurried closer. A pool of loneliness seemed to extend out from them and got thicker the closer they came.

"I've tried diving," the golden one spoke with a rich, soft voice. "I can't reach her."

"Take her to the thirty-sixth floor. The Muses will meet us there," Blair swept an arm toward the elevator.

They did as he bid and we followed silently.

"This is Daniel," Colby spoke quietly. "He will be Amelia's bodyguard, from now until he dies. He will introduce himself to her when she begins classes, but we will ease her into the idea of him being everywhere she is."

"I'll say it's nice to meet you after we make sure she's okay," the woman nodded at me.

"Pleasure to see you again, dragon," James flashed a small smile as the doors opened and the Caretakers directed them to the door on the left side of the hall.

"You two know each other?" the woman rounded on her companion after placing the pixie on the ancient four-post bed.

"You remember why we met? How it wasn't an accident I was on shift that night you brought Amelia to the hospital?"

"Vaguely sounds familiar," she nodded.

"That was supposed to be his sister," James guided her to a seat as the Muses set to work on Amelia. "She was supposed to be your guardian, not me. She would have been able to stay impartial. She wouldn't have fallen in love with you and asked you to marry her."

"What happened to her, then?" the woman was working up a good angry.

"She died," I locked eyes with her. Her red and gold irises lost their anger faster than I could process any emotion.

"I'm sorry," she looked away. "Losing family sucks."

"Four hundred years dulls all pain," I shrugged.

"Only if someone doesn't open up the old scar," she seemed to gather herself, then stood. She held out her hand and introduced herself. "Serenity Colleen Hartley, twenty-four, law student, and heiress to Hartley House of Fashion. My sister is Amelia Mystaya Hartley, seventeen, universe's punching bag. She has no clue what we are, and I would like to keep it that way for as long as fucking possible."

"You know what you are?" I asked, curious.

"I've known since I was four. My mom made me promise not to tell Amelia until we were somewhere that she could be trained."

"Why? Wouldn't knowing help her?"

She shook her head. "When she's stressed, anxious, scared, or any of the related emotions her subconscious sends out a signal that the Hunters have learned how to track. She's always been safer not knowing."

"Interesting. Has she always been like that?"

"Why so many questions?" she was instantly suspicious.

"He needs to know so he can formulate a way to keep her safe when she leaves here," Blair entered our conversation. "The

Muses stabilized her. She's in a light hibernation; she'll wake when she's ready. Now go and sleep. Your suite is across the hall."

"She'll be okay?" Serenity asked.

"She'll be fine. Go rest, you need it."

The Creator and her vampire departed silently; her shrugging away from his touch when he tried to take her hand. When they were gone the Muses undressed the unconscious girl and tucked her under a light sheet. They nodded at us before disappearing.

"Serenity seems to have trust issues," I remarked quietly.

"She used to be so happy. I don't think the paranoia set in until her fiancé killed her," Colby took a seat.

"How is she alive if she has already been murdered?" I also took a chair.

"The curse of their family. It dates back a thousand years, to the original sisters. The short version is that the elder dies within six months of their mother, when the younger is fourteen. She returns as a beast of rage to protect her sister until the younger child of the next generation turns fourteen. Lather, rinse, repeat over hundreds of generations," Blair snapped his fingers and a fire roared to life in the marble fireplace. "Amelia is expected to die when her younger daughter turns fourteen. She will be forty-two."

"So my services will only be needed for twenty-five years?"

"Twenty-five years that we can confirm. She may have a loophole that she can exploit as a Creator, but we won't know until her expected time of death."

"You've kept me alive for four hundred fucking years, for this? Twenty-five years of duty? Don't you remember what happens to my kind once we bond with a charge? We go insane if they die!"

"And we have the ability to kill you if that happens. As a dragon, you were born with a purpose. This is it. She is yours to protect, to nurture, to heal. She will need you more than she will ever understand."

I felt sick. They had known, through the centuries of training. They had lied to me, every single day for four hundred years.

A soft mewing came from the bed, and I turned to look the moment it became a blood-curdling screech. Her eyes were open, and bright red light was radiating from them.

"Death is coming. She will rise and wipe all life from this world. She is mother. She is daughter. She is sister. She is maiden, mother, crone," the demonic, bassy words were ripped from her throat. She let loose another scream before closing her eyes and laying still.

"What in Hades's lowest hall was that?" I blinked slowly.

"Confirmation of a theory," Colby chuckled, seemingly unfazed.

"What theory?"

"The All Mother is returning. You're going to have a very, very long life, Daniel."

"This is what Rylynne couldn't tell me all those years ago?"

"Yes. She knew that if she told a mortal, everyone would find out. She had intended to tell you, when it was time, but dying put a crimp in her plans," Blair nodded.

"Does Amelia know?"

"Not yet. She has a very strong mind, but she shields parts of it from herself. If she let the All Mother's voice in, she'd believe herself to be crazy."

"You'll need to guide her through it," Colby added. "As her guardian you'll be her friend, protector, confidant. Everything except her lover. You can love her, but her body is off-limits."

"Otherwise I'd wind up like James."

They nodded. "Insinuate yourself into her life slowly. If anything happens to bump up our schedule, we'll let you know."

"What should I do until she wakes up?"

"Finish your awakening, and do your duty. Wake up, Daniel. It's time for you to live again."

Important Terms and Creatures

All Mother – Fiona. One of her many epithets as the source of the gods and others.

Lykaoro/lykaora – King/queen of werewolves. Named for Lykaon of Arcadia.
Harpalykos – chief enforcer of Lykaoro/a in a healthy pack.
Akakos/Sokleus – personal guards of the lykaoro/a

Doppelgänger – physical duplicate. 3 known sources.
Valkyrie – female warriors who died in battle. Resurrected by Ares and angels to collect the best of fallen soldiers for wars yet to come.
Fairies – small nature spirits. Pests. Highly skilled seamstresses.
Shapeshifters/weres –

Wolves: One of the only species who can convert humans by bite. Highly frowned upon as all pack members have a purpose. Half-blood and greater can shift. Guardians/protectors.

Leopards: Avoid humans wherever possible. Leader elected to council based on surviving assignments.

Swans: Rare shapeshifters. Leaders, and keepers of all records of the Shifter Council.

Dragons: Also known as draconis. Warrior-guardians. Only protect Creators and gods.

Clairvoyants – Humans with a mutated gene that allows them to see into the unvarnished truth of the ultimate future. So coveted during war-times that they were hunted by other humans (see: Hunters Council), so the "enemy" could not use them to their advantage. Gene became dormant to survive.
Psychokinets – Humans with an exceedingly rare gene sequence resulting from specific bloodlines. Almost all are deemed unstable and a danger to society.
Necromancer – Human who can raise and speak with the dead due to a mutated/advanced gene. Those who carry two or more versions of the mutation can bring the very recently dead all the way back to life so long as their soul is still nearby.

Earth-manipulator – Similar to necromancers; human with one or more mutated genes. Those more connected to the Earth/more powerful can cause earthquakes and shift mountains out of place.
Pyrokinets – see: earth-manipulator/necromancer. If evolved enough, can cause eruption of volcanoes and prevent nearby stars from going supernova, for a short amount of time.
Ghouls – Rotting, sentient corpses that result from improper burial or failure by a necromancer to properly return a person to their grave. NOT ZOMBIES!
Chymera – "Analysts" of supernatural world. Purebloods live an average of 400 years. Kaleidoscope eyes fold and bend in colour when divining true/hidden/unknown things.
Dimme/Lamashtu – Sumerian demon. All are descended from 7 pureblood sisters. Bite cannot convert others. Only female descendants inherit abilities. Human in appearance until violence is provoked. Jaw splits in the middle and a secondary jaw with serrated teeth sits inside the first.
Djinn – Human in appearance. Source of the genie myth. Can be identified by "tattoo" of a snake coiled around their throat, as well as having one green eye and the other purple. Can curse those who wish unjustified harm to another to be djinn until they learn compassion.
Gargoyle – Living stone creatures that protect unofficial sanctuaries for non-humans.
Lazarus (lazari) – Very animalistic in appearance with the head of a wolverine, arms of a beaver, rear legs of a badger, and chest of a koala. Very peaceful, they guard the gateways between dimensions. The shape and colour of their facial markings indicate power/rank, with Laos Niké (Lay-ose Nee-kay) being the matriarch and guardian of Limbo, among other places.
Daeva – Mortal child of two gods. Reason for mortality unknown. Never make it past age 13, if lucky. Do not make it beyond the beginning of puberty.
Vampires – Body cannot produce melanin, resulting in gradual loss of pigment until skin is deathly pale. Absolute control over body temperature allows for stalking of prey in all conditions. Can convert humans, as well as interbreed with them. Chances of half-vampire offspring surviving are slim as not all humans are compatible. Birth defects can be gruesome. Eyes of Originals,

purebloods, halfers and quarters are variants of tri-coloured, though in quarter-bloods only females inherit the colouring. Conversion is selective and is the result of consciously releasing a virus. Blood is not nourishment, but contains the chemicals that are. Euphoria and power result in the most satisfying feed; while fear/terror have a half-life of three days. Vampires were originally created for population control when nature doesn't respond adequately.

Hellhounds – Creation of Ares for unknown reasons. Look like a mix of malamute and jackal with a split lower jaw. Walk on two legs. Bite is poisonous, but cannot convert others.

Laksinki – Demon of unknown origin. Appearance unknown as they can completely alter their shape, size, and colouring. Main targets/prey are humans with abilities. They take the head and whatever physically manifests the human's ability (pyro-hands, necromancer-heart, etc.) Consumption of the parts grants temporary access to ability of the victim.

Succubus – Appear human unless around their own kind. Interbreed with humans often, but purebloods only occur when there is no human ancestry. Always hunt paired; either their mate or a direct blood relation (father, brother, uncle, son, etc.) Are often found working at strip clubs as it allows them to feed discretely. When around others of their kind they have bi-coloured skin, leathery wings, and bone spikes protruding from their heels. Target nymphomaniacs and people who are sexually repressed to stabilise their energy levels.

Incubus – See: succubus.

Nephylem – Angel-vampire hybrids. Warriors who fight for those being unjustly attacked or invaded. In times of peace, they guard the nether space that teleporters move through. Due to their warrior nature they are all tall and strong, but inhumanly agile in regards to delicate hand work.

Seraphym – Mercenaries. They held the leashes of the Malachai for aeons before they became too dangerous. Nephylem-demigod hybrids, they exist in a state of flux. They cannot reproduce, and as such are rare, but they are indestructible. Due to their inability to have children, they are very protective; if ordered to harm a child they will turn on the person who hired them. Can be identified by forest-green eyes and a tattoo/brand of a butterfly on the back of their neck.

Malachai – Laksinki-hellhound hybrids, often called the Dogs of War. Lethal and vicious, the Seraphym were the only ones who could control them. Murder charged their abilities and, the effect being cumulative, all but a handful were destroyed to keep them from destroying the Earth. Appearance unknown as no one is stupid enough to let them out.

Golems – Puppets of sorts. They can only be created/summoned by extremely powerful necromancers and earth-manipulators. The pyrokinetic version is the Ifrit. They can take any shape the creator desires and will perform all tasks ordered.

Angels – Immortal/indestructible. Can regrow any body part removed within seconds, even if decapitated. Ferry souls of the dead to Hades. Can combine their bodies into "berserkers" that can hold off armies for decades.

Hunters/Council – A group of humans who are xenophobic to the point they hunt and kill all non-humans, no matter their allegiance, unless they can use them. Originally trained by Prometheus to disrupt the peaceful lives of non-humans, with minimal killing. Evolution over centuries resulted in a cult-like devotion to ridding the world of all who could protect it. Blue Blood Hunters come from families who have been hunting for generations, sometimes millennia.

Author Bio

K.B. Horricks-King appears to be a borderline nutcase who writes to exercise her demons, because drowning them didn't work (and neither did the exorcism). "If you can't get rid of them, run with them" as she has said when she thinks no one is paying attention. She has the potential to do something good for the world, however, that part isn't guaranteed. Upon awakening most days she believes humans suck, deserve themselves and aren't worth saving. After many cups of coffee, the good stuff that doesn't taste like sewage water, that assessment doesn't change much. She writes, paints, wrangles her daughter, dotes on her father, loves most of the rest of her family while not talking to them all that often and tries to get her two cats to like her. No luck there, yet. An avid gardener, plants seem to like her. At least they don't wither and die in screaming agony when she passes by.

Putting all levity aside, you won't find out much about K.B. as she is as much of an enigma as she is a very private person.

"Alone"is K.B.'s first novel and she is working on the second. She has several short stories in "The UnValentine Anthology" published in 2014.